The Tainted Wars
Reaper

W. J. Grupe Jr

Twin Pines Publishing

ISBN (Paperback) 978-1-952662-10-2

For Marie,
You're every line, you're every word,
you're everything.

The Tainted Wars

Reaper

Chapter One

THE DEMON GLARED AT me across the courtyard of the Minneapolis Federal Reserve Bank with a rage that had been beaten into it over years. We had it surrounded, but its focus was on me alone. Amram Hager stood on my right. The man who had introduced me into this world where every nightmare you have ever heard about was real. Just not in the way you thought. This demon couldn't hop into and out of bodies. It didn't have black eyes and wasn't controlled by a creature from the underworld, and looked like any normal human. It had taken years—maybe even decades—to create such an abomination, but the Tainted had unlimited time.

"Christian, I presume you have this handled?" Hager said in his British accent that always reminded me of Sir John Gielgud. For me, it contradicted his outward appearance. Hager followed the customs of the Hasidic Jew, with all associated accoutrements: wide brimmed black hat, long white beard with those curly sideburns, and a long, black coat that he wore no matter the weather. The only thing missing was the baggy tailoring—not for Hager. Everything fit as if he had been sewn into it. Yet somehow, he still moved with snake-like efficiency. Honestly, the outfit made him look badass.

"Sure," I said. "No problem."

Hager must have detected my lack of conviction and he looked at me askance.

"You *have* dealt with one of these before, haven't you?" Major Lawrence Mangine asked on my left.

A fellow ex-army ranger, he was new to the team though lacked the powers that Bishops like Hager and I have. I hadn't known him during my time in the military, but apparently he'd heard of me.

He'd come with the army Jelena had hired a few months ago, at my direction, and quickly became an invaluable resource. He led all the normal troops on every one of my raids. Lawrence was large. I say that being just over six feet myself. Chairs let out little cries of despair when he sat. At nearly three hundred pounds, I don't think he had an ounce of fat on him. He would have been useful in the battle with Anton, the Hulk sized Tainted I'd faced a month or so back. Lawrence had been the man to kick off our new way of working with the side of humanity that doesn't share our special abilities.

"Hey, this is Christian Bateleur we're talking about."

I tried to sound more confident. I had dealt with a demon before. Once before. There were two that time. I had entered a supernatural fog of war to defeat them. I had no idea what I'd done then, so I wasn't sure if I could repeat it. Before me, no one had ever defeated one. A year ago, they'd been so rare, they were almost a thing of myth. This was the third we'd encountered.

"Shit," Lawrence spat. He knew the devastation these things might unleash. It was all in the briefing we gave the soldiers to teach them the dangers. "Everyone, back off slowly. Do not make any sudden movements. This is a confirmed Crowley."

A ripple of emotion danced through the twenty or so troops filling the courtyard. One especially twitchy soldier pumped a round into his shotgun. The demon jerked toward the sound, her eyes narrowed.

Oh, did I mention the demon was basically a forty-something soccer mom? Her form was not overly muscular, though I would guess she was a regular at the local pilates class. She wore a skirt and a polo shirt as though she'd just returned from a tennis lesson. Her face—well, that was a different story.

In my previous encounter with such a creature, its appearance had aligned with the few books on them. Their faces didn't show any physical abnormalities. But further examination would prove to be like trying to identify the subject of a Picasso. What I saw this time could only be described as the evil underneath. The torment of her soul and those of her victims, both as a human and as a demon, showed in her physical form. This was not something I'd experienced before. My powers were shifting again.

I leaned over a little. "Are you seeing this?"

Hager didn't get a chance to respond. The demon blurred, going after the twitchy soldier playing the moron from every horror film. Blurring was the name we used for moving faster than unaided vision could clearly track. It was one of the powers that all supernatural beings seemed to share. I blurred to intercept. At the last moment, I switched off the speed and gave my muscles an added boost. Using the creature's momentum, I spun her in the opposite direction. She flew into the brick building behind her with a loud crack, then dropped to her knees. The wall had caved in where she'd hit it.

I rounded on the soldier. "Do you need me to define what a sudden movement means?"

His training finally kicked back in "No, sir. Sorry, sir."

I honestly wanted to continue berating him, but I try not to be a dick when possible. Plus, it wasn't my responsibility. The major practically growled behind me. He would set the man straight later.

I redirected my focus to the demon. She was wary now, probably never having encountered someone capable of challenging her.

Hager appeared by my side. "You are getting efficient at switching between powers."

"It would still be easier if we could use more than one power at a time."

"Indeed. To what were you referring in regard to my vision?"

"Huh?"

"You asked me if I 'was seeing this'."

"Oh, her face."

"I see the typical aberration. I presume you do not."

"No." I quickly described what I was seeing.

The demon got to her feet.

"You are not engaging your True Sight?"

"Hell, no. I don't want to witness the darkest depths of *that*."

Apparently, I'd insulted her. She screeched in a tone that reminded me of nails on a blackboard. Some younger readers may need to look it up on YouTube. Going into a frenzy, she blurred towards me. Her pink manicured nails, which came to a sharp point, streaked down at me as fast as a bumblebee's wings. But I was a hummingbird.

As I blocked her strikes, Hager swiveled into a spinning back kick that sent her reeling into a nearby tree well clear of anyone that could get hurt.

"Now, Major!"

"Alpha Team, open fire!"

The sound of multiple automatic rifles echoed off the buildings, drawing screams from the civilians in adjacent areas. She crossed her arms in front of her face as the force of the impacts pushed her back a few steps. Then she got her footing. She pushed out her chest and roared. Then reached up, ripped a huge limb off the tree, and flung it into the team. They scattered.

I didn't let her recover. Blurring to her I added a roundhouse, driving her to the ground on her hands and knees. The demon practically bounced up with a backhand that launched me into a group of soldiers. They caught me—more out of self preservation than concern for my health.

Getting to my feet, I reset my jaw and held it in place while it healed. I heard a few groans from the troops and I think one guy dry-heaved. When the muscles had stitched back together, I tested their range of motion.

"Thanks."

I received a few nods and a couple of thumbs up. I guess they didn't trust their voices.

While I'd been recovering, Hager was going toe-to-toe with the creature in the mini-skirt. He was pummeling her with a barrage of punches and kicks. Each strike pushed her back until she was up against a wall. The stability helped her regain her balance and she caught the next punch. With her other hand, she grabbed him by the throat, lifting him in the air. She spun and slammed him into the building with a snarl. More bricks cracked, mortar raining down on him. I blurred into the fight at near supersonic speed. Just before impact, I hardened myself into a speeding battering ram and plowed into her.

The massive force caused her to release her hold on my mentor. We went down in a tangled heap. Again, she pulled a reversal; flipping me onto my back and sitting on my stomach. She lifted both fists in the air, about to wreak havoc on my face, when Hager swooped in. He grabbed her in a full nelson and wrapped his long legs around her waist. Hauling her backwards on top of himself, he restrained her as she fought to escape. I got up and took a breath.

"Thanks."

The struggling demon had them both hopping about like a Mexican jumping bean. Through gritted teeth, Hager said, "Could we postpone the pleasantries until after we have dispatched the creature from Hell?"

I nodded. "Right."

I kneeled across both of them and grabbed the demon's head in both hands. She froze as I pushed my consciousness into her, delving into her to dispel the Taint within. My success with this was sketchy at best. But I had developed additional skills since the last time I'd tried. The spider web of evil wove itself around her very being; a tapestry of lies, deception, anger, resentment, pain, and death. To my senses, each thread possessed a different texture: smooth, rough, sticky, silky, gritty, cool, or steamy. The slimy ones stood out. I pulled in all the energy I could hold and laid into them like a flamethrower, burning them to cinders.

My vision shifted back into the physical world and I stared down at the soccer mom, who blinked up at me. She had aged ten years without the supernatural boost. I stood up and offered my hand.

"I think it's safe to release her."

Hager did so, if somewhat tentatively.

She accepted my help getting to her feet. "Thank you. I thought I would be stuck as that monster forever."

I smiled, keeping her in my grip. Then, with a twist, I spun her around and secured her wrists with a set of zip ties.

"What are you doing? It wasn't me! It was the demon!"

"I'm not tying you up because of the taint. I took care of that." Over my shoulder I called, "Lawrence."

The big man stepped up.

"Please have her taken to the nearest police station. I believe they will find several outstanding warrants for everything from fraud to murder."

She struggled in my grip, her voice still sweet and innocent. "I'm telling you, it was the creature!"

I turned her to face me.

"I'll give you a pass on the rampage you let loose over the past few months. But you will pay for all the lives you destroyed before trading your soul to keep your ass from sagging."

The woman's expression changed, revealing the actual monster. She curled her lip and spat, which I easily avoided with some super-natural moves.

I met her gaze again and she stared back like she was trying to burn a hole through my head.

"There she is."

Her voice oozed contempt. "I've dodged prison for decades. What makes you think this time will be any different?"

"Because I'll be there as a character witness. The Tainted are not the only ones who can manipulate people."

I gave Lawrence a look, and he motioned a soldier over. The Major walked away with them, explaining what would happen to him should he lose track of his charge.

"Good luck in prison," I called after her.

Hager stepped up next to me, dusting off his hat. He then set it atop his head with grand purpose. "How did you know she was evil to the core?"

"I could see it."

"You are becoming quite adept at that as well."

"You don't know the half." I told him what I had seen in her face.

"Interesting. And you weren't engaging your blessing?"

"Even when I was using other powers, the image never shifted."

"Fascinating." Hager stroked his white beard.

"What do you think it means?"

"I'm sure I have no idea."

"Great."

"And have you also gained the ability to manipulate people's minds like you told the woman?"

"No, I didn't say I could. I said the Tainted were not the only ones. It's not my fault if she misunderstood."

Hager smiled. "Very good."

Lawrence returned. "Is Anderson going to have any trouble with the demon? The kid's about as smart as a sack of wet mice, but I don't want him to be torn to shreds."

"No. She's not supernatural anymore–just a bitch. Can he handle that?"

"I guess we'll find out. We ready to pack up?"

"Yeah, release the troops back to their barracks. Make sure they submit for demon level hazard pay."

"Trust me, they won't forget."

"Any losses, Major?" Hager asked.

"A few minor injuries. But nothing serious, thanks to Christian. Unless you count the number of pushups Anderson will be doing for that shotgun fuckup."

Hager barely even flinched at the F-bomb. Apparently, he was warming up to our new Major who used language in a very George Carlinesque fashion.

"Indeed. Without his ability to cleanse the Taint from a demon, we would have almost no way to stop them."

In an attempt to change the subject, I checked my watch. "We might get back in time to catch the last of the Mets game."

Chapter Two

"NOTHING?" I ASKED AGAIN.

We were huddled around a conference room table in the downtown Manhattan Covenant House. I still felt rumpled from the flight in from Minneapolis on our private jet. The small Bishop community no longer acted as separate units, each focused on defending against local Tainted activity. Since I'd been volun-told into the newly created position of high muckety-muck, we had taken a more global view.

"I'm afraid not," Jelena replied.

She had been promoted from the first non-Bishop, ex-marine sniper on the payroll to general. She now controlled troop movements across the globe—all tracked via satellite. With a brilliant mind for strategy, she was taking to the position remarkably well.

I shook my head. "Twenty-five missions."

"Twenty-seven," Soon-Li corrected.

Soon-Li was one of eight Bishops currently residing at the New York Covenant house. She was an old friend of my mother's, who had died on a mission over twenty years ago. That had taken place before I underwent the ceremony to inherit my God-given powers—better known as First Holy Communion. Thanks to my father, that never transpired. Instead, I ended up falling ass-backwards into this life decades behind schedule with only my military training and no clue. All this had occurred almost a year ago and a lot had happened since. I came into my abilities, saved the city, became the first ever to kill a Tainted, orchestrated a rescue mission for another, and was sworn in as the aforementioned grand poobah.

"Fine, twenty-seven missions and we haven't seen hide nor hair of one of the Tainted, only their minions."

"Yes, but we are gaining ground," Soon-Li continued. "Your strategy has allowed us to take more threats off the board than at any time in history."

"It would be better if we had all the Bishops behind us," I lamented.

"True," Hager added. "But as Soon-Li pointed out, your plan is working."

I looked at him. "Is it? Or did it drive the Tainted into hiding? Did I make it impossible for us to eradicate these creatures?" The frustration built. Closing my eyes I took a deep breath. "Sorry, Jelena, please continue."

"Today's target's name was Kimberly Whitmore. You were right about her background. She was a con-artist, a thief, and a murderer before the Tainted ever got their claws into her."

"May I ask a question?"

This was posed by David, one of the newer Bishops to take up with me. By which I mean that I met him a few days before taking on this leadership position. He was big on rules and regulations—saw the world very black and white. We didn't hit it off right away. He took a little time to warm up to my methods. I live in the gray.

"You just did," I replied.

He pondered that for a second "Then may I ask—"

I stopped him with a look. He grimaced and got to the point.

"I'm not sure how to say this without sounding accusatory."

"Just say it."

"Why did we condemn this woman and let one of the Tainted go free?"

He was referring to the Heretic, the ex-Tainted for whom I'd assembled an army to rescue from the hands of one of her brothers.

I leaned forward. "Valid question, David. Do you believe in redemption?"

"Of course, sir. How could I not? It is a major premise of the Bible."

"Then, you have your answer."

He screwed up his face. "Sorry, I'm not following. Why was one redeemable but the other, not?"

I stared at him for a second, ushering in an uncomfortable silence.

This had been a touchy point in the rumor mill. While those in the ranks wanted to believe their leader was righteous, it was far easier to think that I had fallen under the spell of the pretty little Tainted with the reputation as one of the greatest manipulators ever to walk the earth.

"Because," I said, making myself as clear as possible, "only the Heretic asked for it."

David colored as I gestured to Jelena.

"We'll keep tabs on her to make sure she makes it to trial."

"Don't bother. We have more important things to focus on. So, no useful intel at all?"

"The team did a thorough search of the area. We couldn't determine what her target was. There were several high-profile individuals scheduled to be in the building that day: senators, CEOs, you name it. Without a specific threat, there's no way to narrow it down. Hell, she could have even been after the money."

It was the fifth dead end we had run into. Whoever this Tainted was, they covered their tracks. I sighed. "Any other leads on T-800?"

Everyone sat dejected or shaking their heads.

"Okay, let's cut bait."

Jelena balked. "But all the time and money we put into this operation—"

"Wasn't wasted. As Soon-Li noted, we neutralized multiple targets, including a demon. There are plenty of Tainted still out there. If you follow a player across the map to get one kill, you've probably just passed four others on the way. One might slip in behind you with a finishing move."

Hager's eyebrows came together. "I didn't follow that analogy."

Soon-Li rolled her eyes. "He's talking about Call of Duty."

"Oh, right. I still don't understand."

"Tunnel vision will get you killed," Lawrence offered. He'd been standing quietly in the back of the room, arms folded behind him. He provided his input for two reasons, to move the meeting along or to provide clarification. It was exceptionally rare for him to need any himself.

"Oh, yes. Quite."

I smiled. "What other projects do we have in the queue?"

Jelena glanced at her iPad, then shook her head. "We've been focused on this. It will take us a bit of time to pivot."

"How long?" I asked.

"An hour? Maybe two."

I nodded. "Get to it. I'll be in the gym."

Equipment blurred past me as I streaked around the four hundred meter track in the hidden stadium deep below the house. I imagined that I looked like the ending scene from Superman, the Movie where he orbited the world at hyper speed. Besides it looking cool, I was trying to empty my power reserves. The source of our abilities comes from the waters of the River Jordan, where John the Baptist baptized Jesus. The river itself didn't have power because of that event. It's more of why the holy men chose the spot. Way before Big J showed up, Naaman had been healed by bathing in the same waters. Meaning, someone witnessed a Bishop being recharged after battle. No one knows or remembers where the essence came from, but it has been our font since the dawn of humanity. Since we needed to bathe in it regularly, it was also our greatest weakness. That is, until the Heretic suggested another method.

I felt myself run dry and nearly fell on my face, trying to regain my balance. Like pulling the stop lever while traveling at ludicrous speed. I tucked into a roll and managed to not look too much like a rag doll as I skidded to a stop.

I took a few deep breaths and reset myself. I hated the feeling of being empty, like not eating before putting in a three-hour workout. I felt drained–hollow–like any action would require more energy than I had. The colors of my surroundings had lost their vibrancy, as though I was looking at the world through an old lens filter. It didn't make sense. I didn't have my power on at all times. It was a conscious process to dip into that well of energy. So why did I have this feeling every time I was tapped out?

I shook it off and tried to focus. Lucy—the name the Heretic had asked me to call her—had said that the holy water was just a catalyst. The Tainted had used blood in much the same way. It was where most vampire stories came from. They had perfected a method of draining the body through the carotid artery using double needles. You can probably fill in the blanks from there. After a few centuries, they realized that the power was not coming from the blood but from the powerful emotions that were imbued into it. Pain, fear, horror, sadness. Eventually, they learned to tap in directly. All of their minions, however, still needed that blood.

Lucy had turned the page on that life. She had gained access to an alternative source of power—hope. One that cut her off from her manipulative capabilities but allowed her to do things that no other Bishop could—heal. I had that ability as well, but I seemed to be the exception to every rule. The other Bishops said it was because I was special. I had a different viewpoint. Limitations are self-inflicted.

I took off running, searching for that connection. I went to that place inside where I connected to my powers. It always took on the image of a meadow by a lake. Without my gift, it was a ghost town: hollow, barren, and dry. Once before, when I was low on juju, I had a similar vision with brown grass, wilting trees, and a puddle where the large body of water used to be. That image was mostly caused by the depression I had fallen into. I could mentally shift it back into the beautiful vista I always pictured. This time was different. This wasn't a depreciated mental state. This was death.

I tried to change its appearance; to force life into it. But it didn't budge. I moved onto the obstacle course which was a small simulated town like you might find while playing paintball. I started running through, parkouring onto buildings and through windows before sprinting across rooftops. I leapt from one to another, each time trying to trigger the connection to my power; hoping some subconscious act would restore that link.

I halted on top of the tallest building. Gulping air, I sat on the edge. My feet dangled over, three stories up. I wasn't afraid of heights.

Jumping out of a plane as many times as Ranger School required had squashed that. But most people still have a healthy respect for elevations. I had lost *that* jumping from rooftop to rooftop across downtown Miami, chasing one of the Tainted. Right now, if I fell, I would probably be dead.

"Is that what you call working out? I thought I trained you better than that."

I looked down and saw Soon-Li on the ground a short distance away. She blurred, running up the wall of the neighboring building at a steep angle until she reached a window ledge. Using it as a spring point, she launched herself up, grabbed the ridge of the roof, and swung up next to me.

"Show off."

"Look who's talking. You've been grandstanding since the day you got here." Soon-Li had the smallest touch of an accent, intensified by the fast clipped way she spoke.

"Ha. Is that what you call it?"

"Why are you brooding this time?"

"I'm not brooding."

"So, you came up here to enjoy the view of the track?"

"I'm thinking."

"That's just another word for brooding."

"I am neither brooding nor somber."

"I didn't say you were somber."

"Forget it."

"Was that another quote?"

"Yes. From Star Trek the original series."

"I thought you were into the eighties. Wasn't Star Trek from the sixties?"

"Yes," I said, "but you are forgetting two very important points. I am a geek at heart and the movies were made in the eighties. You can't fully appreciate a movie until you've seen the show. You'll miss all the Easter eggs."

"What does Easter have to do with this?"

"No, not..." I sighed. "Never mind."

Soon-Li slapped the back of my head. "I'm a coder. You think I don't know what an Easter egg is?"

I nudged her playfully. She shoved me back, knocking me off my perch.

"I'm empty!" I yelled, clawing for the roof line as I fell.

Chapter Three

MY FINGERTIPS CAUGHT THE edge but didn't have the strength to stop the momentum. I tried to orient myself. Everything was a tumbling blur. I swiveled, trying desperately to find anything to grab onto. Soon-Li came out of nowhere streaking down to me head first. She grabbed me, then flipped; landing on her feet with me cradled in both arms.

I smiled at her. "Thanks."

She frowned and dropped me.

My spine slammed into the ground as pain shot through me. "What the hell was that for?"

"To try to knock some sense into you. You could have been killed. Believe it or not, you are not invincible."

"Yes," I said, rubbing my back. "That is painfully obvious."

"What were you trying to prove?"

"I was attempting to tap into hope."

"And what was the purpose of doing it three stories up?"

I sat up and leaned against the building from which I had just fallen. "Need. I seem to connect with my power most when it's based on need. It works the best when I'm about to die."

"Were you trying to set up that very scenario?"

"I was doing fine until someone pushed me off the roof."

Soon-Li stared at me for a second, then offered me her hand. I took it and stood, dusting myself off.

"You are really empty?"

I looked back at the distance I'd just fallen. "You think?"

"Good, I brought your sword."

"Soon-Li I'm not sure—"

"You say you need life-or-death stakes? I'll give it to you."

She walked away. I had to either follow her or continue to stand there talking to myself. Thinking of the beating I was about to take, I looked back up at the roof longingly.

"At least that fate would have been swift," I mumbled under my breath.

"I heard that."

I shook my head and followed. On the opposite end of the track was a circle of dirt used for sparring. Spaced around the area, swords, staffs, spears, axes and anything in between were arranged on racks by type. She walked up and grabbed mine. Then handed it to me with both hands and a slight bow. I took it with a mirroring gesture. It was a katana. Modern in its creation, it was crafted to mimic the swords used by the Samurai of feudal Japan. It was a good sword. Nothing special, but Soon-Li wouldn't allow me to get anything better.

"Form first," she said stepping clear. Standing there with her hands behind her back, her expression announced, *Well, I'm waiting.*

I strapped the weapon to my belt and stood at the ready; left hand on the sheath, right on the pommel. She nodded, and I drew it in one swift motion. Soon-Li disappeared, as did the ring. There was only me and my sword. Swipe, swipe, stab. My two hands gripped the pommel; one high near the guard, one low, acting as a pivot point to increase speed and strength to each strike. Turn, stab, step back, dodge, swipe, block, swipe. The kata covered the entire area of the circle. My sliding steps kicked up dirt. Nearing the end of the exercise, I stabbed. Then I immediately leapt in the opposite direction, slashing an arc that would have severed several heads had they been unlucky enough to be there. I landed in a defensive position. My foot traced a hundred and eighty degree arc in the dirt. When I spun my body to realign with it, I was facing Soon-Li again. I finished with a salute. Then with a snap, I slid the weapon back into its sheath.

My breathing was elevated but I wasn't panting. A thin sheen of sweat coated my skin. I gave a smile, thinking I had done well.

Soon-Li stood silently staring at me. "Sloppy."

My face fell.

"You need to put more power into all of your strikes, not just the fancy ones. Every slash, every stab must have full commitment. Just performing the moves is not enough. You must be fierce. Strike fear into any on-lookers."

"Maybe if I had a better sword."

I didn't even see her move. I felt the tug on my belt and she was standing there with my sword in her hand. She held the tip at my chest and gently pushed me backwards until I stepped out of the circle. She strode back to the center and faced me. Fire burned in her eyes as she stared at me. Soon-Li went through the same form but it looked nothing like mine. Each swipe cut the air with a whistle. Each stab may as well been stuck in a tree for how little the tip wavered. I watched her dance. It was beautiful. Yet, subconscious fear gripped my spine. My fight-or-flight response screamed at me so I had to focus to keep my feet planted. When she finished, I found I was holding my breath. I let it out, trying not to be too obvious. She stepped up to me, spun the sword, and slid it back into the scabbard on my belt.

"Seems fine to me."

"My mistake."

She took up her weapon, which differed from mine in almost every way. It was Chinese, ancient—maybe centuries old—straight, and double-bladed. The guard was carved in the shape of a dragon's face and a long red tassel hung from the hilt.

We faced each other, saluted, then slipped into our ready stances. I stood with one foot forward, both hands gripping the sword in front. She held hers in a reverse grip so that the blade rested against the back of her arm, sticking up over her right shoulder. I attacked and she batted the blow away as she would a fly, her sword flicking out like it moved on its own. I struck anew—this time low, aiming for her legs. She side-stepped easily and, again, smacked my sword away. I was using two hands against her one-handed weapon and she redirected my strikes like it was nothing. When she parried my stab attempt, I spun— intending to attack from the other direction. Halfway around, she hit me hard enough to send me flying. I dropped to my knees but still hung onto my sword.

"Had you been an actual opponent, I would have used my sword instead of my foot. Spins look great in the movies but all they do is leave your back vulnerable."

Leaping to my feet, I turned and stabbed again. She wasn't there. I caught sight of her in my periphery right before she slapped the flat of her blade against my wrists—then my forehead. I dropped the weapon and grabbed my head, checking for blood.

"No fair, using powers."

She raised her eyebrows. "I didn't."

"Wow, I really suck at this."

"Actually, you are improving quickly."

I rubbed my head again. "It doesn't feel like that."

Her sword shot out and flipped mine off the ground, launching it into the air. It fell into her other hand like someone had placed it there.

I got to my feet. "Still no powers?"

Soon-Li shook her head. "I have had over twenty thousand hours of practice with my sword."

"That doesn't sound right," I said, skeptical.

"Two hours a day for over thirty years. Do the math."

I didn't have to. The number appeared to me as she proposed the calculation. "I don't have that kind of time."

"You don't need it. At the rate you are progressing, with focus and diligence, you will be able to match me in ten."

She handed me my sword.

I took it. "Is that all?"

"Come. Let's go once more."

We did. Then again and again. For the next hour, she flicked and slapped me until I was bruised all over I couldn't spare any focus on trying to connect with the alternative source and it didn't appear to me out of need either. However, by the end, Soon-Li needed to concentrate more to prevent my sword from sneaking its way through her defense. I even blocked some of her strikes.

After the last exchange, I was panting and held my hand up. "I've had enough."

"Agreed. You are becoming sloppy again."

"Again?"

"There was a point where I wasn't completely displeased."

"Stop with the compliments. You're going to make me blush."

"Sir?"

I turned and found Jeremy Stark, my personal assistant. He'd once compared his position to a yeoman aboard a ship. Kirk had one, so I deemed the role acceptable.

"Yes, Jeremy?"

"The team is ready for you."

"Thank you."

"I also took the liberty of preparing the items for your shower and laid out your immersion robes."

"Efficient as ever."

"Thank you, sir. I will leave you to it."

Stark turned ceremoniously and strode back across the grounds like he was a one man parade.

Soon-Li inclined her head towards his retreating form. "How are you two getting along?"

"Great. At first, I couldn't imagine what he was going to do all day. Now I don't know how I would do all this without him. He doesn't hover, but somehow knows when he's required. He appears out of nowhere with exactly what I need. Usually, before I know I need it. Besides the whole thing being a little creepy, and him needing to loosen up a tad, I can't complain."

"He's not making you soft?" Soon-Li asked.

I barked out a laugh. "He is the first one to suggest hitting the gym or the shower."

"I don't disagree with him there." She smacked me on the ass with the flat of her blade. "You stink."

The secret lower level had a whole other set of accommodations from upstairs. A small kitchen with dry and canned goods connected to five sleeping quarters. Bishops sometimes used them for overflow during large gatherings or as a napping area while working on a project. They were also helpful when the house went into lockdown, as I discovered during our recent activity in New Orleans. There was a lab for studying anything from forensics to engineering, an arsenal that could support a minor war, and a garage filled with whatever vehicle might be needed. But the main reason for all the security was the immersion pool. The source of a Bishop's power. For now.

I showered and put on my dousing robes. They were ceremonial in nature—white with red fringes and rope belt—and not very conducive to soaking in a pond of holy water. They became saturated and had to be wrung back out into the pool for fear of it running dry. But I understood the necessity of tradition— the familiarity and the comfort. If I was to change this practice, it wouldn't be now. There were far more important things going on. Plus, I was trying to make this all obsolete.

The door opened at my subcutaneous chip that our AI matched with my voice, facial recognition, recorded stride markers, ear shape, and about five other variables. Recently, the chances of me being alone for a recharge had become slim. This time was no different.

"Hello, Christian."

"Hey, Tira."

Tira Gupta was one of the first Bishops I had been introduced to and we'd had an immediate attraction. We danced around that connection during my first few weeks until it became evident that I wasn't your normal, everyday supernatural hero. When I started doing things others couldn't and were thought impossible, neither of us handled it very well. She became distant and I moved to Florida.

"Glad you're here," I said. "I could use a spotter."

"Do you need me to get back in with you?"

"No, that's not necessary. I'm empty and this may take a while. Just make sure that I come up. On the off chance I have a vision, I may be too engrossed."

Visions were a new thing for me and started a few months ago when we were trying to find John's kidnapped father. I hadn't even known they existed before I experienced my first one. Apparently, they were common enough but too brief for most Bishops to glean any information. My recharge time was dramatically longer than the typical Bishop. So the visions often provided direction. I hadn't had one since that first time.

Tira smiled "Sure."

I made my way into the shallow water, which came just above my waist. I took several deep breaths, taking twice as long on the exhale as the inhale in order to expel as much carbon dioxide as possible. Then I sank under. Once my head was fully submerged, the lightning show started. Thick bolts of power arced into me in zig-zagging patterns. My muscles convulsed randomly—leg, back, arm, shoulder. I ignored the dance and focused on my mental palace. My happy place, if you will.

I'm not sure where it originated but it was where I went to in my head whenever I attempted anything new with my powers. I stood on the shoreline of a lake. Its waters barely covered the bottom, but they were rising fast, as though a great deluge were filling it. The sky, however, was clear, and the sun bright. A light breeze drifted past. Behind me, a meadow extended as far as I could see. I smelled grass and wild flora.

I heard a faint buzzing sound in the distance, deeper than that of a bumblebee, and a jolt of excitement shot up my spine. Or maybe it was just the recharge coming in with an especially powerful shock. Out from over the rising lake waters, a familiar bug made its way to me— a dragonfly. It had appeared to me the first time I visited this place in my mind and came back on the occasions when I found myself at a crossroads. I'd waited for its arrival for a while but it had been absent since my first vision.

It skipped across the lake, making small ripples in the water. When it finally reached me, it hovered in front of me as though waiting.

"Sorry, you must be tired after that long flight." I stuck out my index finger as a perch and it landed lightly. We stared at each other. "Well, nothing to say?"

Another shock arced through me, causing my back to spasm, and the vision turned white.

Kimberly Stone left Carwash with a solid buzz derived from one part dancing, one part loud music, and two parts alcohol. It was late and she knew she would regret it tomorrow morning. But we were talking about a retro disco club with a round, colorful stage and a swimming pool. A damn swimming pool! She needed to blow off steam, act out, rebel against the straight-laced businesswoman role she played daily. It was time to let her hair down, literally. She giggled at her own joke, thinking about the tight bun she wore that usually gave her a headache by four. Checking the rideshare app again, she saw her driver would arrive in three minutes. The night air held a crisp feeling to it as well, probably due to the stereotypical fog.

Yes, it had been a good evening. She had danced with several guys— even snogged one of them in the corner. If her stuck-up mentor could only see the new vice president now, he would be shocked or maybe excited. Horny? She laughed again, this time out loud.

She checked her phone.

"What the fuck?"

The car had turned from Davies onto Brook Street. Which meant in order to get to her, they would have to go around Hanover Square. If the idiot had gone up to Oxford, he could have turned on to Dering and been brought right in front of the club. Apparently, the driver figured out the mistake as well because he stopped at the corner of Brook and New Bond Street and triggered the 'arrived' prompt.

"My ass."

She keyed the call driver button.

"Hello?"

"I've got news for you Jeff. You haven't arrived."

"Just come through the Watchhouse corridor."

"Bullshit. I'm not walking through there at two in the morning. Drive around to where I am."

"Yeah, that's not happening, love. Do you want this ride or not?"

"I want it where I asked for it, where I'm fucking standing. Not around the corner through some barely lit alleys."

"Suit yourself."

Jeff hung up and she looked at the app. It read 'ride declined' as the icon of the car drove away.

"FUCK!"

Her mood went south fast. She considered calling for a new lift then fleetingly thought of walking to the underground. She decided, instead, to walk to Oxford Street then try again with another rideshare.

As she walked, she let her mind drift back to the club—the music, the dancing, the taste of the apple martinis. Not to mention the hot guy's lips. His beard had tickled her face while he kissed her. She didn't even know his name. The warm glow returned, as did her smile. Her thickly heeled shoes clicked against the cobblestone street, echoing off the buildings. She wasn't a fan of these streets—too many places a person could lurk.

The rattle of metal cans spooked her. She fumbled into her clutch for her small can of mace. She fought with the zipper, too scared to even curse. Then, just as she had gotten it open, a cat screeched and shot out of an alley.

"Shit. Little pet cemetery reject. I knew I shouldn't have watched that movie."

A hand touched her shoulder. She jumped, turning and flapping her arms at whatever was behind her. It was the bearded guy from the club.

"What the hell, man? You can't go sneaking up on a girl like that."

He held up his hands. "Sorry, I was trying to catch up with you so I could get your number."

Seriously? Why were guys *this* clueless?

"Yeah, listen, if I wanted you to have it, I would have given it to you."

"But...uh..." He pointed back towards the club.

"You're sweet, and a decent kisser. But I only wanted a fun night."

He pursed his lips and rubbed the stubble on his cheek. "We could finish what we started in there."

"Thanks, but I have to get up early." She walked away, leaving him standing there.

"What the hell? Talk about leading—"

Jesus, this guy couldn't even complete a full sentence. He'd ruined what would have been perfect fantasy fodder with his bumbling attempts at getting in her pants. She tried to be nice, or at least not entirely rude, but now she was pissed again. She whirled around with a litany of insults ready to fly but they all got caught in her throat.

The guy wasn't alone. Behind him lurked a dark figure. The dome of light cast from the street lamp cut across the bearded man, leaving the other obscured in darkness. The appearance of the person hadn't been what caused her to stop, nor anything her recent stalker was doing. It was the air of menace that emanated from the newcomer. It had a weight all its own that oozed off its owner and drifted toward her. The only thing she could see clearly were the eyes as they burned with hatred.

The bearded man moved his lips as though trying to speak. No words came forth, but what did was a flow of blood. She wanted to scream, but like him, nothing came out. She fought with herself to move her feet but they felt cemented in place.

He fell face-first onto the cobblestones and she heard the crack as his skull shattered. Now she could see the weapon. It was a chef's knife, the kind found in almost any kitchen. A long, wide blade dripped with the man's blood.

Finally finding her footing. She turned to run but was yanked back by her free flowing hair. Her first strange thought was to wonder how he could have possibly caught up to her so quickly. The question disappeared in the wave of panic that took hold. She cursed and yelled and fought but it dragged her, still by the hair, into the alley the cat had recently vacated. She could feel that this wasn't a person, not really. This held more evil than any one human could embody. She continued to flail and scratch but it did nothing to slow her captor. When they were deep within the alleyway, he pulled her head up and she looked into his face for the first time. Now, she screamed.

Chapter Four

INHALED SHARPLY, SWALLOWING water. Breaching like an orca, I splashed the contents of the pool all around the chamber as I knocked Tira, backward. I climbed onto the grass, hacking and sputtering and vomiting holy water. She was by my side in an instant, rubbing my back and encouraging me to continue coughing. She needn't have bothered. I couldn't have stopped even if my life had depended on it. It took me a few minutes to clear out my lungs enough to talk.

"I'm okay."

"Are you sure? I can get some oxygen."

I gave her a thumbs up, still gulping air like a drowning victim. Which I guess I was.

"What happened?" Tira continued to rub my back. I rolled over and stared up at the carved rock ceiling.

"I had a vision. How long was I down there? Did I finish?" I had to stop for a breath between each question, though not giving her enough time to answer. I focused on slowing my breathing.

"Almost three minutes. The replenishing had stopped for nearly thirty seconds but you didn't seem to be in any distress. I came back in just in case. What did you see?"

"A nightmare."

In the locker room, I changed into the clothes that Jeremy had left for me. Not an army uniform, but not jeans and a t-shirt referencing some movie. This was slacks and a button down with a collar. *Ugh.* The only thing worse would be a polo, which is just a dress shirt that identifies as a tee. But I digress. He also included a tie, which I threw in the trash as I walked out. I would find it back in my room tomorrow, dry-cleaned and pressed.

Tira was already waiting for me in the hallway. "Ready to talk yet?"

"Nope."

"Talking about a traumatic experience reduces its hold on you."

"Thanks, doc, but you can put all three of your PhDs away. I won't be needing them."

She shrugged. "Suit yourself."

"Jeremy keeps trying but I'm not having any of that either."

In my periphery, I caught Tira's eyebrows scrunching together But she didn't ask.

We took the super secret elevator that led up to the pantry near the kitchen. Meaning the large number of troops residing at the house were all aware of it. It was kind of hard to keep it hidden with the hallway never empty. However, none of them were authorized for the lower level. They knew it existed but that was the extent of it.

Stark was standing by a plate with a metal cover for keeping the contents warm.

"No time for lunch right now."

"I anticipated that, sir, so I acquired something you could consume quickly."

"Great."

I tried to keep the sarcasm out of my voice but didn't think I was successful. My yeoman had an obsession with getting me to eat healthy. I pictured a green shake or a granola bar made from pressed kale. He raised the lid and two hot dogs stared at me. My breath caught. The misshapen buns barely contained the long cylindrical all-beef—at least, that's what I told myself—frankfurter, mustard and sauerkraut haphazardly applied. All this could only indicate one thing that I dared not hope for.

I glanced at Jeremy. "Are they?"

"I believe you refer to them as—" The corners of his lips pulled down into a grimace, as though the words themselves had a foul taste. "—dirty water dogs."

I stepped up to Jeremy and put a hand on his shoulder. I took a shivering, melodramatic breath, keeping eye contact.

"You complete me."

He rolled his eyes as I grabbed one, fearing they might be snatched away. My first bite took out half, requiring a bit of effort to chew the large wad. Condiment residue stuck to either side of my mouth and Tira handed me a napkin, a smirk on her face. I wiped away the remnant after swallowing.

"Now, that's good."

Jeremy handed me a bottle of water, cap already removed. I regarded it.

"I'm not even going to complain about this."

"How very big of you, sir."

I ignored his comment, took a swig, and started walking.

"Let's eat and walk," I called back, then halved the dog again. We took the route through the library and up the spiral staircase to the second floor. As a book nerd, it was my favorite path to my office.

We ran into one of the Bishops that had recently joined me in Manhattan after I assumed command. There were many like him that wanted to be in the new global headquarters. Closer to me, I guess, though I still found that hard to believe. Hager and Speranza rigorously vetted anyone that applied.

"Hey, Nathan."

Hearing me, he stood up quickly, practically knocking over his chair. I considered the man a walking dichotomy. Picture a buff blonde surfer, a perpetual three day scruff, and the temperament of a socially awkward geek. I can say that since I identify as one myself.

"Mr. Bateleur. It's good to see you."

"Christian, remember," I reminded him.

"Yes, of course."

"What are you studying?"

"Demons."

I rubbed my shoulder remembering the most recent encounter. "Ask Tira for book suggestions. She has done in-depth research."

"I will, thanks."

I continued on and, midway between the first and second floor,
I reached back for the other slice of heaven in a bun. I took more
human bites, savoring the flavors that could only be obtained on the
streets of Manhattan. By the time we arrived at the war room, I had
finished, wiped my mouth, and deposited the napkin on the now
empty plate—save for some residual kraut and globs of mustard. I
showed restraint by not licking the plate.

"Thanks, Stark."

"Certainly, sir. But please understand this will not be added to
your routine."

"Of course. We must restrict my happiness at all costs." I stepped
into the meeting room before he could reply. "What do we got?"

The next half hour contained a catalogue, highlighting the deprav-
ity of humanity to a point where only the Grinch could have walked
away nonplussed. You know, before the heart growing incident. Wars,
skirmishes, revolutions, drugs, human trafficking, gang violence, orga-
nized crime. Depressing.

"What else?" I asked.

They all looked at each other.

"Isn't that enough?" Jelena finally said.

"Oh, it's more than enough, just not…"

I couldn't articulate what I was looking for, just that I would know
when it hit me.

"There was one other thing I found," Adam said, "though it seemed
small scale compared to the rest."

I inclined my head. "Go."

"There has been some unusually violent deaths leaving no forensic
evidence and no witnesses despite taking place in very public places.
I tracked the M.O. and there have been similar crimes going back
hundreds of years in batches of twelve."

"What is the current count?" Jelena asked.

Adam hesitated. "Two."

She made her distinctive sound which communicated exactly what she thought of the statement. But she didn't leave it there.

"We have criminal activity that is leaving a path of destruction behind it of hundreds, even thousands, and you want us to investigate two deaths?"

"But if you include all the deaths over time—" Adam argued.

"We can't waste —"

Adam was one of the few who would go toe to toe with Jelena. Probably because they were dating and this was all just foreplay.

Where?" I interrupted.

She frowned at me. "Christian, I don't think—"

I ignored her and focused on Adam.

"London."

I nodded. "A man and woman a few blocks away from the night-club? Carwash?"

He checked his tablet and his eyebrows knitted together.

"Yes, a couple that had just come from a place called Carwash. How could you possibly know that?"

"He had a beard?"

"Christian, what the hell?" Adam exclaimed.

"They weren't a couple." I looked at Jelena. "We have our target."

"But, Christian, what are two people compared to an entire country at war?"

I held her gaze. "To the families of people who were killed? A great deal."

I checked the rest of the faces and could see their confusion and doubt. They'd come here to follow me. Why didn't they trust my judgement?

I let out a long sigh. "I had a vision just before I came up here. A man and a woman being brutally murdered by a malevolent force. I viewed it through the woman's eyes. I could feel all of her terror and pain. That's why we are going."

Everyone's resolve solidified and a few heads bobbed.

I frowned. "Jelena, make preparations. I will be in the library."

✝

"What's troubling you?"

I looked up at Hager. He had recruited me a year ago, and now I held a position above him. One that both he and the head of the high council requested I take up.

I closed one book, moved it to the side, and opened another. "Nothing."

Hager pulled out a chair and sat, facing me in silence. When I finally glanced up again he said, "I believe the current turn of phrase is 'tell that to your face.'"

"It's nothing."

"It is obviously anything but."

I flipped the page but wasn't really reading it. "Let it go Hager."

"Is that an order?"

"Will that get you to drop it?"

"It will not."

I sighed. "It's not important."

Hager stroked his beard. "The leader of a group of supernaturally powerful beings having a bee in his bonnet warrants a conversation."

"Why, do you believe I'll go rogue?"

"You've already done so. Quite successfully, I might add."

"Wonderful, crisis averted. Discussion over."

I turned another unread page. He continued to sit there, staring at me in silence.

"Take a picture. It'll last longer."

"You are very adept at being an ass when needed."

Hager cursing, even at such a minor level, caused me to stop. I closed the book and peered around.

"I assure you, there is no one here. I had the library cleared. Discretely."

"It's stupid."

"Human emotions generally are. But that doesn't make them any less real or valid."

I took a deep breath. "I feel like they don't trust me."

"The Bishop contingent or the hired army?"

I shrugged. "Some of both."

"Why do you expect that is?"

I considered that for a few seconds. "I get the impression they are waiting for the next miracle. My decisions don't carry as much weight as when they think they're coming from a higher power. Everyone thought my idea of pursuing the two deaths strange until I revealed my vision. Then they were on board."

Hager leaned back. "I see."

"What do you see?"

"You want them to follow Christian the man, not Christian the messiah."

"I'm not a messiah."

"What would you call yourself?"

"Just a guy trying to do the right thing."

"You wish to separate the two. Like a wealthy man trying to determine if the women courting him are doing so because of who he is or what he has."

I scratched at the stubble on my jaw. "I guess."

"Then you are honorable."

My brow furrowed and one side of my mouth contracted.

Hager smiled at my confusion. "Some people in your position would take advantage of their status. Revel in the attention, regardless of whether it was for the persona or the person. You want them to like and follow you for who you were. The man you were before being blessed with abilities far beyond that of other men or even other Bishops."

"Is that too much to ask?"

"Yes."

I threw my arms up. "Great."

"Tell me something. Do you like me?"

"What kind of stupid question is that?"

"Humor me. Do you like me?"

"Yes, of course."

Hager tugged the lapels of his jacket. "Do you like my clothes?"

"What?"

"Just answer the question."

"Sure."

His eyes narrowed. "Answer it honestly."

"Fine, not particularly."

"Do you like my views on religion?"

"No."

"My views on sports?"

"Hell, no."

He nodded. "There are a lot of parts of me you either dislike or disagree with. Does that diminish your fondness for me?"

I sighed. "No, of course not."

"Why?"

I narrowed my eyes at him. "Because all your annoying elements make up who you are."

Hager stood up straighter but took the insult in stride.

"You cannot separate your abilities from yourself. They are one part of who you are. But the best thing about you is that your powers don't define you. You would be making the same choices whether you had them or not. Everyone here knows and accepts that as fact. That is why they follow you. They don't hitch themselves with Christian the almighty but Christian the man who does the right thing at all costs."

"I guess."

"You know I abhor that word. It is used as a replacement for disagreement without a defensible argument."

My mouth quirked in a half smile. "I suppose."

Hager's eyebrows met in the middle of his forehead and I had to laugh. I stood up and offered my hand.

"If you're done with your pep talk, we need to get moving."

"Did it work?"

My eyes narrowed. "I guess."

Chapter Five

W E ARRIVED IN LONDON on the red eye. It was the best time to hop the pond. You can catch forty winks, pretend you got a whole night's sleep, and your internal clock isn't FUBAR. I'm complaining, but it wasn't that bad. Not like Kandahar, where day was night, night was day, and the only thing keeping me from falling asleep in my soup was being surrounded by an entire country trying to kill me. Good times.

We landed at London City Airport, a small airport with an even smaller runway, which sat on the Thames right near Canary Wharf. I normally fly out of LaGuardia, with its famously short runways at just over seven thousand feet. Taking off from there required the pilot to climb faster on a steeper than normal angle. At London City Airport, the angle was nearly double the norm. Needless to say, I was anticipating our flight home for many reasons.

We had to charter a specific plane since only a handful were rated to land at this airport. On the plus side, we eliminated an hour of city driving from Heathrow. Our private plane had its own VIP customs check. The guy sitting behind the glass seemed disappointed with our lack of celebrity status and was trying to decipher why we merited the royal treatment. See what I did there.

"You guys making a movie or what?"

"Yeah," I said. "It's about an immortal race of puppet masters who have been pushing the human race into conflict since the beginning of time. A small band of supernaturally enhanced heroes battle against them in a desperate struggle to save the planet from their own shortsightedness."

Hager looked askance at me. The Border Force Officer glanced back at me, raised an eyebrow and said, "Sounds stupid."

"Pretty farfetched, right?"

He flipped through my passport, chose an empty page, stamped it, and handed it back to me.

I took it and waited. The man behind the glass raised his eyebrows at me.

"No welcome to the United Kingdom?"

He continued to stare at me without a reaction.

I said to Hager, "I told you we should have filmed this in Germany."

I picked up my bags and moved on.

"What happened to keeping a low profile?" Hager asked as he caught up with me.

"That was a low profile."

"Your fake movie struck a little close to the mark."

"Bah. It could have been the plot to Star Trek Fifteen,"

We gathered our group and exited the VIP area to be met by three members of the UK team. I recognized them from their files. Edward Thorne was past his middle years, wearing a three-piece suit and carrying a cane. He'd been the London Covenant Head for about seven years since his predecessor met his demise in a skirmish. The Bishop with him was Francesca Deluca, a young woman probably in her late twenties. She was tall and had a bold nose that seemed to work for her. She stared at me like I might take flight at any moment. Lieutenant Harris was small in stature but looked like she could bench-press me. Her tight, curly black hair was trimmed close to her scalp. She wore black fatigues and, I shit you not, a raspberry beret. I would have said something stupid but my brain was caught between the Prince song and; Aren't you a little short for a storm trooper?'

"Mr. Bateleur, I presume."

Edward Thorne flipped his cane into the crook of his arm, held out his hand with a smile, and introduced himself and his protégé.

"Great to meet you. Call me Christian." I grasped his hand and he captured it between the two of his.

"Christian. Fabulous, I will do so. And please call me Edward."

"Of course, thank you." His demonstrative mannerisms gave me pause. After a moment, I remembered my manners. "This is—"

"Mr. Hager needs no introduction. He led the London Covenant when I was just a lad. We must find time for a proper tea while you are here."

"Thank you, Edward, that would be lovely. I do hope we can find the time."

"Of course, of course."

"And this must be the famous John McCaw, son of the Creole Knight. One might say the public name to be a breach of the rules of secrecy but then our friend here has made that point moot."

John's eyes narrowed and his hand stopped half way in its proffered shake. Thorne reached out and grasped it with both hands, anyway. There was nothing in the Englishman's demeanor that suggested him to be anything but genuine. He finished pumping John's arm and moved quickly along.

"Soon-Li, how wonderful to see you again. How long has it been?" He captured her hand as he had the rest.

"Too many years to put a number to it."

The tightening of her facial muscles, and her grip, showed just what he was in for if he did put a number to it.

"I would not dare chance the ire of one who bested Tai-Fan."

He held her gaze for a few more heartbeats then glanced over at Lawrence.

Being somewhat new, I presumed Thorne was not as familiar with him. "This is Major Lawrence Mangine. He will be leading the military aspects of this mission."

Edward Thorne bobbed his head and casually motioned towards the woman dressed in black. "And that is Lieutenant Harris. Though I doubt we will be requiring their services, he can coordinate everything through her." Removing the cane from under his arm, he stepped up to me. "I have arranged a small repast back at the Covenant House, if you will follow me."

He pivoted on the toe of one of his highly polished Oxfords and headed for the exit. Francesca followed in step.

I looked at Hager who raised his eyebrows, the equivalent of calling him a dick. I was inclined to agree.

"I would rather we went to the scene of the crime."

He waved away my suggestion with the hand not swinging the cane, never looking back. "We have plenty of time for that later."

Edward Thorne never slowed, giving me the choice of following or yelling after him.

Lawrence leaned over to whisper in my ear. "The cars you requested are here."

Thorne stopped in his tracks.

I smiled and spoke in a normal volume to Lawrence. "Excellent, please get our gear stowed and everyone settled. I will be along in a minute."

Harris was a deer in the headlights, torn between following her superior officer or following the local head she was assigned to.

I solved her problem with one sentence. "Lieutenant, you're with us."

My team moved towards the two vehicles as Thorne finally turned to face me. I stood stock still, waiting, arms clasped behind my back. Other travelers passed around us and the twenty-foot gap he had created while he ran through his options. After a moment, a frown splayed across his face that he very nearly repressed. He leaned over to Francesca and mumbled something I didn't bother trying to hear. She nodded and continued in the direction they had been heading. Then he strode over to me as casually as he could. I could sense the tension radiating from him. By the time he reached me, he was once again in control of himself. Though he stopped so close as to be invading my personal space.

"I wish I had known you had arranged your own transportation."

I didn't step back and let the silence drag on for a hair too long. "We will be visiting the crime scene. You may follow if you wish."

✝

I wasn't tired, but I was hungry and had a caffeine withdrawal headache. However, since I had made visiting the scene into a thing, I couldn't give Thorne the satisfaction of showing it. Though he could probably hear my stomach growling, even without his enhanced senses.

The alley was not as deserted as I remembered from my vision but neither did it compare with the sea of people typically on a midtown Manhattan street.

He pointed with his cane. "There we are."

The image in my head blended with the location. This was definitely the place, though a few unimportant details had changed. The boxes that had been stacked were absent and the dumpster was pushed further back out of the way of the investigation. Crime scene tape barred entry to the alley, but it was blue with white writing instead of the black on yellow I was used to. The message didn't change: POLICE LINE - DO NOT CROSS. I ignored it just as quickly.

"Are you looking for anything in particular?" Thorne asked.

"I will know it when I see it," I answered without glancing at him. *Was that true?*

Hager's voice intruded on my concentration. I silently cursed myself for showing him how to project his thoughts into another's consciousness. It was a trick I'd picked up while buried alive in New Orleans. It appeared that most Bishops had the capability to some degree, though so far, no one could communicate past line of sight. The problem was, Hager usually held his tongue in mixed company. He no longer had that restriction.

I'm hoping I will know it when I see it, I sent back to him.

Oh, my.

That was the other issue with my new discovery. The connection was kind of like a mental phone call. Whatever a person thought came through until they hung up. I had greater control but everyone else sent through random thoughts as well as what they intended. Thankfully, it acted as a deterrent from overuse.

I reached out, letting the source of my power fill me up. It brought a familiar warmth, like bathing in sunlight on a cold winter's day. I had used my talents in the past to invoke true sight which allowed me to see other-worldly influences overlaid onto places within the physical world. Buildings used for nefarious activities would show decay and rot while those supporting more positive effects, like outreach programs, schools, and *some* churches (don't ask) would shine with an inner radiance.

For the most part, it didn't work on people. Humans are way too complex, evoking a myriad of points across the philosophical good to evil scale. Generally, trying to look at someone with true sight made me dizzy and nauseated. It rarely provided me with any useful insight. My hope was that my vision would extend to wicked presences that had recently passed by. I squeezed my eyelids shut and focused on pulling up said ability. When I thought I had it right, keeping my focus on the ground, I opened them.

I could see minor visual markers but little else. I steadied myself against the building and peered up at the city street, trying to avoid looking directly at anyone. The telltale signs manifested themselves here and there. The clearest depiction was a law firm that was split right down the middle. One side appeared post apocalyptic while the other was a lamp shade in the shape of a store front. I redirected my gaze back down the alley but didn't see anything suggesting either good or otherwise.

Look harder.

This voice was internal, I think. Though it did sound like the baboon from the Lion King. Where ever it came from, I thought the suggestion had merit. Could I increase the intensity of my view? I'd used a version of true sight to identify the veil separating dimensions when I created a portal to travel across Miami via the divine realm. Not something I'd done often since it required that I memorize the harmonic resonance of the place I was going. I had spent time doing just that in the underground stadium of the Manhattan Covenant. Being trapped in a cave is a great catalyst for re-prioritizing activities you haven't found time for before.

I focused on the ground and concentrated, trying to dial into the level of sight that would show me what I was looking for—almost like adjusting the focus on a camera or microscope. At least that's what I told my subconscious, hoping it would translate to the current application. A crimson splotch appeared, then vanished. I thought attempting to reverse the process would be more difficult so I just reset myself and started again. For a second time, the smudge came and went.

"Shit."

"Is there something specifically interesting about that spot on the pavement?" Thorne asked.

"Just give me a minute."

I put a little too much venom in my reply and then cursed my lack of restraint. I took a deep breath, trying to calm my anxiousness to find a clue quickly so I could claim victory. Speed would just make me miss it again.

Concentrate, slow, easy.

I started over, inching my way through the levels of sight. This time, I saw it coming. First it appeared like a decades old stain, then one more recent that had been scrubbed at. Finally, the dark red spill took on a hue like red wine on a white carpet.

"Got it!"

"Got what?" John asked.

"I can see the aura of what happened here."

"That's not possible," Thorne mocked.

Hager jumped to my defense. "You will find that being impossible does not seem to deter Mr. Bateleur."

I had to force myself not to smile and, instead, concentrate on the task at hand, not wanting to spoil the minor win by losing it. Looking around, I found this particular supernatural lens didn't have the dizzying effect that most of the others did. It was like using a filter to see a hidden word in a puzzle game. It just showed what was invisible to the naked eye.

The scene had been transformed into something out of Texas Chainsaw Massacre. There were red stains everywhere around the opening to the alley. Not blood, more like the remnants of a heinous act. The metaphysical manifestation of the violence that occurred on that spot. It was grotesque. My stomach lurched in a way that made me happy I had missed breakfast.

Dammit.

The first brick-colored blotch was a few paces before the alleyway's entrance. Further out, on the other side of it, was a large splash of dark purple intermingled with the crimson in a path leading deep into the darkened area between the buildings. Having witnessed this firsthand, I had an advantage and could extrapolate the meanings of the colors. Time to put on a show.

"The first victim died here." I pointed to the bright red spray in my view. "He was surprised, meaning his attacker came at him from behind. The second victim stood there and witnessed it. I'm seeing a massive amount of fear, panic even. Whomever was being controlled by the Tainted must have grabbed her because the path leading into the alley is filled with fear mixing with hate. Then it turns into a Jackson Pollock of death."

The team stared at me.

Thorne crossed his arms and frowned. "That aligns with the police report I received from my contact. They could find no other tracks out, however. They presume the perpetrator wore some kind of coverall that he removed after the fact."

"No," I said simply.

Thorne's eyes narrowed. "How do you mean?"

"He did leave tracks but they didn't go out." I redirected everyone's attention with a pointed finger. "He went up."

Chapter Six

"**I**'M GOING TO FOLLOW the trail," I said. "Soon-Li, care to join me?"

"Love to," she smiled.

Then she leapfrogged from wall to wall up the three stories until she was perched on the edge of one roof.

"Hager, take the rest of the team and trail us on the ground. I believe two people roof-hopping across London is plenty."

He stroked his beard. "Agreed."

Not to be outdone, I leapt straight up and gently stepped onto the roof just as gravity was about to take hold again.

"Show off," Soon-Li said as she climbed to her feet.

I didn't respond but, instead, connected to her mentally.

"*I have a feeling Thorne will be listening in.*"

"*Cōngmíng de.*"

"*English.*"

"*Gàisĭ. Sorry. You don't know how hard it is to think in another language. I said, smart.*"

"*I can imagine, and thanks.*"

"*Your jumping finesse has greatly improved. Is that the limit of your height?*"

"*No.*"

"*Lā shĭ. I guess I'm not the roof queen anymore.*"

"*You are still the queen.*" I put extra emphasis on the last word.

"*Hmph,*" she said audibly.

"*You told me Thorne was political and judgmental but I didn't realize it was to this degree.*"

"*His family is immensely wealthy, not including the Covenants' deep pockets, and he is connected to the royal house. His sense of superiority would be astonishing without the addition of his powers, His line would have intentions on the crown*" *if it wasn't expressly forbidden in our mandates."*

We continued leaping between roofs, following the invisible trail. London's views were not like those of New York or Miami. I apparently do this kind of thing a lot. There was something regal about the architecture. Even smaller buildings were created with the same care as their kin who stood tall, defining themselves against the skyline. Or I could have just been romanticizing the activity. Still, I felt the urge to break into a verse of Step In Time.

We were traveling west. This, luckily, didn't take us across any major roads that would have been difficult to cross. I was actually enjoying myself. This was freedom. Like skydiving, it was leaving the shackles of reality behind for a few brief moments—even gravity. We went soaring over buildings, trying to keep out of sight of people on their balconies. Well, less their view and more their phones.

"Any idea what we are dealing with?" Soon-Li switched to her outside voice.

"I'm not sure. I don't think we are following one of the Tainted. Maybe a minion of some kind. *Since this is my first time, I would only be guessing from there."* I added the last part through the mind meld. Hey, I figured out the power. I got to name it.

"How are you watching the trail and jumping?"

We landed and sprinted towards the other side.

"I'm not. I memorized the frequency of the vision and switched to it at the apex of our leap." We reached the edge and vaulted into the air again. Dropping lightly on the next building, I motioned for us to halt. "The tracks end."

"Here?"

I pointed at a small balcony across the street. It held two chairs with a small table between them and a large plant in one corner. A sliding glass door led into the apartment.

She regarded the area. "I'm sensing two people in there."

"I don't know why I've never asked this before but can you tell if one is a Converted?"

She met my gaze and her thin eyebrows pulled together. "No. Your trail is the closest we have come."

I smirked. "I'll have to work on that."

"Our bigger problem is that no matter how softly we land on that balcony, it will make noise. I wish we could unlock that door from here."

"Already done."

Soon-Li looked at me askance. "You've been doing more than a little training. You need to give yourself a break occasionally."

I ignored the statement. "You ready?"

She frowned but inclined her head. I counted down on my fingers. We jumped when I made a fist. In mid-air, I switched from putting energy into my leap to reaching out with a lick of force to yank open the door. As soon as our feet hit, we dashed into the apartment.

The scene was ghastly. Blood painted the walls from arterial spray. Other than that, there were no signs of a struggle. The source of this addition to the decor was prone on the floor. He was still twitching.

I spun around in time to see a figure in the frame of the open glass door.

"Are you kidding me?"

She was a person I could never forget. There she was in her red sari with its black hood, wearing a grin that I saw in my nightmares. She dropped off the balcony and disappeared. I moved to follow but Soon-Li grabbed me.

"What are you doing? I can't let her escape!"

She pointed at the man lying in a pool of his own blood. "Wounded first."

"Then you go after her."

"So she can slip back in and stick a knife in you? I don't think so."

"But—"

"Christian, stop arguing. Your most important directive is protecting life, even those touched by the Tainted. Stop wasting time."

I ground my teeth, knowing she was right. "Fine."

I knelt down next to the man, placing one hand on his head and the other over the slash across his throat. I had healed enough people that, while not completely muscle memory, it wasn't the struggle it had once been. The man stopped twitching and, with his windpipe now whole, he started breathing again.

"He'll live." I stood up and walked to the sink to wash my hands.

"He doesn't look so good."

"He lost a lot of blood. I can stitch together bone and tissue but I can't increase the production of hemoglobin. At least not that I know of." I scrubbed at my hands with more force than necessary. "That was Kali, wasn't it?"

Soon-Li didn't answer. I looked at her and she nodded.

"I wasn't sure if you would remember her."

"You don't forget someone who throws a dumpster at you." I rinsed off and tore a paper towel off the roll next to the sink, then turned to face her. "I didn't connect their resemblance till now."

She pressed her lips into a thin line, unable or unwilling to speak. I pulled out my phone and called Hager. When he answered, I gave him the address that I read off a stack of mail on the table.

"We are almost there."

"One more thing. Someone needs to call Tira and let her know that her sister is in the UK. She just tried to kill the suspect."

Chapter Seven

THE UK COVENANT WAS unlike anything I had experienced as a house of Bishops. For one thing, the building itself predated the United States. In fact, at nine hundred years it was as old as Yoda. The kicker was that its name was St. Bartholomew the Great. I'll say it again, you can't make this shit up. John Candy would be so proud.

The church itself was massive, with a bell tower consisting of five bells. It had been featured in many movies, including Four Weddings and a Funeral, Shakespeare in Love, and Avengers: Age of Ultron, to name a few.

Even with the masses, the tours, and the filming, the secrecy of the Covenant was maintained thanks to an off-limits, cramped circular staircase. They kept random stonework dating back to the twelfth century in the small room at the top. At the far end, behind caution tape, a hidden elevator took you to the catacombs deep below the church. Dug out at the same time as Great St. Barts, the impeccably tiled catacombs were maze-like. So, getting lost was a real possibility.

We did a deep dive into our suspect while he recovered in the medical wing. Donald Johnson was a bank executive who had done well for himself. He made a comfortable living, though he never left London. He was engaged up until about two months before. Based on social media, he and Sabrina had been dating since they were in grade school. They had grown up, gone to separate colleges—sorry, universities—but still maintained their relationship and moved in together shortly thereafter. He had found his career in the banking industry and she had pursued photography.

About a year ago, she began traveling for work and, obviously, fell in love with it. You could see the passion lighting up her face with each new post. The subjects of her pictures included buildings, landscapes, and local people in their daily grind. Not being much of a critic, I considered them okay.

"It's exquisite." Soon-Li apparently was more adept than I was.

"It's a guy smoking in a bar."

"See the way she captures the mood? She uses the natural light coming in through the only window. Rays piercing the dark interior. The smoke has an ethereal effect as it drifts around his face."

I squinted, hoping it would reveal the mysteries of the photo. It did not. "Looks like a Marlboro ad."

She sighed.

Not long after, Sabrina had changed her relationship status to single. It took Donald another two weeks before he did likewise. Soon-Li swiveled in her chair.

"So, we have a woman who was engaged to the same man she played with as a child. Her career brought her to new places where she experienced life outside of what could be found in the streets of London. Mr. Johnson was tied to his job or had no interest in things beyond the city where he grew up. She wanted more than he could give her, so she left."

"Wait, so he became so pissed at losing her he killed two people?"

Soon-Li shrugged. "Possible."

"I'm not buying it. *Donald*—" I said the name in a whiny voice. "—had one parking ticket in his life. I challenge anyone to go through life without at least that." I scrolled further through the file. "The guy was a literal boy-scout."

"King's Scout Award recipient," Soon-Li corrected.

"Whatever. I can't see how he went from that to double homicide, even with a murder whisperer in your ear."

"Did you ever go through a breakup?"

"Too many to count."

"No dark thoughts afterwards?"

"Why? You make a connection and hope it will work out but the odds are against it. When it ends, you move on."

Soon-Li cocked her head at me. "Sounds like something we should dig into a little deeper at some point."

I frowned at her.

"Have you been madly in love with someone, and without warning, they've left you?"

"Oh. Well, no."

"Because you were never that invested in the relationship."

I shrugged.

"What if Marie left you?"

I opened my mouth to speak but found no words available. Ours had been a very fast developing romance, at least for me. I sometimes wondered if it was the same for her but never put any deep thought into it. I considered her leaving and it scared me— gave me an actual shiver.

Soon-Li could see I was following her. "Take that feeling and add a decade getting comfortable with someone. This is not just some person you met in a bar."

Or who arrested you, I mentally added.

"This is someone you grew up with; a person who was always by your side. Both families presumed marriage. They most likely talked about it over dinner, making plans for years. One day you see your life all plotted out, a clear path leading you to your supposed nirvana, and the next—everything has changed. You start to question who you are without the person that you thought made you complete. Now, are you getting it?"

"I suppose. But when it comes down to it, she didn't want him. Why expend so much energy on someone who doesn't feel the same? If she was a con artist that robbed him of all his money, fine. If she abused him physically or mentally, understandable. But she just rejected him."

"And sometimes that can hurt worse than anything."

I sighed. "If I took rejection that hard, I would have to kill half the women in Manhattan."

"Then, for their sake, I'm glad you are so well adjusted."

I pursed my lips. The door opened and Tira stepped in with Hager and John. Soon-Li stood up and pulled her into an embrace.

"How are you doing?"

"I'm okay. At least we found her again."

I waited for what I thought was an appropriate amount of time before saying, "Can someone catch me up?"

Soon-Li gave me the side eye that told me it hadn't been long enough.

Tira sat, the rest of us following suit.

"This is your sister? The one married to Rich?"

She shook her head.

"I'm confused. How many sisters do you have?"

"Two."

"And one of them is a Converted?"

Hager put a hand on my shoulder. I took a deep breath and said, "Maybe you should start from the beginning."

Tira needed a few moments to collect her thoughts, then met my gaze.

"We are triplets. I was born first. Kamala—Kali as you know her—was second. Matrika was last."

"Kamala? Isn't that the name of your niece?"

"Her namesake. My sister was a good child; selfless, caring but incredibly ambitious and competitive. It turned into a jealous streak that rivaled Indra. She always complained that she should have been born two minutes earlier.

"She wanted your power?"

"Yes. Were it possible, I would have gladly given it to her. She graduated high school at fifteen and Harvard at seventeen. By thirty, she was one of the richest women on the planet. None of it made her happy. She disappeared for a few years shortly after. The next time we ran into her was during an op that both my father and I were on together. The creepy smile she wore told me our encounter was not by chance. She named herself after the Hindu God of destruction. A fitting name since I have rarely spoken to any of my family since." She stared off into space for a few seconds before regaining control of herself. "We never could figure out which of the Tainted had converted her."

"Since we found her in New York last year, could she have aligned herself with Baldemar?"

"Possibly," Hager said. "That was what we were trying to determine when you...bumped into her."

That had been my first contact with the Tainted when I followed him into an alley and nearly got myself killed. "Which is when you lost her, thanks to me."

He didn't deny it. Hager wasn't the type to wave off culpability simply to spare someone's feelings, though he didn't rub my nose in it, either. When had he stopped doing that?

"More likely, she just latched on to a plan that might have put an end to both her siblings."

"She wants you dead?"

Tira shrugged. She fiddled with something in her hands, drawing my attention. It was a laminated, folded piece of paper—a bookmark. It took me a minute to remember where I had seen it before. A security guard had used it six months ago. It had been the final puzzle piece that allowed us to foil Baldemar's plans. The guard she had been forced to kill, and whose eyes she had stared into while he died. The repercussions of one of my plans that had gone awry.

"What are the chances we can convince her to reconsider?" I asked.

Tira looked away.

Hager said, "There is always hope."

A knock came at the door and Major Mangine stuck his head in. "Our guest is awake."

I glanced at Hager. "Let's see what he has to say."

The holding rooms on this side of the pond were even more comfortable than in the States. Both versions doubled as overflow for visiting Bishops—basically, bedrooms that locked from either side. These also had built-in drawers and televisions mounted behind bullet-proof glass.

The Major didn't bother to knock. Mr. Johnson was not a guest. He didn't lack culpability anymore than someone did when they drove while under the influence. He was a murder suspect who was as close to being caught red-handed as was possible.

Donald sat up. A portable IV pump was standing by his bedside, feeding a saline solution into his veins to replace the fluids he'd lost. There wasn't a scar, thanks to the healing I had performed. At least not a physical one.

Mangine stepped in and dragged the only chair to face the bed, before standing off to the side. He was close enough to intervene should our guest get squirrely, I sat.

"Mr. Johnson, my name is Christian. How are you feeling?"

"Okay, I guess. Am I in a hospital?"

"Not quite. But let's hold off on that question for a bit. Do you remember what happened to you?"

His hand went unconsciously to his throat. "I was attacked."

"Do you know by whom?"

His eyes darted from me to the Major and back, attempting to suss out what we knew. It was clear he was not in a hospital. Mangine's uniform was militaristic in its design but wasn't police issued. Nor was he handcuffed to the bed. I suspected he was trying to find an answer without implicating himself. I wondered how much he was really aware of.

"Some woman I met in a bar."

"Which bar?" I probed.

"Carwash."

"What was her name?"

He hesitated. "Not sure."

"What happened then?"

"I took her back to my place."

I set my elbow on the arm of the chair and cupped my chin with three fingers. "So, you bumped into this lady at a bar, didn't ask for her name, and suggested moving the party back to your place."

"Yeah…I mean, no."

"Which is it?"

Blinking, he glanced to the right. "We had a few drinks first."

"Ah. Any dancing?"

He gave me a confused look but answered anyway, "Some."

"Got it. So, drinking, dancing, then off to your place for a nightcap."

"Yes."

"You and Jackie."

"Kali." He closed his eyes and bit his lip at the slip.

"So you did know her name?"

"Uh, yeah. I had forgotten until now."

I tapped my forehead. "Of course, what with all that drinking and dancing you were doing."

"Right."

"Then you and Kali retired to your apartment."

He nodded.

"Was that before or after you killed your ex-fiancé?"

"After."

"Thank you." I stood up.

"Wait, no."

I halted my exit.

"Oh, it was before? Jaunt home for a little nookie, then, while the passions were high, you cooked up the scheme to kill her."

"No!"

"See, now I'm confused." I turned to the Major. "Are you confused?"

He stared back at me without responding.

"See, he's speechless. There are only two options. You either came up with a plan to kill her in cold blood or you shot her in the heat of passion."

"Stabbed. NO! I mean, I didn't kill her!"

"Look, Mr. Johnson, can I call you Don?"

He blinked at me. I took it as acceptance.

"Great. So, Don, you have admitted to Sabrina's murder. You confirmed the method she was killed and that you know the woman who supposedly tried to kill you. And the best part is we have it all on record."

I pointed at the small camera in the corner. Don found it and looked like he was about to cry.

"At this point, I can simply hand you and the recording over to the police. Most of the information connecting the two of you came from them anyway. I'm pretty sure the DA, or whatever they are called here, will have a slam dunk of a case. We even have a motive. She dumped you, throwing you into a rage. If you couldn't have her, no one could. Right?"

"NO!"

"Oh, so you are going with the Clinton version of the truth. Deny, deny, deny." I performed the last with a poor impression of the ex-president.

"I killed her but it wasn't me!"

"Well, that makes perfect sense. Major, release him."

Mangine made no move to follow through on my request.

Donald let his head drop into his hands. "You don't understand."

"You're right, Don." I sat back down. "How about you start from the beginning? This time make it a good story—one with all the facts."

He wiped at his eyes and sniffed. I grabbed a tissue out of the box on the nightstand and handed it to him. He took it without acknowledgement, blew his nose, and threw it in the small trash bin next to the bed.

"Sabrina broke up with me. You were right about that. I couldn't believe it. We had spent nearly our whole lives together and she wanted to throw that all away."

"And that made you angry," I prompted.

Don shook his head. "Not at first. Mostly sad. That's what led me to going out at night. I just couldn't stand being alone in our apartment."

"You could move," I suggested.

"We had just renewed our lease." There was venom in that statement. "Let's do it for two years." He said in a mocking, high-pitched voice. "It'll lock in the price and we love this place so much. I can't imagine moving." Don coughed out a laugh.

"Three months later, she was gone." He pulled another tissue from the box and dabbed at his nose. "Anyway, like I said, that was when I started going out. Most nights, I sat at the bar and nursed a beer. One night I was really hurting and chugged it as soon as the bartender handed it over. Then I followed it up with a few more. It was the first time I felt good in a while. When I got home, I was too drunk to notice all the little reminders of her. In the morning, I was too sick. It became a ritual. Work, bar, sleep."

"When did it change?"

"When I met Kali. She treated me like the most interesting person in the world. Hung on every word, laughed at all my stupid jokes. She was gorgeous and into me. *Me.* The banker. Night after night, I would talk about how sad I was about Sabrina leaving and she never said a word against her. She was shocked as to why she would do it. I started to feel the same way. If this beautiful, interesting woman was into me, what was wrong with Sabrina? Kali traveled for work, too, but she still seemed excited to return to me."

"She wasn't with you every night?"

"No, she was a flight attendant. She would be gone days at a time and bring me back little trinkets from wherever she had been."

I looked at Soon-Li, who raised her eyebrows.

"Major, package the prisoner up and pass him over to the constabulary with all the evidence we collected."

I thought Don's jaw would actually hit the table. "What? I assumed you were going to help me?"

"I did. You are alive and I have given you the opportunity to unburden your soul to us. Don't you feel better?"

"I will go to jail."

"Well, yeah. You murdered two people."

"But that wasn't me!"

"While you may have been helped along the way, the person that shoved the knife into Sabrina was definitely you."

Soon-Li and I left the room. Don continued to declare that it wasn't his fault and would probably continue to do so well into his incarceration. The Major never said a word while cuffing him.

Out in the hall, Soon-Li said, "She has several fish on the line."

"My thoughts exactly. We need to find her before she finishes corrupting them."

I started walking and Soon-Li matched my pace.

"What if we did it the other way?"

"How would we do that?"

"I've been working with other technically savvy Bishops over the past few months. We have been creating an open source AI."

I looked at her askance. "Open source? Us?"

"Well, open source among the Bishop community."

"That's more like it."

"We'll share with law enforcement at some point, especially since we included all of their data in teaching the model."

"What's the plan?"

"We can build a profile from Don's social media and use it to find men who are in similar circumstances."

"Very good, Number One. Make it so."

Soon-Li stopped and regarded me, forcing me to stop and face her.

"It was a reference to Star Trek, the Next Generation."

She shook her head. "I was thinking how like your mother you are."

"She quoted movies, too?"

"God, no. Or at least not to your obsessive degree."

"I wouldn't call it obsessive."

"I meant in your demeanor. How you deal with people. You knew what I intended all along, didn't you? Or had the same thought yourself? But you allowed me to present the information to you, then complimented me on my insight."

"While my powers are growing, I cannot yet read minds."

"Stop talking like Amram and that is not a denial."

I put a hand on her shoulder and smiled. "I would be a fool to try to manipulate you." Leaving her standing in the hall, I called back, "Let me know when you have something."

"That's still not a denial."

Chapter Eight

"I STOOD ON THE block watching the quiet house on Private Drive with a feeling that all of this had happened before."

"This is Meadway, in Barnet. North of London," Soon-Li pointed out. "And why are you narrating our search with a British accent?"

I put my hands on my hips. "Because it's fun."

We had just arrived via a Covenant car: a Mercedes S class which Soon-Li drove, as she had more experience driving on the left. Though, I didn't see how anyone could screw it up. Every street had little blue signs with thick white arrows reminding drivers which side to stay on.

"This is my first trip to the UK and I haven't even had time to visit Big Ben or Stonehenge. I've got to see *that* before I leave."

Soon-Li shrugged. "Why? It was just a failed experiment."

"I'm sorry, what?"

"Back in the early days, we thought aligning the stones with the summer solstice would allow us to communicate with the Heavens."

"So they made a radio for speaking to God?"

Soon-Li shook her head. "You should set up more sessions with Tira."

"I don't need psychotherapy. With the financial backing of the Covenant, I'm just eccentric."

"And what were you before?"

"A blue-collar worker."

"Speaking of Tira, was it a good idea to leave her behind?"

"We haven't confirmed if this guy is connected to her sister yet. I would rather not drag her through the mire until it's absolutely necessary."

"So nice of you. Maybe you should have asked her?"

I ignored her. "Shall we drop in on..." I checked the list. "Frank?"

We crossed the street, approaching the small brick and white stucco cross gabled house with a large bay window that almost seemed ill-fitting. The manicured lawn was framed with flagstones and the cobblestone drive was in a losing battle against weeds. It was nearly indistinguishable from the houses on either side, with minor variations. What stood out the most were the telephone poles. There were only two and they weren't connected. Wires streamed out in all directions like a giant maypole. It made this scene familiar, yet foreign.

Walking up the drive, around the bushes that hid the walkway in front, we got to the door and I knocked.

"What is our cover story?" Soon-Li asked.

"How about the truth?"

"That will work. Hi, Frank, you don't know us, but we think a pretty girl is coercing you to kill your ex-girlfriend."

"Maybe not that much truth."

He didn't answer. So, I extended my senses to see if he was pretending not to be home. According to people where he worked, he had COVID and wasn't expected to return for a few days. I heard nothing, but...

Soon-Li met my gaze. "I think we're too late."

"You smell it too?"

She nodded.

"Let's go around the back."

The rear was meticulously maintained, with an outdoor kitchen and multiple seating areas. I took it all in.

"Nice yard."

"Garden," Soon-Li corrected.

"Yeah, I see the garden. It's nice too."

"No, in the UK, the area surrounding the house is the garden."

"They don't say yard?"

"They do, but it refers to an area that has been covered with concrete."

"So, a patio."

Soon-Li shrugged.

"Weird country."

"They would say the same about the US."

A sliding glass door looked into the kitchen. The smell's origin became obvious. Frank was hanging from the exposed rafters. The hangman's noose was fashioned out of a long, red extension cord. I pulled out my phone and called the UK Covenant so they could notify the authorities. I didn't want to get pulled in with the locals.

"At least he had a better concept of hanging than most," Soon-Li said.

I put my phone away. "Why do you say that?"

"The step ladder."

"I need more."

"It gave him more height," a voice answered from behind us.

It was Tira.

I frowned at her. "Are you following us?"

Tira crossed her arms. "No, I asked Confucius to inform me of the results of any analysis Soon-Li was doing."

"I'm sorry, who?" I asked, screwing up my face.

"My new AI," Soon-Li added, still examining the body without touching it.

"You named your AI Confucius?"

She shrugged. "I thought it appropriate."

To Tira, I said, "Sneaky."

"No more so than you leaving to investigate Kali without me."

"You can't investigate your sister."

"This isn't a cop show. There is no evidence to contaminate. We aren't trying to bring charges against her. And she ceased to be my sister when she was converted."

I tried to come up with an argument but none seemed viable.

"You think the ladder is some kind of connection to Kali?" Soon-Li prompted.

Tira touched her lip with the tip of a finger. "She went through a phase where capital punishment fascinated her—the different types employed throughout the ages and across the world."

"Still not getting it."

"There is a calculation for the optimal drop distance depending on the victim's weight. Most people use a chair, which results in stran-gulation rather than a broken neck. There were plenty of chairs and counters he could have used. So, he was more informed."

"He could have just looked it up online."

She didn't quite roll her eyes at me but the sentiment was the same. "Why don't we go before the police arrive?"

The next house on the list was even further along in an investiga-tion, as it had police tape across the front door. Tira had joined our carpool since she had taken a rideshare to the previous location.

I glanced at the two ladies. "Shall we see what we can find?"

Tira frowned. "Why bother? Kali will not be back here; it's a dead end."

I nearly drew blood from biting my tongue as Soon-Li pulled away from the curb. As we approached the next house, a green BMW backed out of the driveway.

I pointed. "That's him. Can you follow discreetly?"

Soon-Li's eyebrow lifted. "Is it the fact that I'm a woman or Asian that is making you question my ability? Maybe the combination?"

I rolled my eyes. "In this case, I'm using *can you* as a replacement for *would you, please*."

She sniffed and began tailing the car loosely. The last few months as Veil Warden (I have John to thank for that colorful title) had me working in close quarters with her. As she was an old friend of my mother, I had the benefit of being regaled with story after story from their youth. This was good and bad. Some stories included portions that no child should learn about their mother. She skipped those parts once she realized where the tale was going but she was usually too engrossed in the telling to remember who her audience was. Mom was, apparently, a free spirit before settling down with my father.

It also became clear that Soon-Li was on a mission to stamp out unconscious bias. She lived through times where her gender, beauty, and heritage were all used against her. She didn't appear angered by the blindness of her fellow humans, but tried to remind people it existed and needed attention. I was used to it now and could hear when my statements failed to express my true meaning. I was a believer in the whole sticks and stones philosophy, sure. But that didn't mean I should toss words around with careless abandon. Neither words nor bullets could pierce my skin. Not everyone was so fortunate.

"Where ever he's going, it's in a hurry," Soon-Li said.

"Did he notice us?" Tira asked.

"I don't think so. He has been pretty consistent, just driving fast and impatiently."

We passed out of the suburbs and into a more urban environment with a gritty edge to it. Turning down Albany Road, he pulled onto Haywood Street—more of a mini alley. We passed him and parked in what used to be a driveway but was now blocked by short-term fencing. The tan and ivory, twelve story building to our left looked to have been the pinnacle of high end living forty or fifty years ago. The grime, graffiti, and overgrown planting beds told a different story. Two additional buildings in similar disrepair framed the large courtyard which held the vestiges of a community garden. Now, what was left of a greenhouse, random furniture, shipping pallets, and the occasional shopping cart created a haven for nocturnal creatures. Some of them walked on two feet.

I stared at him through the passenger window. "He's kidding, right?" I glanced at my two companions. "This is clearly a trap. There might as well be ominous music playing in the background."

Tira shrugged. "Men are infamous for poor decisions when blood flow has been redirected away from their brains."

"Can't argue there. I'll follow. You two stay close but keep out of sight. I don't want to spook Kali."

We all hopped out. Soon-Li spied a walkway that ran along the first set of apartments fifteen feet above street level.

"I'll keep lookout from there."

With that, she took a few steps, leapt, bounded off a pillar, and vaulted over the parapet.

"I'm going to circle around and come in from the other side," Tira informed me.

She blurred out of sight before I could respond. I glanced about for witnesses to her departure but, of course, she was too smart for that.

I tried to walk nonchalantly, though I'm not sure I was selling it. Kali wasn't just another Converted to me. Ignoring the fact that she was Tira's sister, she was my introduction to the supernatural: the pivot point from which my world had shifted, never to right itself. I had built her up in my mind as an unstoppable force. Logically, I knew she didn't stand up to any of the Tainted I had already faced. She had to be a pale comparison to Uji's skill, Anton's strength, or Baldemar's evil. Though, I had never encountered the last in anything besides a game of wits—which I'd won, of course.

But Kali was my boogie man; my monster under the bed. Confronting her would be like facing my inadequacies in persona. It was irrational but it didn't stop the sweat from rolling down my spine. All this without considering her kinship to Tira, which meant that when I confronted her this time, I couldn't kill her. I had removed the taint from a few people, with mixed results. In most cases where the victim survived, they had an underlying wish to be free of the influence. I didn't know if Kali wanted freedom. Based on Tira's description, she seemed to have pursued this path. Was she an addict helpless against the pull or a deranged killer whose lust for power existed separately from the blood that gave it to her?

"What was this guy's name again?" I asked into the com in my ear.

"Mark Stay."

"Really? Did his ancestors not travel? Here are the Millers. They have ground wheat into flour for hundreds of years. Next to them are the Bakers whose prowess with their craft has kept us salivating for generations and, finally, the Stays…who didn't go anywhere."

"Or maybe it's referencing the strong rope that supports a ship's mast. A critical part of every sailing vessel." Tira offered.

I blinked. "That's not as funny."

"Are you done?" Soon-Li asked.

"For now."

Mark turned right and I crept up behind, peeking around the

corner. He made his way to the open-air stairway of the building on the right. I waited, watching him as he came into view on each floor before climbing to the next. Most of the doors and windows were covered by large pieces of sheet metal. On the fourth floor, he started down the walkway, checking the apartment numbers of those still visible.

"Soon-Li, do you see anyone?"

"No one from my position."

"Nor here. I would think there'd be someone around," Tira chimed in before I asked.

I sprinted forward and leapt to the fourth floor railing, hopping over and putting my back against the wall of the stairwell.

"He didn't hear you," Soon-Li informed me.

I glanced down the walkway. Then I blurred to the nearest pillar, continuing that way as I moved closer. I was only one column behind him when he finally reached the unit he was looking for at about the midpoint of the building. He took a second to adjust his appearance, checking his breath. I engaged my enhanced senses just as his hand reached out to knock.

"Kali, it's Mark. What was so urgent?"

His solid rap on the door was followed by the distinctive *slick-slick* of a pump-action shotgun. Tira yelled my name as I kicked into another blur. I tackled Mark a hair's breadth before the shotgun rang out. I was able to get *him* clear at least, just not both of us.

Chapter Nine

P AIN BLOOMED ON MY side as the force of the blast sent me reeling. I landed next to Mark instead of on top of him. He stared at me uncomprehendingly. His lips formed the word 'who' as three more rounds tore through the door. He decided he didn't care and did his first smart thing. He started running. Unfortunately, it was in the wrong direction, away from his car and into the warren that was the local gang's sanctuary.

"Christian, are you okay?"

Soon-Li's panicked voice crackled over the com. I wasn't but neither was I admitting that. I could already feel my body healing.

I said through gritted teeth, "Fine, get after Mark."

More gunfire followed his progression down the hall, which meant that these apartments were filled with gang members tasked with ending Mr. Stay's life.

"Great."

The guy who shot me stared through the gaping hole in the door.

"Who da fuck is dis? He not da guy in da picture." He opened it and stepped out, seeing his quarry fleeing down the walkway. "There's da fuck nut."

As he raised the shotgun, I back-armed him in the shins. His legs were swept out from under him and he landed on his face. Cursing again, he looked over at me.

I scowled at him. "You shot me. It hurt."

I grabbed him by the hair and slammed his head into the floor, knocking him out. Three guys followed him out of the apartment, taking in the scene without grasping what was happening. In their eyes, two guys were down. One was a member of their gang and their supposedly easy target was sprinting away like a jackrabbit pursued by a fox.

I got to my feet slowly so as not to spook them. They didn't see who'd neutralized their friend and I was lying on my side, so not yet labeled a threat. I wobbled a little more than my injuries warranted as I stood. One of the three stepped in close and stuck a MAC-10 under my chin. It was an optimal sub-machine gun for gangs in this area because of its compact design for easy concealment and its eleven-hundred round per minute firing rate. I was still healing, so superpowers were off for now. I seriously needed to find a way around this one power at a time bullshit.

But here's the thing; despite Major Mangine's accusations to the contrary, I am not just a Bishop. I'm a highly trained member of the Airborne Rangers. Gangs ruled by intimidation. Stick an automatic weapon in a normal person's face you get panic and compliance. Do that to a Ranger and you get a pissed off Ranger. The Washington Crips gang found that out in 1989. The UK gangs were about to learn the same lesson.

I had my attacker disarmed and on his knees before the pain from my first strike could register. One hand held him in a wrist-lock while the other gripped his MAC-10. I kicked the guy behind him in the chest, launching him and his mate back into the room they had just left. Before they landed, I smacked my captive in the face with his own gun, then tossed it over the railing. Other members were coming out of the remaining rooms. So I started after Mark, nearly slipping in the pool of my blood. I cold-cocked the first one out, who crumpled in a semi-conscious heap. After a quick glance, I realized who I had punched and sucked in air through my teeth.

"Sorry, lady."

I didn't feel too bad since she was holding a forty-five and cursing me like Eminem in a rap battle. The residents of the following unit were already out on the walkway. I threw one off the balcony, making sure he had a grip on the railing, and elbowed the guy coming to his rescue. The two women with them weren't armed as far as I could see and I didn't have time to search them.

I pointed backwards. "You may want to help your friend."

They both gave me the finger.

"Stop flirting and get moving," Soon-Li reprimanded over the com. "They are almost on him. The only thing saving him from a bullet is that people keep getting in the way."

Weeding through the throng of adversaries was taking too much time. An idea had come into my head and I didn't want to contemplate its epic degree of stupidity. I hopped up on the railing, careful of the guy dangling, and jumped, scrambling up to the next level. Pain shot through my side and back, which was filled with pellets. The door had slowed the bullets enough to limit the damage somewhat. Fortunately, all the training I had been doing saved me from plummeting to my demise. I was almost healed but there was no guarantee I'd be able to engage any other powers before I went splat. My feet hit the floor and I took off at a sprint.

"Are you still healing?" Soon-Li asked.

"Yeah. Frigging buck shot takes forever."

"You're crazy."

"No argument there. Tira, where are you?"

"Coming around the other way. Almost to you."

Soon-Li informed me, "You are catching up to Mark. How are you going to get to him?"

"You probably don't want to know."

"You're not going to try to fly again, are you? You just said you're still healing and you can't glide consistently."

"Sometimes, you just have to say, what the fuck, make your move."

"That doesn't apply to jumping off a five story balcony and hoping a set of faith wings will catch you."

I picked up speed. "Just give me a countdown."

She grunted in frustration. "Three."

Another hole closed. I felt the steel pellet drop into my shirt. I thought there were two left but couldn't be sure. The pain was all but gone.

"Two."

I calculated a launch point ahead of me and focused on it. Another slug fell.

"One!"

I hopped up onto the railing and launched myself out into the air, fixing an image in my mind of two gossamer wings unfurling off of my back and catching the air. I reached the apex of my jump and dropped.

The curse was just forming on my lips when the last steel ball dropped out and my wings popped open like a parachute. Riding the air, I streaked into the horde of assassins pursuing Mark. Apparently, just shooting him was not good enough anymore. Hitting them from above, I took down those in front and the rest tripped over them. I tucked and rolled, coming back up and into a blur. It took no time to catch up to Mark.

I yanked him back by the collar. "Where the hell are you going?"

He turned around. His panicked expression changed to shock when he saw me instead of someone pointing a gun,

"What...?"

His question was cut off by what sounded like a platoon of guns being cocked simultaneously. My brain went into overdrive, outlining options. *I* could escape the hail of bullets but I couldn't drag Mark with me. My defenses could shield against some but I didn't have the reserves to deflect them all. No other options came to mind. I pulled Mark to me and hardened my skin, waiting for the pummeling. Bon Jovi played in my head.

Chapter Ten

A CRASH CAME FROM behind me a moment before the firing started. I turned to see Tira holding a metal door blocking the assault.

"I can't hold them forever."

I picked up Mark, who was incoherently babbling while pointing at my fellow Bishop, and slung him over my shoulder.

"What are you doing? Put me down!"

I hopped over the short wall as Mark let out a very feminine screech. I stopped our fall at each floor by grabbing the balustrade, forcing a grunt out of my passenger. We hit the ground as Tira landed next to me in a crouch.

"Thanks for the assist."

She curled her lip as if she found my statement unnecessary. Then, stepping up to the nearest door, kicked it in. I put Mark back on his feet and he tried to rabbit again.

I grabbed his arm and yanked him back. "You want to stay alive, you stay with us."

Tira glanced back at me and I shrugged.

"I always wanted to say that."

I pushed our guest through the door. The apartment was occupied despite the blocked entrance. Two gang members came around the corner brandishing automatic weapons. A twist of Tira's wrist and one was disarmed; his hand held palm up over his head, straining against the pain in his elbow. The other, she punched in the throat. He dropped his gun and grabbed at his neck. Her foot snaked out, catching him across the face dropping him to the floor. She glanced at the guy who was still trying to relieve the pressure on his arm. He visibly paled and started shaking. Another manipulation of his arm and the remaining guy was on his back. She kicked him, knocking him out cold. Mark stood there, openmouthed.

I said, "I thought doctors were supposed to do no harm."

"They'll be fine in a few hours. They won't feel any worse than they would've otherwise."

She flipped a hand towards the alcohol and drugs sitting in the corner before navigating her way through the apartment.

Mark shook his head. "I'm not sure who is worse, you people or the gang."

I pushed him to follow. "They are, trust me."

"Why should I?"

"'Cause we're the good guys."

He looked back at the men lying on the floor.

"Okay, we're the less bad guys."

We exited into an interior hallway as more opponents thundered out of a nearby stairwell. Tira ripped the door across from us off the hinges and slid it down the hall. It hit the jumble of people at ankle height, causing them to be tossed around like bowling pins.

Mark frowned at me

"What? Everyone loves a good antihero."

I nudged him through the now doorless opening. This apartment was occupied as well, but the residents were not in, luckily for them. We made our way towards the door to Ravenstone, a tiny street in front of the building meant for accessing the garages. Soon-Li screeched to a stop on Bagshot Street, which ran parallel. Tira jumped in the front seat and I shoved Mark forcefully into the back and climbed in after him. We took a right on Mina Road before making our way back to the Covenant House. Mark swiveled to look through the back window, watching his nightmare shrink in the distance.

"You can drop me anywhere. I will make my way home on my own." He had a whiney way of speaking that, now that we were clear of the danger, was annoying me.

Tira cocked her head towards him. "You aren't going anywhere just yet. First, you need to tell us what you know about Kali."

He settled back in his seat and took on an air of fake confusion.

"Kali? Indian goddess, I believe. I don't have any more information than Wikipedia. Maybe try there." He pointed out the side window. "This spot looks tickety boo. How about you pull over here?"

I tried to shift my role to good cop since Tira apparently had chosen her role. It was not my area of expertise, sure, but I gave it a shot.

"Mr. Stay, I appreciate you wanting to get back home, especially after this harrowing experience. However, we believe you do know Kali."

"I'm not sure why you would come to that conclusion."

I huffed. "How about that when you saw her twin sister, you almost swallowed your tongue?"

Tira waved from the front.

"Or, I don't know, it could have been that you called out her name before you knocked."

I needed to work on my good cop. Mr. Stay studied his hands as he fiddled with his tie.

Soon-Li glanced in the rearview mirror. "All that will have to wait. They're back."

I checked out the rear window at two cars and three motorcycles coming up fast. "Can you lose them?"

"Probably, but not without alerting every cop in the city. And I can't scrub our trail while driving."

"Tira, can you switch with her?"

She rolled her eyes. "I'm a doctor, not a race car driver."

"Did you say that on purpose?"

"What?"

"It's just that—"

"Christian!" Soon-Li hollered

"Sorry."

Thinking for a second, I came up with a quick solution.

"Soon-Li open your window."

I hit the toggle button for mine. She glanced at me in the mirror with a perplexed expression. Then her eyes went wide.

"This is crazy."

"No time for a better plan. Throw it into cruise and put your seat back all the way. Mark?"

Mr. Stay was staring back at the approaching vehicles, fear etched on his face.

"Mark!"

He glanced at me.

"When I get out, move into my spot."

"Get out? Where are you going?"

"Don't ask questions. Just do it." I grabbed his shoulder to make sure I still had his attention. "Okay?"

He nodded. His glasses bobbed with the rapid movement.

"Ready?" I asked Soon-Li.

"As much as I can be."

Tira reached over and put a hand on the steering wheel.

"Now!"

I climbed out onto the roof of the car as Soon-Li tilted her seat back. She grabbed the handle over the window and pulled herself into the backseat. Two gang members pulled alongside on a motorcycle. The passenger was about to bash in the rear window when he noticed me. I slid across the roof, kicked the rider, and swung into the driver's seat. The bike wobbled as the driver tried to regain control but went down. I punched the gas and struggled not to fall backwards. Then I triggered the seat back while trying to keep the car on the road.

I gave thanks for this being one of the few automatic transmission cars in Europe. High speed driving on the opposite side of the road in a foreign country was going to be tough enough. If I had to shift with my left hand, I would really be screwed.

I made a hard left onto the A2 and was nearly creamed by a huge, red double-decker bus. The driver slammed on their brakes, letting loose a string of curses including several variations I hadn't heard before. I filed them away for future use. Pulling the wheel in the opposite direction, I jetted over two lanes and angled across traffic. We shot passed a brick building with white highlights on the left. Its cornerstone sign identified it as The Dun Cow Surgery. I would have taken a second glance if I hadn't been trying not to kill a pedestrian. Something bothered me but I couldn't pinpoint what. Happily, though, this was a one-way street. I hoped I was going in the right

direction. Behind me, traffic ground to a halt. The cars following us
got tangled while two motorcycles serpentined their way through. I
screamed past white signs displaying a big twenty with a red circle
around it. I presumed it was the speed limit, though I couldn't be sure.
Since I was going fifty, I didn't want to think about it too much. I was
rapidly approaching a small Tesco gas station on my right, followed
by another intersection.

I called into the back, "Which way?"

Soon-Li's fingers were pecking away at the keys of the laptop she
had pulled from somewhere.

"You should have stayed on the A2 instead of shooting past it."

The road was splitting, directing traffic to either side of a small
island where a light was clearly red.

"That's not helpful. You need to decide in three, two—"

"Left!"

I gunned it as I heard a final tap on the keyboard behind me. The
light changed to green in the heartbeat before I zipped through it,
pulling hard on the steering wheel and going into a drift.

Tira grabbed the seat with one hand and the dashboard with the
other. "Left, left, LEFT!"

A stinging reply rose to my lips until I realized she meant the direction of traffic. I tapped the brakes to catch the wheels and gunned
the accelerator, shooting over to the *correct* lane. Maybe they should
make those blue and white arrows bigger.

"Sorry, habit. Friggin' UK."

A few more keystrokes and the light in the rearview mirror turned
green again. It took the bikes time to maneuver through the chaos,
increasing our lead. This car was fast but it wasn't about to beat out
a motorcycle. We zipped along, zig-zagging around traffic which was,
thankfully, light. The bikes, as predicted, were gaining quickly. I was
an okay driver but I was no John. On our first mission, he'd skidded
across a railroad crossing a foot and a half in front of a train to lose a
line of cops. I, however, was not familiar with the area, was driving on
the opposite side of the road—usually—and most of my experience
was in an Econovan I used for my old heating and cooling company.

I glanced at the rearview mirror. "Any idea where this is taking us?"

"Back to the A2. They should be less likely to continue the chase on such a main road."

Tira added, "Hopefully, they agree."

"When I get to the A2, which way do I turn?"

"Right."

Mark cleared his throat. "Um, excuse me."

"Not now, Mark," I replied. "I'm a little busy and we're not stopping to let you off."

"No, what I was going to say—"

"Shut up, Mark!" Tira snapped.

The gang was almost on top of us and both second riders were pulling out shotguns. "I thought the UK had a policy about guns."

"They do. For the police," Soon-Li informed me.

"Great."

I slammed on the brakes just as the two bikes were coming alongside. They shot forward as I pulled hard on the wheel in both directions. The left bike was pushed into a steel fence and went down hard. The one on the right hit a parked car so both riders were launched over the handlebars.

"Nice move!" Soon-Li complimented.

"A little more violent than I would have liked, but they weren't leaving me much choice."

I eased back on the accelerator until I checked the rearview mirror and saw two cars were barreling down on us.

"I think this would be an excellent opportunity—"

"Shut up, Mark!" we all yelled in unison.

I stomped down on the gas as the road curved towards the A2. As the main road came into view, my panic started to rise.

"Soon-Li, we have a problem. I can't make a right."

"What do you mean, you can't?"

Tira, who had been preoccupied looking at the cars tailing us, checked our predicament and answered.

"There's an island in the way. And there's a fence on it."

"That's what I've been trying to say," Mark said with a distinct whine.

I glanced in the mirrors at the cars. A man climbed out of each, balancing on the doors while preparing their automatic weapons. I stared at the stream of traffic that would take us back towards the building from which we were trying to flee. I made a decision and settled down into my seat.

"Hold on."

I received glances from both of my compatriots. Soon-Li stowed her laptop and yanked Mark down onto the seat, covering him with her body. Tira braced herself. I kicked in my enhanced senses a moment before I reached the road. Time slowed to a crawl. I analyzed the situation, picked my path, and returned to normal speed. Then I pulled a hard right, pumped the brake, and hit the gas again. Our car slipped into a drift and slid across the first lane, passing in front of an oncoming vehicle and into the second. I steered into the drift, the tires caught and we rocketed forward, going the wrong way down a two lane, one-way street.

I reengaged my supernatural senses and everything slowed down again. Once more, I plotted a path through the chaos of cars, then let normal time slam back into place. We zigzagged back and forth then shot left under the overpass where the New Kent Road funneled in. We dodged between people, dogs, cars, and support pylons, before barreling onto the walking path of the small park which was encircled by all the roads. I found out later in the formal, written complaint that it was named Ring Road Square. The street I was on led to a tall, grassy knoll dotted with trees. I did the unheard of in this country—leaned on my horn. The blaring acted like a siren. Everyone stopped. We hit the hill and were launched into the air. As we landed, hard, we skidded through the last few perpendicular lanes until we slid nicely into the traffic of the A2. We each took a moment to catch our breath. Mark stuck his head out of the window and vomited.

Chapter Eleven

We arrived back at St. Bartholomew the Great without further incident. Though Mark could have led them straight to us with the trail of regurgitation he provided. After we had gotten clear, Tira gave him a sedative. He didn't seem like the most trustworthy person and he showed some signs of intelligence. So showing him the best kept secret in London would have been a bad idea. Getting an unconscious man into a public church, however, proved to be no picnic. Major Mangine met us as we pulled into the garage with a puss on his face. Lieutenant Harris stood next to him with two members of her team. They hauled our new guest out of the car and half dragged him in front of us.

I followed and the Major fell in alongside me. "What is my role?"

"Isn't that a better question for your wife?" I replied.

"I'm being serious."

"Yes, and I've warned you about that before."

"If you continually go off on your own, I can't protect you."

"While I appreciate the sentiment, I think I can handle myself."

"Until you run out of juice."

I stopped and regarded Lawrence.

"I'm not stupid. It's obvious you go into the only room that's off limits to—"

"Major! That will be quite enough." I shook my head.

He continued. "The fact is, while you are powerful, you cannot handle every situation. Especially since you seem to have an issue using lethal force."

"Is that a bad thing?"

"No, but it hamstrings you."

Lawrence tugged at my bloody shirt with the buckshot holes. I pulled away and continued walking, as did he.

"Now I understand you went up against an entire gang with submachine guns."

"Two super humans had my back."

"Only because Ms. Gupta beat you to the first location."

I glanced at Soon-Li. "Is that what you were tapping out on your keyboard? Ratting me out?"

She grinned. "I needed something to distract me from your driving."

"Fine."

"Fine, what?" the Major pushed.

I flipped my hand. "You can tag along next time."

"It's not a matter of me tagging along—"

Tira touched his shoulder from behind. "Take the win."

The Major took a deep breath, but stayed quiet. The team had sat Mark at the table of an interrogation room, where he lay snoring with his head in his arms like a kindergartener during quiet time. Tira gave him a stimulant to wake him up.

His first words were, "I would like to speak with my lawyer."

Mark's grating, whiny voice was getting to me. I sat on the edge of the table.

"Mr. Stay. I'm not sure if you've figured it out but we're not cops. We don't follow the same rules and regulations here. You might as well be in Gitmo. You know what that is, right? The Military prison in Guantanamo Bay, Cuba? The place where terrorists disappear to? Sound familiar?"

"I'm not a terrorist."

"And I'm not a federal agent or an agent of the crown." No one knows you're here. You don't even know where here is." I motioned behind me at the two-way mirror. Hopping off my perch, I stepped behind Mark's chair. The door opened and Tira entered. "Remember her? Remind you of anyone?"

Mark's breathing increased and sweat formed at his temples.

"A lover, perhaps?"

Mark glanced at me and laughed a big belly laugh that lifted his head towards the ceiling. "You guys really have no idea what's going on, do you? What, did you just stumble on me as I was leaving my house?"

Tira and I exchanged confused glances before we could stop ourselves.

Mark rubber necked between us. "I'm gay."

I walked around the table to stand next to Tira.

"Then how do you know my sister?"

"She's paying me!"

I frowned. "For what?"

He shook his head.

I eased myself into a chair. "Mark, I'm getting the feeling that you may not know the entire story here. Maybe Kali got you involved with something you assumed was harmless. Let's presume you didn't know people were getting killed."

His head shot up at that. It looked like he wanted to speak but decided to remain silent. This guy was smart but he'd made some really stupid choices. No, that's not right. He made choices based on passion.

"Tira, would you excuse us?"

She glanced at me with words on her lips. I understood. This guy had information that might bring her closer to her sister. Feeling responsible for Kali's actions, Tira needed to stop her. If need be, she would beat the knowledge out of him. Our eye contact lasted three whole seconds. Then she whirled and walked out.

I spoke over my shoulder at the two-way mirror. "Can we get a drink for Mr. Stay?"

The Major walked in with a water bottle. Placing it on the table, he turned and left as well. Mark looked at it, licking his lips but making no move to take it. Shrugging, I opened it and poured some in my mouth without letting it touch my lips. I swallowed, recapped it, and slid it closer to him. He grabbed the bottle, and took a long drink.

"Let's start from the beginning. We found you because you fit the profile of someone who recently broke up from a lengthy relationship." I wanted to say dumped but figured that might've hampered the conversation. "Want to talk about it?"

"Not really."

"Were you guys fighting?"

Mark didn't respond.

"Was he stepping out on you?"

"Jeffrey wouldn't do that."

"You?"

"No! I didn't do it. I love him."

I leaned back. "But he thought you had."

Mark nodded before taking another sip and absently wiping a tear away.

"Why?"

"Someone had sent him pictures. They were supposedly taken during days I worked late but I didn't do it."

It seemed like a defense he had repeated often. "When did Kali approach you?"

"We shared a table at my local coffee shop. She worked on a TV show about getting couples back together. Second chance at love, she called it. But she had trouble finding enough couples to focus on for the first season."

I rubbed the stubble on my chin. "You volunteered?"

"More than that, I told her I could get her all the couples she needed."

I sat up straighter. "How?"

Mark looked at me as if that was the stupidest question he'd ever heard. "I am the foremost expert in data analysis. I hold the Guy Metal in Gold from the RSS."

"RSS?"

Mark rolled his eyes. "The Royal Statistical Society. I built my entire business around that expertise."

"So that's what she was paying you for."

"Yes."

"Why didn't you just tell us that?"

"It wasn't exactly legal. I scraped data sets from multiple social media accounts, private dating sites, and other proprietary information."

"And in return, she would help you get back together with Jeffrey."

He lowered his gaze. "That's why I went to that building. She messaged that she had a plan to reunite us and to meet her there."

Someone tapped on the mirror.

"Excuse me for a second, Mark."

He nodded absently and wiped at another tear. I left and entered the adjoining room where Mangine, Harris, Tira and Soon-Li sat.

"I don't know if I buy this," Soon-Li said. She held a cup of tea in one hand and saucer in the other. "Are we saying that neither Kali nor the Tainted she's working for have the resources to do a little data analysis?"

Tira replied, "Kali could probably do it herself. Or else she would have contacts."

I took on the thinking man pose. "Maybe she did and he was one of them? What if she knew about his relationship and which buttons to push? Mark said he didn't cheat on Jeffery."

"They all say that," Soon-Li pointed out.

"Yes, but perhaps Kali was priming him as one of her next meals. Think of the power that would come from someone so obviously innocent. She used his desperation to get him to break the law. Just a little at first, to provide her with some needed intel. Then subtly increasing what's required until he almost doesn't recognize himself anymore. The ultimate betrayal would be when she convinces him to kill Jefferey."

They all looked at me; arms crossed, derisive expressions on their faces.

Finally, Lieutenant Harris turned to the others. "Is this how he usually works? Just makes things up?"

Tira said, "Pretty much."

Lawrence added, "Unfortunately, he frequently ends up being right."

"If we accept your premise, why kill him? Why the big show of sending him to gangland?" Soon-Li asked.

I considered it. "That was a little over the top."

"You think?" the Major replied. "They had enough people and enough firepower to take on a small insurgency, Plus, they chased you for two miles."

Tira shook her head. "She knew we would follow him. The trap was for us."

"But he was definitely the primary target." Soon-Li added. "They were just prepared for resistance."

Harris pointed through the mirror. "But why so much effort for that guy?"

We all followed her direction and watched in silence as Mark picked something out of his ear and smelled it.

Soon-Li dropped her head into her hand. "He has to know something."

I snapped my fingers. "Lawrence, have you ever taken covert training?"

"Of course."

"What was the biggest rule for improvising a backstory?"

"Stick to half truths. It is easier than trying to make up things on the fly."

I smiled. "Especially names."

I returned to the interrogation room and sat down. Mark seemed to have no idea I was there. I'm not sure if he even realized I had left. His introspection had put him in an almost catatonic state.

"Mark?"

No response.

"Mark." I didn't raise my voice, but was more direct.

He looked up.

"I have one last question for you and it's important. Ready?"

He maintained eye contact but didn't offer any acknowledgement.

"Did Kali speak of anyone else during your conversations?"

"I don't think so."

"Think," I urged. "This is crucial. Did she bring up the name Baldemar?"

His brow furrowed and he raised his eyes. "No, not that I can recall."

I sighed. "Okay. Well, it was worth a shot."

I pushed myself up from the chair and started for the door.

"Though, she did say the name of her producer. Euryale, I believe it was."

Something broke in the next room.

Chapter Twelve

"EURYALE IS THE MOST elusive of all the Tainted." Soon-Li remarked.

Francesca and Soon-Li were providing the intel as we sat around the briefing room table.

"She's always been a recluse, as far back as documentation shows," Francesca continued. "She rarely leaves wherever she has set up camp. Any extremely rare sightings have always been at night. It is said she becomes the shadows."

"What is she, Dracula?" Lawrence scoffed.

"In a way," Soon-Li replied. "The Converted account for the blood sucking parts of those legends. She was the essence of Dracula."

"Wasn't that Vlad the Impaler?" I said.

"That was who Bram Stoker *believed* to be his inspiration. We planted that bit of information in his subconscious."

"We can do that?" I asked.

"Some," Francesca replied. "Though it is rare. Anyway, she chooses one of the Converted as her go-between. That person rounds up her victims. It makes her killing seem random these days."

"These days?" Lawerence asked.

Soon-Li nodded. "Euryale is the embodiment of a serial killer. She isn't interested in mass destruction, wars, or genocide. Her emotion of choice is fear. She's behind many of the mass killings since the discovery of serial killers: Jeffery Dahmer, Ted Bundy, the Zodiac Killer, John Wayne Gacy."

"Jack the Ripper," I added.

Soon-Li met my gaze. "That's why I didn't consider her for these deaths. The man was killed from behind. Not her usual M.O."

"Maybe he wasn't her target," I offered.

"How do you mean?" asked Francesca

"Euryale works through people. It was Donald being manipulated. The point of the attack was to kill Sabrina. The other guy was just in the way. She probably goaded Don into killing him, knowing it would cause his fiancée to panic. When you see your attacker kill someone right in front of you, it removes the possibility of hope."

My statement pulled at a memory, and just like that, the conference room disappeared.

I was in Shorabak in the southern part of Kandahar, near the border of Pakistan. Myself, along with two of my unit, had been captured when an op went sideways. We were in a mud-brick house. My hands tied behind me and a rag was shoved in my mouth that seemed to be made of dirt and sand. I didn't have a blindfold, which was stupid of them. To my arrogant mind, this would be their undoing. I remember thinking: you don't capture a Ranger, you dumb shit. You kill them. Or else you can bet your ass they will kill you when you least expect it.

The harsh daylight streamed around the fabric covering the tiny window. It was blisteringly hot outside but the wall was cool on my back. The pungent odor of goats wafted in from the small courtyard in the center of the house. Mosquitos buzzed around my face and in my ear. Annoying, but not as bad as the sandflies. Those had a bite on them that rivaled most bee stings.

The four men holding us were Taliban. They stalked around with AK-47s slung over their shoulders, mumbling to each other in Pashto. I only caught dribs and drabs but my buddy, Josh, could speak it fluently. With any luck, these morons would feed us all the intel we'd need before the rest of the team tracked us to this little shit hole. Then the tables would turn.

A high-ranking member walked in and started screaming at them. Their self confident airs collapsed. From what I could translate, they were trying to explain how they had done a good thing in capturing us. The new guy, terrorist, dickhead, seemed to agree with my previous analysis. Capturing a Ranger is a good way to become crow fodder. That's when I started getting worried. This guy was smart. He held his assault rifle at the ready. He paid attention and he didn't underestimate his enemy. I knew we were really fucked when he didn't point the rifle at Josh. He pulled a Makarov PM, a compact Soviet pistol, from his holster. He put two bullets in Josh's chest and one in his head. Blood sprayed me in the face, dripping into my eyes and mouth despite the gag. I stared at what was left of my friend and wanted to scream, but nothing would come out. I looked at the man who had killed him and knew with complete clarity that I was next. Shifting his aim to me, he met my eyes and said one word; kāfir. It was one I knew. It meant infidel,

He smiled just before his head exploded. A 50 BMG bullet from a Barrett M107 tore through it. The small sonic boom from when it had pierced the sound barrier came a moment after.

I shook my head to pull myself back into the here and now. Everyone was staring at me. I wasn't sure how long my trip down memory hell had taken.

What was I talking about? Right, Euryale's first victim. I cleared my throat. "You can't rationalize whether they would go through with it. The proof is right there, staring you in the face."

My words were hollow. Josh's dead stare hovered in my vision still. I could taste his blood in my mouth. Swallowing hard, I excused myself. Only one person could vanquish these demons. I retreated to the small office set aside for me, pulled out my cell phone, and dialed.

"Hey, how's London?" Marie asked.

"It's okay. I miss you."

"I miss you too, but it's only been a day and we already talked today. What's going on?"

"Nothing."

"Try again."

I didn't respond.

"Are the Brits being mean to you? I will fly over right now and kick their asses."

I laughed. "What's on the agenda for today?"

"What else? More paperwork. I'm not sure accepting this promotion was a good idea."

"It's what you wanted; what you've been working towards since you became a fed."

"Yeah, but it's like working with a bunch of children. Half of them think they can do the job better. The others won't make a move without checking first. Then there are the schmucks playing the optics game. No one wants to simply do the job."

"You do," I reminded her.

"Yeah and I'm in the minority. I'm thinking of packing it all in and fighting demons full time."

"I think I can find a position for you," I teased, using my best seventies porno voice.

"Oh, I'm sure you can. It might make the Major jealous."

"I'm willing to risk it."

"Just remember, if you see the new Deadpool movie without me, you'll never see me naked again."

"So, we keep the lights off from now on?"

"You think I'm kidding." Her tone became dangerous.

"No. No, sir. I mean no, ma'am. I wouldn't chance it."

"That's better."

I couldn't help but smile. "Thanks."

"Anytime."

"I've gotta go. I left a meeting to call."

"You'll tell me about it when you get home, right? The real reason you called?"

"You're pretty smart for a fed."

"And you're an ass."

"I love you, too."

Marie was quiet for a moment. "I do, you know."

"I know."

"Talk later?"

"If I'm still awake."

She scoffed, "Old man."

We said our goodbyes and hung up. A knock came at the door. "Come."

John walked in. "Hey, you good?"

"Yeah, thanks."

He came and sat down. "Sand-land replays?"

I regarded him for a second, then nodded.

"Fuckin' place. I wish it would stay where it is and leave us the hell alone."

"Amen to that. What do we got?"

John leaned his hip against the desk. "Soon-Li is getting the rest of the intel that Mark provided on Kali. Tira is going to delve into his mind to see if he's been compromised."

"Good, we don't need another Denise incident."

On my first mission with the team, we'd encountered someone controlled by Baldemar. He was the current head of the Tainted, if there actually was one. They didn't work together well, each having their own agendas. Let's just say he was the one leading the stampede. Anyway, Tira had declared Denise clean of outside influence. That wasn't the case. Since then, she had dedicated countless hours to her craft and had buttoned up her cleaning methods, I hoped.

John pointed out, "It's just a precaution. We don't think he was actually infected."

"I would agree with that. Have you met him? I wouldn't want to take up residency in that mind.

Chapter Thirteen

"**D**O YOU THINK ALL of this is really necessary?" Thorne asked.

I wondered if the British accent made him sound so pompous or if a Jersey one would do the same.

I stopped what I was doing and studied him. "You believe that, after the last encounter, added precaution is a bad thing?"

"Not at all. However, I think our time would be better spent in quiet prayer."

"I'll tell you what, you pray. We'll go see if we can get to this next victim before they are bled dry."

To the Major, I said, "We ready?"

He slid a magazine into the MK18 and pulled the loading bolt as he watched the round enter the barrel. Meeting my gaze, he replied, "Hu-rah."

We were taking everyone this time. Well, those currently on team Christian. That included John, Hager, and Major Mangine with me in one vehicle Soon-Li, Tira, and Lieutenant Harris would be in a second while the small company of four soldiers occupied the last car. I'm not quite sure why we had a boys against girls team up. It's just the way it worked out.

John peeled out, leaving the odor of burned rubber in our wake. I caught Thorne's reflection in the side mirror wrinkling his nose, which made me smile.

"We are guests in his country and his house," Hager pointed out from the back seat.

He had relinquished the shotgun position to me shortly after I had taken over leadership of more Covenants than had been under one umbrella since...Well, you know.

"Your point?"

I knew it but I wasn't in the mood to acknowledge my current lack of emotional intelligence silently.

"Politeness costs you nothing but gains you a great deal."

"Hager, he's a pompous ass that would rather spend his days on his knees than out in the field actually making a difference."

John tried to hide his smirk.

"Praying. I meant praying," I clarified.

Hager continued, ignoring the juvenile banter. "Prayer is not always a passive activity."

"Now you are just trying to sound wise."

I was being an ass, but I couldn't help it.

I caught his raised eyebrow in the rearview mirror. "While I agree, some of the human race has used it as a crutch to abdicate responsibility. However, that was never its true intention."

"How do you mean?" Despite myself, I was intrigued.

"Prayer is a form of meditation. Many use a mantra to aid in concentration. The repetition helps to clear the mind and is a trigger for entering into a state of centered awareness. Prayer is a similar process. It opens the person up to things they may not be receptive to otherwise. If one's thoughts are a hurricane of concerns and emotions, it is impossible to focus on a particular problem. Prayer helps to quiet the mind and focus the emotions. Epiphanies are often experienced. Many attribute it to God speaking to them and providing the answer when it always resided within them. They were just unable to see it. Like cleaning out the closet and finding a garment you assumed lost. There is also a hypothesis that large scale communal focus on something can actually affect the physical world. Prayer groups may actually work, just not in the way they think."

John and I exchanged glances.

"Did you hear what I did?" he asked

I gave a slow nod, not able to stop my mouth from hanging open. "Hager quoted Eminem."

"I knew he was a prophet."

We both started laughing. I desperately needed it at that moment.

Hager sighed. "I should have ridden with the ladies."

Still smiling, John said, "Hey, I noticed *you* didn't meditate before going out."

Meditating was also our code word for taking a holy dip in the sacred waters while there were non-Bishops in earshot.

I motioned towards the back. "The Major is privy to our recharge process. Not the particulars, but the general idea."

"Your continued discretion is appreciated," Hager noted to Mangine

He never stopped looking out the side window as he spoke. "I have military secrets that will follow me to my grave. This one won't be an issue."

His answer made me smile. "As for my recharge, I was looking to do a little more experimentation later on. I need to work off some energy."

John shook his head. "Even after your last incident?"

"Tira did most of the work. I was in charge of keeping Mark from getting away. It didn't require a whole lot of power."

Actually, I was down to half of my reserves. But I felt confident that, with everyone in the party, I could manage.

"I'm not sure if experimentation during an active operation is the best of ideas," Hager pointed out.

"When are we not in an active operation?" I countered.

"How do you put up with him?" Lawrence said to Hager. "If you set him on the yellow brick road, he would be off first chance he got to stick his head in a hornet's nest."

"It is trying, but he usually has the uncanny habit of finding what we're searching for in that nest."

I grinned at Lawrence who just rolled his eyes.

We parked next to a Bentley in a small permit-only lot near Kings Bench Walk, which of course we had a sticker for, and took the footpath around Temple Church to the address. We stared at the building.

John sighed. "Not this again."

We were looking at a rectory.

He huffed. "If there's a secret entrance in the basement, you're on your own."

"Maybe we send Thorne, instead."

The last time we ventured through the hidden passage in a strange rectory, the results were less than ideal. I usually get a bad taste in my mouth when I almost buy the farm. Then I spent a few seconds wondering where that phrase originated.

Soon-Li said, "I already double checked. This is the correct address."

I rubbed the stubble on my jaw as I considered our options. "Okay, here's how it's going to go. Soon-Li, the Major, and I will go in and check it out."

Hager grumbled, Tira tried to argue and the soldiers shuffled their feet. John smiled. I don't mind occasionally explaining my decisions, but I really enjoy it when I get to point out something that should be blatantly obvious.

To Hager, I said, "You are not dressed for a visit to this type of church."

In response, he merely adjusted his hat.

I glanced at Tira. "You're too close to this and you're going into confrontations way too hot. As for the rest of you, I'm not taking an entire team into a priest's sanctuary. Lawrence, leave the rifle. You can take a side arm if you can conceal it. You're not normally trigger happy but take extra care here." To the group, I said, "I will radio if there are any issues. Any more questions?"

Lawrence went to Harris and handed over his assault rifle. Then he removed his belt and holster, withdrew his Glock, and gave it to her as well. He double checked that a round was in the chamber before he slid it into the small of his back. During this preparation, he rattled off his own instructions.

"Form a perimeter. Keep an eye out for any superhuman activity. Radio in with anything that seems off."

Harris saluted. "Wilco."

The three of us crossed the street and entered the rectory. This one looked like a typical office building hallway. The first door on the right was open. The desk inside was positioned so that whoever was behind it could see guests arriving.

Behind a too-small desk sat a rotund gentleman. No, that's not right. All of his proportions were those of a man weighing under two hundred pounds except around his middle, front and back, making him look like a weeble-wobble.

"Mornin', folks. What can I do for you?"

"Goo mornin'." Soon-Li piled on to her accent until her English was almost unrecognizable while asking for the priest.

"I'm sorry, did you say Father Elias Kane?"

"Yah. Where he?"

Still smiling, Mr. Wobble said, "Do you have an appointment?"

Soon-Li gave a curt nod.

"What is the name?"

Soon-Li repeated the priests barely intelligible name.

"No, I mean your name."

Another nod. He glanced at Lawrence and me, hoping we could elaborate. I smiled and mimicked Soon-Li's head nod. The Major just stared through him as if he wasn't there.

The weeble's smile slipped. "Oh, for the love of God."

"Yes," Soon-Li repeated the name again.

He shook his head and wrote a note, handing it over to Soon-Li. "Bring to Father Kane. Fifth floor." He held up his hand with fingers extended. "Room D." He looked at his improvised sign language, trying to puzzle out how he was going to communicate a letter. He opted for writing it on another piece of paper, which he circled six times. "D," he repeated. He gave the second note to her.

She peered at both and said in her actual voice, "Thank you very much." Then walked away.

I bowed and hurried after her.

"Why did you bow? That's Japanese." She threw the notes into the garbage outside the door to the stairs.

"I panicked. What did the note say?"

"'I have no idea what these people are saying. Hopefully, you will have more luck.'"

"Cute trick."

"Yeah, it only works in English-speaking countries. Most others are multilingual."

"Ouch."

We took the stairs two at a time and made it to the fifth floor in under a minute. Soon-Li and I could supplement our reserves with some supernatural support. So we weren't winded. The Major, despite not having the same advantage, wasn't phased by the climb in the least. Then again, I wasn't sure if Soon-Li needed the help either. Was I the only slacker?

Father Kane's room was at the far end of the hallway. I knocked, then took in the intimidating figure of Major Mangine. "Maybe you should wait in the hall?"

The words were just out of my mouth when something felt wrong. The air felt thin. Then the world exploded around us.

Chapter Fourteen

THE SHIELD OF AIR I created for the three of us held. However, the explosion still had enough force to throw us against the far wall. Pain radiated across my back from the impact and I coughed out the dust and fine debris that filled the air. The door disintegrated into wooden shrapnel that pelted the hallway all around our protective barrier.

"What the fuck was that?" When I finally got my head together, I glanced toward the apartment, expecting to see devastation. Instead, two women stood there. They wore skin tight outfits made up of straps in a zig-zag pattern that concealed as much as they revealed. The designs were opposites of each other, which gave me the impression of bookends. Their hair had been woven into thick braids, ending at their lower back. They wiggled their fingers at me flirtatiously. One stretched her arms out.

Soon-Li looked up a second or two after me and gasped. "Move!"

She punctuated her statement by shoving me to one side and blurring in the other direction. I pushed the Major ahead with me and blurred to keep up. The surrounding air turned arid, like we'd stepped out into the desert. Hundreds of ice needles pounded into the wall where we had been, ripping it to shreds.

I tried to get my breathing under control. "I repeat: what the fuck was that?"

I looked over at Soon-Li, who keyed her com unit. "Amram, the twins are here." There was a slight tremble to her voice.

"*Oh, my.*"

"Who the hell are the twins?"

John chimed in, "*Let's just say very dangerous. You need to get out of there.*"

"Not without the priest."

Lawrence, closer to the apartment entrance, drew his Glock. "Can I shoot back now?"

"Just don't hit the priest."

From another pocket, he withdrew a small mirror on a telescopic handle, which he extended so that it hovered by his foot. He eased it over until he could see into the room. Then he stuck his gun in the doorway and started blasting. The Major fired six rounds before he checked the reflection and said, "Go."

I blurred off the floor and through what was left of the doorway. My breath caught as I tripped over one of the twins' legs. The other grabbed me mid air and slammed me onto my back causing another blooming of pain. She hopped on my chest and straddled me, putting a dagger to my neck. It all happened in the space of a few heartbeats. I lay barely inside the doorway. I watched past my eyebrows as Soon-Li tried to follow but was deterred by another ice storm.

The chest sitter called out, "I have a red-hot knife at your savior's throat."

I thought she was being dramatic until I felt the heat and smelled the burning flesh.

"Speaking of hot." She ran her nails through my hair and yanked my head across the floor, craning my neck. She ground her hips on my stomach. "I could have fun with this one."

"Sorry," I croaked out. "But I'm spoken for. I can introduce you to my friend, John. The ladies seem to like him."

I was buying time to figure a way out of this without losing my head, pun intended. I had plenty of options but none that I could accomplish before she sliced my carotid artery, I thought about hardening my skin but I honestly didn't know if she could sense it, giving her time to do sufficient damage.

"Ember, enough of that. Time to withdraw."

I strained my eyes to see the speaker but I already knew that raspy voice. It was Kali.

Father Kane sat on a couch with his head in his palms. "I'm still not sure."

Kali's voice softened, its hiss all but disappeared.

"Baby, it's okay. We can talk about it, but we need to go." She took him by the hands and guided him to his feet. "Crystal."

The other twin grabbed a water bottle off the counter and uncapped it, aiming at the door. She squeezed with both hands. The water came shooting out, becoming a sheet of ice that covered the doorway. Tossing the empty, crinkled plastic over her shoulder, she stepped over to me. Then she drew her own seven-inch knife from a sheath on the inside of her thigh. She slid her cold blade next to her sister's until I could feel the blood in my capillaries withdrawing painfully. Then, with the other hand, she grasped my crotch with way more force than necessary.

"You're right, Ember, he's scrumptious." She caught my now widened eyes, "Don't try anything, Olof. I'll be able to tell if you get *hard*."

I blinked and tried to ignore her grip. "I don't suppose you're related to Nadia Popov, are you?"

She was one of my clients who kept trying to coax me into bed with double entendres that were closer to sexual harassment. She smiled at me and increased her pressure on my neck, and… elsewhere.

Ember leaned over and kissed Crystal on the mouth, quickly but sensuously. So, maybe they weren't sisters. She went to the rear wall, opened a window, and stepped back a few paces at the edge of my periphery. Crossing her arms in front of her chest, she pulled them apart as if she were stretching an enormous ball of pizza dough. The curtains billowed as air flowed into the apartment. It became harder to breathe.

Crystal practically purred into my ear, "Isn't she sexy?"

Ember slapped her hands together with a loud crack and the back wall blew out in a thunderous explosion. I took the opportunity to extract myself from the uncomfortable position with a palm strike to Crystal's sternum. It cleared me of her knife enough to roll away.

"I'm free. Get in here," I said into the coms.

She recovered quickly and leapt at me, knife in a stabbing grip. In a blurring motion, I swiveled my body like a breakdancer; extending my leg out in a sidekick that met her in the air. The momentum sent her across the room, crashing into the opposite wall.

"We can't," Soon-Li replied. "There is something about this ice that won't break."

Ember witnessed the bitch slapping I'd given her sister, and screamed with rage. The two of them blurred in and attacked at once. It was all I could do to keep their strikes from landing. They weren't two people. They fought with a single mind. If one used speed, the other employed strength. Only the hours of practice at slipping from one enhancement to another kept me from being immediately overwhelmed. Somewhere in a flurry of movements, they caught both of my wrists. One sent shivers down my spine while the other scalded me like being splashed with a pot of hot coffee. As one, they drove their knives into my shoulders, sending me onto my back. The blades penetrated completely through, pinning me to the floor. A wave of dizziness crashed over me and I could hear my heartbeat in my ears. I was stuck, bleeding profusely, and I couldn't heal with the blades still in me. One of them must have nicked my lung because I struggled to breathe.

"That was sweet, Ember," Crystal said as she stared into the other's eyes.

"Mmmm," Ember trilled.

"We are going *now!*" Kali said from her position in front of the hole in the wall. "There are more outside."

They leaned down together, kissing me on the lips. Then they said in unison, "We'll finish this later."

They got up, leaving their knives in me. All three of them leapt through the hole, dragging Father Kane with them. I heard rifle fire as the team on the ground tried to take them out as they bounded from roof to roof, escaping into the night.

"*Christian, are you clear of the door?*" Lawrence asked.

I lifted my head, looking past the two knife handles. I was on the other side of the room.

"You could say that." My voice sounded raspy. Had it not been for the coms, they wouldn't have heard me. A few seconds later, an explosion took out the door frame and Soon-Li came flying through.

"Oh my God, Christian!"

She dropped next to me. The Major came in with two other soldiers and cleared the room. I noticed he had his assault rifle back.

"Tira," Soon-Li said into the coms, "Christian is hurt. Get up here." To me, she said, "What can I do?"

She viewed herself in a maternal role. I presumed that was why a highly trained superhuman was asking such stupid questions.

I took in a long, slow, painful breath. "See those knives? Pull them out."

She sucked in a breath through her teeth. "Of course."

She grabbed them and yanked without warning. I half grunted and half growled as I grabbed both shoulders and rolled onto my left side. I felt the small tear in my lung close and I inhaled deeply. Lifting myself off the floor with one hand, I leaned back to prop myself up—but fell. Cursing, I attempted to get up but my right arm wouldn't move. The normal tingling feeling accompanied my wounds closing but I had no movement on the right side. I tried to wiggle my fingers but they just sat there as if saying, *fuck you.* If I'm honest, this gave me a considerable amount of anxiety. I told myself this wasn't an issue. The healing process was doing its thing and the feeling would return when complete. Then, I ran out of juice.

"Uh, I think I have a problem."

Tira sprinted into the room, followed by the rest of the team. "What happened?"

Soon-Li held up the two daggers. "He was stabbed."

"Is that all?" John asked. "He'll be fine. I've been stabbed plenty of times."

I tried again. "Uh, guys."

Soon-Li shoved the daggers in John's face.

"They pinned him to the floor. Have you ever had that done to you?"

"The floor? No."

"Guys!"

They all looked at me.

"My well is dry and I can't move my arm." My voice quivered and I cursed my lack of stoicism. Tira kneeled down next to me.

Hager pulled the Major in close to whisper in his ear. They exchanged glances.

Then, Lawrence said, "Beta Team, perimeter check."

They saluted and moved out. Once they were clear, Tira ripped my shirt where the knife had left a hole. The wound had closed but was still red and inflamed. She placed a hand over it and closed her eyes. Waves of power tickled over my skin and burrowed deep into my surrounding muscles. Though she had done this kind of delving before, I never experienced that reaction. The tingling stopped.

"The central set of nerves going into your arm is severed. It looks like it started to reconnect when you ran out of power. We need to get you back to the Covenant House,"

I sat up with some help and leaned against the back of the couch and took in the scene. The apartment was disheveled as if someone had bumped into a dollhouse and knocked everything over. Scorch marks climbed to the ceiling by the door and out from the large hole in the exterior wall.

Tira produced a sling from one of her tactical uniform's pockets and used it to secure my arm.

"How is the other shoulder?" Tira probed.

"It's sore but functional."

She nodded as if it was to be expected.

I leaned around her. "So who the hell are these twins?"

Hager sighed. "No one knows if they are actually twins. They are referred as such because of how they dress and their similar features."

"Ow. I think I'm good, thanks Tira. They are more than just similar. I had a closeup look at both of them and they seem to be mirror images. Each has the same birthmark on the opposite side of their faces.

The Major's voice came over the coms. *"Police are two minutes out. The team is already by the car. We need to move."*

"I suggest we not use the stairs again," Hager said, looking at the large hole in the wall.

They all looked at me. I knew what it meant.

"Fine," I huffed.

Tira held out her arms. "Fancy a lift, govna?"

I narrowed my eyes. "Funny. But leave the comedy to the experts."

"Is *that* what you consider yourself?" Hager asked.

John led the way, hopping through the opening while Tira picked me up like a sleeping child.

"This is humiliating. Can we make sure that none of the team sees this?"

Hager smiled and leapt down to make sure we were clear. He knew the power of imagery. This would not help our growing supporters.

"Stop complaining," Tira replied. "If you're good, we can stop and get ice cream."

"You can do me the courtesy of not enjoying this so much."

"Sorry." She unsuccessfully tried to hide her smile.

"I'm injured, you know."

"Don't be so dramatic. You just need a quick dip to finish healing. We will get you back in plenty of time."

I didn't want to extend the amount of time being cradled in Tira's arms but I couldn't let that comment go. "What does that mean?"

I bounced as she shrugged.

"Tira, spill it."

She shook her head in what I assume was frustration at her slip. "There have been cases where injuries like this have become permanent when the subject was separated from their source for an extended period."

"How long?"

"Days, usually."

"Usually?"

"There have been cases where it was shorter."

I sighed. "What are you waiting for?"

"You to stop asking questions."

I gave her a head bob and she stepped up to the edge.

"Ready?"

"Probably not, but let's go."

In an emergency, I once swept Marie off her feet and jumped rooftops I needed to call and apologize.

Chapter Fifteen

B ACK IN THE CHANGING room of London's Covenant House, John helped me into my immersion robes. They were similar to ours in the States but more elaborate. These had filigree stitched into the usual red trim and accompanying belt. They were a tradition, not a requirement for the immersion process but Bishops took traditions very seriously—especially in the British colonies. Tradition also called for a loincloth but I wasn't asking for help with that. I stuck with my trusty boxer briefs.

Men, at least those I've known, are not comfortable providing and accepting help. We could provide aid in almost any other way, including dragging another man through a minefield, with less self-consciousness. Had this been my wedding and he was helping me with my tie or cuff links? Sure, no biggie. But this level of vulnerability made us both uncomfortable. So we needed a distraction.

"What happened with the twins?" John asked.

"Dude! Had I not been on the receiving end, I would have said they were the coolest thing I had ever seen."

I described what went on in graphic detail. He would respond with the occasional, "Seriously?... Oh, man!" Or, "That's fucked up."

In the end, he got me dressed with minimal embarrassment on both our parts.

"Ready?" he asked as he tied my belt.

"Hell yes, this one armed thing sucks."

In the London Covenant, the immersion chamber was more like a shrine. It had its own wing with an entrance through a bookcase. With the decor, I wouldn't have been surprised if we entered through a live painting. So yeah, I was a little jealous. The stone lined corridor, which looked like it had been built the same time as the great pyramids, led us deeper. At points, I expected to see a talking skull warning that dead men tell no tales. The final archway before the pool was ornately carved with symbols and gargoyles. They appeared to be pagan. The inner chamber contained carvings as well but these were intricate depictions of battles. I didn't recognize any of them so I presumed they were part of The Tainted Wars. One scene caught my eye and I walked across the cobblestone floor to inspect it more closely. It showed a divine entity bestowing his grace on a group of people.

"The first blessing," Hager pointed out. "I don't know if it had a different name but that's what it has been called in any text I've read."

Symbols were carved off to one side.

"What does that say?"

Hager paused for a moment, then sighed. "To defend those who cannot defend themselves. To guide the lost. To bring light to the darkness."

I blinked, staring at him.

He nodded. "The answer you provided during your initiation ceremony. The words you could not possibly have known but recited verbatim."

I peered at them, running my fingers along the designs. I felt a connection to them I could not explain.

"Shall we?"

Hager motioned towards the pool. I wanted to continue perusing the carvings but preferred the use of my right arm more. Hager took my good arm and Soon-Li put a hand on the opposite shoulder. Amazingly, even balancing in the water was more difficult. With their help, I immersed myself up to my ribs.

I went into my pre-submersion routine. This would be a long one. Not only was I completely tapped out but I was injured. Would I heal as soon as the recharge started, extending the process? Would I have to wait until fully charged to be fixed, then recharge again? Would I have any visions with the extended charging time? How would those visions affect the healing? Too many questions that I didn't have answers to. I needed to leap and see what happened.

Finishing my breathing exercises, I gave a thumbs up to my support team. The light show that accompanied my recharging could be extensive and startling. I closed my eyes, bent my knees, and sank below the water. I clamped my teeth together in preparation for the shocks about to go through my body.

I felt nothing. I tentatively opened my eyes, not wanting to be blinded by the underwater lightning storm. There was only dimly lit water. I looked up, thinking I wasn't completely submerged, but it was a good foot to the surface. I could hear the confused mumbling coming from both Hager and Soon-Li. Standing back up, I breached the still pool. Pulling my hand away from Hager's grip, I awkwardly wiped the water out of my face.

"What's going on? Is there something wrong with the pool?"

Hager replied, "Soon-Li and I were just discussing that very possibility."

"Hold on, I'll check."

Soon-Li dipped below and, immediately, white and blue lights danced across her skin. It only took a few seconds for her to get topped off before standing.

"Water seems fine. Amram, maybe you should check? See if it's a male thing."

"Why would it be a male thing?" I asked, a bit too aggressively.

Soon-Li shrugged. "I don't know of anything that would cause an immersion to fail. I'm just eliminating possibilities."

John waded in quickly, causing some splashing and heavy ripples. Customarily, we moved with care in the pool. One did not splash around in the sacred waters. It showed his level of concern.

"I'll check. I probably used more power today."

He submerged himself without preamble and the plasma ball effects started up anew.

"Shit," I blurted out, before I could stop myself which earned a reproachful stare from Hager. John reemerged.

"Try again," Soon-Li said to me.

I let out a heavy sigh and did so. Once again, nothing happened so I resurfaced. It took all my resolve not to let out another vile curse.

Hager tilted his head towards the ceiling. "Arthur, please ask Tira to join us."

"Certainly, sir," the disembodied AI responded. Then, after a few moments it added, "She is on the way."

"Thank you, Arthur."

"You are most welcome, Mr. Hager."

Frigging British politeness. I wanted nothing more at that moment than to drop a few F-bombs. It wouldn't help. Other than temporarily making me feel better it would raise the stress level in the room. One of those annoying things you had to acknowledge as a leader. You need to make it seem like the shit storm you were in the middle of was not only manageable, but expected.

I breathed deeply. "Hager, if you would assist me, I see no need for Tira to wade into the pool to examine me."

"Of course, my boy."

Soon-Li and Hager helped me out of the water and to a stone bench along one wall. I tried to keep a dignified appearance as I sloshed down with my wet robes. I'm not sure I succeeded.

After a minute of awkward silence, Tira came in. "What's going on?"

Soon-Li spoke up first, "Christian couldn't recharge."

She looked to me. "What do you mean?"

What the fuck do you think it means?

I sighed. "I got in the water but nothing happened."

She cocked her head. "Nothing?"

"I got wet."

She strode over. "Lay back and open your robe."

I swung my feet onto the bench and laid across it, pulling at the hems of my robe to give her access to my chest. Tira kneeled down next to me, placing one hand on my sternum and one on the top of my head, as though palming a basketball. She closed her eyes as I watched her as she delved into the source of my power. The thing that made me a Bishop. We didn't have any organs that you wouldn't find in a typical human. But there existed a metaphysical font somewhere between our hearts and our heads. Its size varied for everyone.

With the large number of Bishops coming and going in the New York Covenant, Tira had been doing research on the depths of everyone's talent. It was an interest she had taken up. Some had vast wells of power. Others' were very shallow. It seemed to be random. For example, John's was fairly shallow while his father had one of the deepest among the Bishops. Before I came along, that is. She had said that comparing mine to his would be like comparing an Olympic sized pool to a lake. It could be sensed, even when empty, like the hole from a dry well.

I watched Tira's eyes flick back and forth beneath her closed eyelids. With each passing second, her eyebrows got closer together. She needn't have bothered. When you use the power long enough, you get a sense of it within you. I didn't need anyone to tell me what I already divined. Everyone else, though, would need to hear it from someone other than me.

It took another second and her eyes shot open and she met my gaze. Her mouth gaped until she remembered to close it. Her eyes darted to the side in a silent request to reveal her findings. I nodded almost imperceptibly. She stood and faced them.

"Christian's divine well is gone."

Chapter Sixteen

"WHAT DO YOU MEAN, it's gone? You mean empty, right?" Soon-Li asked.

Tira shook her head. "It's not there. I can't find any indication that Christian is anything but a normal man."

Hager looked from me to Soon-Li to Tira. "Not possible. No one has ever simply lost their blessing. How would something like that even occur?"

"I don't know," Tira replied. "I've never heard of it either. At least nothing was referenced in our library. Luckily, London's is more substantial."

"Maybe we should call Speranza and check if there's anything in the Jordan Library?" John suggested as he wrung out his robe.

Hager rested an elbow on his opposite arm and stroked his beard. "I don't know that I would trust communications at this point. Our opposition will see this as a weakness to exploit."

I stood up. "I'm going to my room. John, can you give me a hand again?"

All eyes were back on me, as if they had forgotten I was in there.

John stepped over. "Of course."

Once again, I was dry, groomed, and in the office assigned to me. It was off the beaten path but not quite a broom closet. Thorne didn't want to insult me outright but neither was he laying the place at my feet. I spent my time going through the ton of paperwork that accompanied this position. It was all electronic and highly encrypted. I needed to be on my beefed up laptop if I didn't want to wait an hour to read one email. I figured this was something I could actually do. Though, typing with one hand was proving problematic. Luckily, I didn't have to sign anything since my signature was my fingerprint from my right index finger. It took only three tries at that before I spent the next half hour figuring out how to add my left hand to the registry. That was after the twenty minutes it took to change the mouse configuration and become skillful enough to function with only minor frustration. Someone knocked on the door.

"Come."

John stuck his head in. "How's it going?"

"Awesome, I always wanted to know how Rocky felt in the second movie."

Smiling, John came in. He was carrying a bottle of scotch and two glasses. He chortled at my shocked expression.

"I hope you are not bringing me news as bad as the last time you drank scotch."

The previous occurrence had been his sister's funeral, the first time I had witnessed him drink something other than beer or water.

"Nah. Just thought you could use the pick-me-up and, to be honest, I'm not a fan of British beers."

"They keep them in the refrigerator."

"That's not the problem." He put the glasses down and poured two fingers worth in each. The scotch was an eighteen-year-old Macallan that was aged in Sherry seasoned oak casks and had a price tag of about five hundred dollars. "There are a few I like but none of them are here. Now you give me a good, hand-pumped bitter. I'm all in."

He handed me a glass, then took the other. I brought it to my nose and breathed in the notes of ginger and cinnamon.

"Then, before we leave, we need to find us a proper pub."

"I'll drink to that."

We clinked glasses and I savored the liquid swirling around my tongue before swallowing.

John looked at his glass. "Damn, you may convert me yet."

"I will keep trying. Did you guys find anything about my..." I lifted my right shoulder, which was about the extent of its movement.

He shook his head. "Nothing conclusive, but there are a few avenues that we are looking to go down."

"Like?"

"Soon-Li thought it might have something to do with the Twins' knives."

"How would that make a difference?"

"There was a Bishop who could imbue items and weapons with her blessing."

"That's a thing?" I sat upright. The possibilities of such instruments of power were pinging around my brain like Ricochet Rabbit. I tried to move my arm. "Why would anyone create a weapon that took away someone's gift?"

"She didn't. Her's had very simple applications. Some could make you stronger, jump higher, run faster. But Soon-Li believes that if a Bishop could do it, why not one of the Tainted?"

"Seems logical, I guess. Did this Bishop..." I pointed my glass towards John.

"China May."

"Interesting name. Did China create anything that increased the well? Or that allowed you to use less power."

John shook his head. "She wasn't able to manipulate the blessing itself."

"What happened to the talisman?"

"They were called Shèngpiàn. She recorded every one that she handed out. There is also a book somewhere that documents the method she used to create them. Though, I'm not sure it's been translated."

"What language was it written in?" I took another sip.

"Sumerian."

I nearly had a spit take. "Damn. And no one has been able to replicate it?"

"Many have tried, but none have been successful. After a while, people just stopped."

I sighed "It's almost sad how fast people give up on worthwhile endeavors simply because they run into difficulty."

"Even Bishops suffer from the human condition."

I grunted. "You've been hanging around Hager too much."

John swirled his drink, staring down into the sun-kissed amber liquid. "I have another reason for stopping by."

I frowned at him. "You've never had a problem telling me things straight out."

"You've never been…"

"Handicapped "

"I wouldn't use that word."

"Handicapped : Having a physical or mental disability that substantially limits activity. So sayeth Webster." I took a sip to punctuate the statement.

He frowned. "Did it say anything else?"

"Only that it's outdated,"

"I agree with that. You went to a dark place pretty quickly."

I stared at my glass, maneuvering it around with my fingers like a pitcher with a baseball. "I've never been physically incomplete."

"I'm not following."

"The one thing I always had was my body. While I never thought I looked perfect, I felt it worked perfectly. It was something I could count on. Whatever I put it through, it would take with barely any repercussions."

"You can't be serious. You were a Ranger—put through the wringer and thrown into combat situations that most people would crumble under. Are you saying you never broke any bones? Never got a sprained ankle, a fractured finger?"

I put my glass on the desk. "My physical stamina was like my a super power before I had actual ones. My nickname in the squad was Iron Man. While the other guys would wrap their knees or shoulders, or take long soaks in an ice bath, all I needed was a hot shower and I was good as new. Now…" I lifted my hand in the sling and let it drop. "I've not only lost the thing that made me a Bishop, I've lost the thing that made me Iron Man."

John leaned forward. "But you didn't lose what makes you Christian. That is something no one can take from you."

I barked a laugh. "Yeah, what's that? Sarcasm and the ability to quote random movie lines at will?"

"Yes."

I frowned at him.

"It is also your big heart that won't give up on anyone, including those that have willingly gone over to the other side. Your intelligence that always seems to come up with the exact right plan just when we need it. It's your leadership that has brought more Bishops together under one banner than in all of history." He stood and put his hand on my good shoulder. "It's almost sad how fast people give up on worthwhile endeavors, simply because they run into difficulty."

I looked up at him. "Even Bishops suffer from the human condition."

"Done feeling sorry for yourself?"

I stood. "For now."

"Good, Soon-Li and Tira want to run some tests on you."

We started for the door. "Great from invalid to lab rat."

"Stop bitching."

"See, that's better. You were becoming kind of sappy back there."

"Watch what you say. I can kick your ass now."

"Oh, now I *am* getting my power back."

Chapter Seventeen

"SIR, PERMISSION TO SPEAK freely."
I waved away his statement like a buzzing fly. "Major, cut that shit out. You can always speak your mind, but no matter what you say, I am going on this op."

It had been three days: three days of being scanned, prodded, poked. You would think a supernatural organization with the resources of a small kingdom would have methods more advanced than the local country doctor. Tira even checked my blood and… other liquids. Then, there were the psychological examinations, conducted of course by Dr. Gupta. She asked me about everything from my relationship with my father to sex with Marie. It was frustrating, embarrassing, and not helping.

Luckily, Jelena was making more headway. With the help of Soon-Li's new AI, she had been trying to identify viable locations where Euryale might be hiding out. She had narrowed these down to five and we were performing reconnaissance, I was determined to go, knowing it wasn't the right thing to do. So, trying to convince me of the illogic would not have dissuaded me. Nevertheless, that's what Mangine, Hager, and Tira were trying to do. I needed to do something to stop feeling useless. It was this or install air conditioning in my temporary office. Honestly, the latter almost won out.

"Do you know why generals don't fight?" the Major asked.

"Too old and fat? Too weighed down by those stars. Oh, oh, I know, plantar fasciitis."

He crossed his arms. "That's not a thing."

"Sure it is. Basketball players get it. And I think my cousin Charles has it, too., Though, that is another mystery."

Hager closed his eyes for a moment and took a deep, calming

breath. "I believe the point Major Mangine is trying to make is that you are far too important to risk further injury. This movement that we have built with the Bishops who have chosen to join your cause, the traction we have finally started to make after millennia, would all crumble without you driving it."

I leaned forward on my desk with my one good arm, my eyes drilling holes into Hager. "Do you really think that anyone would want to follow me *now*? Like this?"

"You sell yourself short."

"No, I am looking at the reality of it." I pushed off the desk to stand tall. "The reason everyone followed me was because I was special. I could do things no one else could. See things no one else could see. Everything else was just luck—a soldier playing the part of a demigod and thinking he was a general. Well, I'm not special anymore. I am not even a complete person. But I am still a soldier. Rangers are first to battle and that's where I'm going. Until you guys relieve me of my command, I'm still in charge. So do me the final courtesy of getting the hell out of my way."

The Major and Soon-Li filed out but Hager didn't move. His eyes never left mine. When the room was clear, he said, "You're right. You aren't complete. But it has nothing to do with your arm or your lack of powers."

He shook his head and left the room. I leaned on the desk and let out the breath I had been holding. I needed this. Why didn't they see that? I was sliding and needed a handhold. I had done what was asked of me since the day I was forced into this war. I'd taken on the responsibility when it was laid at my feet. I'd fought things I couldn't comprehend with little more than my wits, sarcasm, and a few movie lines. Why couldn't they just let me do what I did best?

A knock came at the open door. I looked up and Soon-Li was half in the doorway.

"Come for one final attempt to talk me out of it?"

She shook her head and her long braid wobbled. "I know you too well. You are stubborn like your mother. Once you set your mind to something, no one can divert you."

"Come to give me advice, then?"

She stepped fully into the room. "I came to give you this."

She withdrew a sheathed sword from behind her back and held it out with two hands. It was an arming sword like one might expect a knight to carry.

I reached out hesitantly, then stopped, looking up from the sword into her eyes. She nodded and I took it in both my hands. The ends of the golden cross guard were reminiscent of talons. Its black leather-wrapped handle was longer than normal for a single-handed weapon and the pommel was the shape of the top of a bishop chess piece. The sheath was white with red, intertwining leaves and flowers. In the middle, prominently displayed, was a dragonfly. I gently pulled the sword free of the scabbard a few inches so I could examine the blade. Intricate runes were etched onto the blade, and, where it widened slightly next to the hilt, another dragonfly was emblazoned in gold.

Soon-Li smiled. "It was the sword your mother carried, and her father before her. All the way back to Roland."

My brows knit together at that name and it took me a second to connect the dots. It was from a story my mother had regaled me with, "Roland the Paladin?"

"The same."

"Then this is—"

"Durendal," Soon-Li finished.

This wasn't just a sword. Durendal the Unbreakable was said to contain a tooth from Saint Peter, blood from Saint Basil, hair of Saint Denis, and a piece of the Virgin Mary's robe,

I fought to control my voice. "I thought you said I wasn't ready for a real sword yet."

"You're not. But it is ready for you. Plus, you need something to protect that soft head of yours."

The sword on my back felt good, like it was supposed to be there.

Its strength battled against the lack of feeling in my arm, switching my mood back and forth from elation to frustration. I would lean forward and feel the strap on my shoulder and a rush of adrenaline would flow through me. Then I would get an itch on my cheek that I would try to scratch with my dead arm and my mood would plummet.

I watched through binoculars. A compromise that the Major, Hager, and I had come to. The target was a house in the country and I was in a tree about two hundred yards away. I carried enough technology to make a black ops team jealous while perched forty feet in the air on a climbing tree stand.

While on the injured list, I had taken over from Soon-Li as tech operator. This basically meant I ran pre-written programs she set up for specific scenarios. *To override a security system, click here.* Not completely idiot proof, but enough that I could manage the process with minimal training. The climb to my lofty perch had been enjoyable, though frustrating with my current limited mobility. Surprisingly, my nurse-maids allowed it without encasing me in bubble wrap.

I knew I was being stubborn and cranky but I honestly couldn't stop myself. A different person had taken the helm and kept barging in with obnoxious comments when I tried to speak. The team was sensitive to my situation and, therefore, tolerant of my outbursts. However, it wouldn't be long before the last straw fell. I needed to get out of this funk but I struggled with knowing how. It was like being in the middle of a hedge maze; knowing the direction of the exit but not being able to navigate to it.

"Eagle, this is Honey Badger. Can I get a sitrep?" Mangine's voice over the coms pulled me back from my introspection.

I realized that the view through my thermal imaging field glasses was no longer aimed at the house as it should have been, but at the horizon where the sun dipped below the tree line. I adjusted my line of site and clicked the com's button.

"Copy, Honey Badger. Crows are blind. Be advised the primary target still looks to be secured on the second floor. Secondary target is on the first floor. Deploy."

The blind crows meant I had disabled the security system. In my current situation, I felt kind of bad for them. Cameras were only positioned on the outside. So taking them over would not have yielded anything. Infrared gave me a clear picture, but I had no way of confirming identities. They were just red figures who, sometimes, could be identified as male or female from an anatomical perspective, at least. The primary target was the priest. The secondary target was Kali. Euryale would be the jackpot.

"*Copy, moving in,*" reported the Major.

I watched as the small band of military troops and Bishops double-timed it from the tree line. As they neared the house, the team split. The Covenant members would focus on Kali while military personnel would be the rescue team. According to the floor plans, an alternate stairway could be accessed at the back. The retrieval would happen through there while the others would engage in a frontal assault. I had several nagging questions. Where was Euryale? Where are all the Converted and mercenaries that were usually crawling all over a place like this? Where were the wonder twins?

What, like you didn't know that name was coming?

"*Honey Badger in position,*" the Major reported.

"*Gandalf in position.*" I could hear the frustration in Hager's voice at my chosen call sign for him.

Smiling, I said, "Deploy."

The red outlines at the front of the building blurred into the room while the ones in the back doubled timed it up the stairs. I held my breath, waiting for the surprise. I was expecting anything that I hadn't calculated, including a portal opening up and a horde of Converted pouring through. They encountered no resistance. Kali was down in less than a second.

"Uh, Mr. Bateleur, I do believe we have made a mistake."

By the time Hager had finished his sentence, the Major and his team were up the stairs and in the room where the priest was being held.

"Yeah, this guy is no priest and this room was not built for torture, at least not the bad kind."

We had raided the house of Margot Blythe, also known as Mistress Ventress' House of Domination, Hey, it fit the profile. Plus, there was a guy tied up in there. He'd just paid to be that way. No harm, no foul, right? Except that her client, Mr. Linimyer, had wet himself during the unfortunate mixup. I guess there were no hard feelings since the dominatrix asked if we were available for hire.

The ride back was quiet. I felt myself slipping back into depression. All of my worst fears were coming true, one on top of the other: losing my powers, the inability to lead, failing to move the investigation forward. My imposter syndrome was at an all-time high. Why did I think I could lead a band of super humans against demigods and their minions? It was ludicrous. Since I had taken over, we had spent an inordinate amount of money, gotten half the Bishop community's hopes up, and pitted the other half against us, but that was about it.

When we returned to the London Covenant, I went to the place where I could find solace—the library. The ones in New York and Pennsylvania, which were the first two established in the States before they were actually states, were impressive enough. Neither could hold a candle to London. It was larger, of course, since it was considerably older, but that wasn't what pulled at me. These were not simply rows of shelves built to hold books. This was a celebration of the printed word. The stonework, the arches, the torches, (unlit for obvious reasons) the gargoyles carved into the stone, the fireplaces large enough to walk into without bumping your head. All of it lent itself to the romance of the page like an ornately appointed hardcover book. Such a thing doesn't add to the book's content but creates an aura of majesty around the volume. In the same way, this library's atmosphere transformed the simple act of reading into something magical.

This was the one place I felt at home in this foreign land. Yes, they all spoke English—probably in greater percentages than back in the States. And yes, I could walk out and step into a Starbucks or a McDonalds but I could do that in Dubai too. Everywhere reminded me I was not home. I was not in my element, especially with the loss of my powers. But here, I could forget all that for a while and delve into other worlds, other times. These were not stories made up for my entertainment, though the characters and tales they told were no less gripping. Probably more so, since it had all actually happened.

It was here that Francesca DeLuca found me. "Am I disturbing you?"

I glanced up from the page, taking a moment to pull myself back into the present. "Oh, hey. No, not at all."

The one thing I learned from terrible leaders was the way to make a person feel unwelcome. I pushed the book away and motioned to the chair next to me, which looked a few hundred years old if it was a day.

She took it and sat. "How is your arm?"

"It doesn't hurt a bit." It was a knee jerk reaction and I regretted it as soon as it left my lips. "Sorry, bad habit. It's the same. It's not getting better and I'm not sure it will. But thanks for asking."

I could see she was concerned for me but didn't know how to express it, both for me and for what was to come with the Bishops. "Is there anything I can do?"

The simple answer was no. It would save me from having to talk about my issue; save the explanation for my search and avoid the inevitable chit-chat that accompanies working with someone. I wasn't in the mood for conversation, explanations, or the pitiful expressions that people gave when they were in the company of a disabled person. But that wasn't what a good leader did, Dammit.

"As a matter of fact, yes, if you're serious." I watched her eyes. I had a task ready that would send her to the other side of the city if her expression told me that her offer wasn't sincere. They widened and she held back a smile. I nodded towards the pile of books. "Grab a stack. The neat ones are to be reviewed."

"The others are the discard piles?"

"Correct."

She pulled a pile over to her and slipped the top book off it, "What are we looking for?"

"Any record of a Bishop losing contact with his well of power."

She gawked more openly. "So, it's true."

"Did you think I was faking? Or maybe I was using the sling as a fashion statement?"

"Sorry, that was stupid."

"No, it wasn't. I'm just busting your chops."

Francesca actually looked flattered.

"Besides, this is only a temporary setback."

"That's a good attitude to have."

"It's not a mindset. It's a fact."

The confused look on her face was clear as day.

"Have you heard the story of how I beat Uji? Or how we took down Anton?"

This time she did smile and nodded vigorously. "But I would love to hear your version."

"I'll tell you what, if you find me a solid lead, I will regale you with both. But for now, I have a question. What happened in each case before we were victorious?"

"You almost died."

"I was going to say we were at a low point but sure, let's go with that. The point is, sometimes you need to lose everything before you can see the truth. Life has a tendency to obscure the important things. You spend your time doing what is required every day. You eat, you go to work, you pay your bills, you go to sleep. Then, you wake up and do it all over again. The phrase stop and smell the roses has been overused so the message has been garbled. It doesn't mean to take time to relax. It means to pay attention to what is around you. Don't be so focused on the destination that you lose sight of the beauty of the journey."

Her eyebrows got closer together, reminding me of Hager.

"Okay, let's try it a different way. Many of the best inventions were created because of an epic failure."

"How is your lack of power from a failure?"

"I failed to protect Father Kane. I failed in combat against the wonder twins." Her lips pursed but I just kept going. "I didn't capture Kali. I could go on, but you get the picture. It doesn't matter how badly we fail or that we fail at all. It matters that we have the emotional intelligence to acknowledge our failures and try to learn from them. The more we deny our shortcomings, the more of them we collect."

"You seem almost happy about this."

It took me a moment to realize she was right. I needed to assure another that things were not as bleak as they looked for it to click for me. Go figure.

"I also believe that the bigger the setback, the greater the advancement." Wiggling the shoulder of my dead arm, I added, "I think we have a big discovery on the horizon. Now let's get to it, shall we?"

Chapter Eighteen

ESIDES SUNDAY MORNINGS, THE occasional wedding, and Wednesday evenings during practice, the bell tower of St. Bartholomew's church was the quietest place to be. One was undisturbed except by pigeons and parakeets. The latter may be descendants of the ones owned by Jimi Hendrix. It wasn't on the inside that I chose to perch, however, but the outside. A small walkway surrounded the enclosure for the bell, which afforded a spectacular view of London. I brought a towel, since the birds left something behind that I didn't wish to convalesce upon. The corner had just enough room for me to sit cross-legged.

The early morning sun peeked over the horizon, coaxing the city out of its slumber. Listening to the rising city was something I had done even before all of this craziness began. My favorite locations included small parks where the business and residential life crossed. I would sit with my coffee and watch the world go by. At the time, it felt like watching a beloved show where each episode had all new characters. I felt separated from them, then and now, but for other reasons.

The research that Francesca and I had delved into the day before had yielded nothing. No one in the history of the Bishops, according to the London archives, had ever lost their well of power. Though, plenty had lost the ability to connect with it. A problem that, in all cases, was found to be psychological. Kind of like when Peter Parker got disconnected from his spider powers. But none of them had a missing well. There hadn't always been a Bishop around able to detect it but the subject always could. They described it as being similar to an initiate's first attempts, just beyond reach.

I didn't have that problem. It had taken me a while to recognize mine. But once I did, it was like a watch; forgotten until I wanted to know the time. Without it, I felt naked.

Settling into my position, I made myself comfortable; laying my hands palms up on my knees. Practice had made me decent at meditating. Tira would probably have disagreed with my assessment. I could relax my body and clear my mind dramatically quicker than almost a year ago. Now, being far above the rising city, I let myself take in the world. The breeze rustled the nearby trees and brushed across my skin, tousling my hair. Birds of various types called to each other, a symphony of chirps and coos. The smell of a wood fire from a neighboring restaurant drifted on the air with the accompanying fragrance of cooking eggs and sausage. A train far off in the distance clanged rhythmically as it rattled over the rails.

I alternated deep inhalations with long, drawn out exhalations. Within moments, I found myself in the meadow; the starting point for all of my meditation sessions and the spot where I tried anything new with my gift. The lake—the mental image of my well of power—was gone. There wasn't a hole, as one might find, from it having dried up. Its passing didn't even leave an indentation in the ground. The meadow simply went on and on. I sighed as I looked around. Was I even in the right place? My doubts were fleeting. I was connected here and, no matter how it changed, I would still recognize it. So be it. If there was one thing that my life had in great abundance, it was change. The speech I had given Francesca yesterday had not been total BS. I would embrace this recent transition and see where it brought me.

As if summoned by my decision, a buzzing sound cut the air. Off in the distance, I saw a small creature bobbing and weaving as it made its way to me. It was a dragonfly. Not just any, but the one that had been with me on this journey from the start. My spirit animal if you believed in those things. Any doubts I had of its supernatural connection were erased when I found it prominently positioned on my ancestral sword. It was my harbinger. Not of doom and destruction but of change, of evolution. I felt a sudden rush of exultation. This would be the bridge I needed to regain my powers, to restore my well.

The large insect stopped. I waited but it just hovered, raising higher or dipping lower. But it never moved forward. I frowned, puzzled. Maybe it was tired of coming to me. Perhaps I had to go to it. I started walking, my footfalls crunching on the high grass. It took me a minute before I realized I wasn't getting any closer and came to a stop. Confused, I looked around as though I might find myself on a treadmill. I tried running towards it, but only succeeded in going nowhere faster. I wondered briefly if the person who came up with that saying had been under similar circumstances. I paused to focus on the problem. I was moving without moving. The real problem was trying to correct a spiritual issue with physical solutions. I wasn't really standing in a field at all. I took a deep breath and thought., *do you think that's air you're breathing?*

While this was my sojourn to this metaphysical realm, it hadn't always been the case. I remembered back to the first time I'd found this meadow during my initial guided meditation. Granted, that session had not gone according to plan. Especially when I was nearly consumed by forces I could not fathom, much less control. But I wasn't focused on that aspect. What triggered my recollection was that I had entered this field for the first time from somewhere else. I had felt this spot and moved myself to it.

I didn't believe my actions in this realm had anything to do with the power bestowed upon us as Bishops. People with no supernatural abilities built memory castles for themselves all the time; elaborate residences where they placed specific memories for quick retrieval. This was a version of that. Some could also manipulate their dreams.

I concentrated on what I wanted to do, trying desperately to vanquish the song "Dreamweaver" from my head. I pictured my destination and willed myself to be there. My surroundings blurred until I stood in front of the dragonfly.

"There you are. Sorry it took me so long to get here. You know how thick I can be."

I reached out with my finger to give it a place to perch and ran into a wall. I cursed causing the dragonfly to look reproachful, though I'm not sure how it conveyed it.

"Sorry."

I placed a palm gingerly on the invisible barrier between myself and my guide. It was smooth. I pushed at it and it yielded somewhat, feeling like the inside of a balloon. Well, a balloon could be popped. I balled up my fist and gave it everything I had. This time it didn't give. My knuckles felt like I had just punched a brick wall. The shock reverberated up my arm and I nearly drew blood trying to keep the string of expletives under wraps. How this barrier had changed from flexible to solid had me stumped. So did the level of pain I was experiencing from a mental exercise.

I encountered an invisible barrier once before. It had separated me from moving at a speed nearing or at the point where time stopped. I had punctured that barrier with my gift, which I now no longer had. Staring at the ground, I wondered if I could dig my way around it but immediately dismissed the idea. As much as this place felt real, it was not. Therefore, the ground would have no limiting factors. The buzzing increased in volume and intensity. The dragonfly looked to be attempting to get my attention.

"What?"

The deep vibrations of its wings modulated as though trying to communicate through frequency changes.

"This would be a lot easier if you could talk."

It gave me the impression of sighing and settled into a deeper, low frequency buzzing. Then it slowly moved forward and placed its head on the barrier at my eye level. I caught on after a second. I placed both hands on my side and slowly leaned forward, touching my forehead to the opposite spot.

A thunderclap accompanied a blinding flash and a concussive wave shot out in a ring from the connection point. The grass rippled and the trees that dotted the area shook, causing a few leaves to break away and float slowly to the ground. I didn't see any of that. It was an impression I had whenever I looked back on that moment later, including the slow motion backwards fall into the turf.

My mind had been transported, similar to an out-of-body experience I had on a Miami rooftop while trying to find Krissi. The key difference was that, at that time, I had to "walk" everywhere. Now the concussive force shoved me back into my physical form on the bell tower, where my metaphysical self was summarily launched like an ICBM. I traveled too fast to track exactly where I was going beyond a simple directional path. Not to mention, the shock of the entire process had me reeling. I caught a few landmarks but, besides that, everything was a blur.

Within seconds, the compact streets of London gave way to more rural areas which dispersed even further until my target became obvious. It was a large manor house with sprawling, manicured lawns surrounded by a forest and accessible by a singular road cut out of the tree line. I streaked down into the minor castle through a window and down several hallways; past tapestries, paintings, chairs, and suits of armor that all shifted slightly in the wake of my passing. I came to rest, finally, in a small room after I bounced off the wall and into a corner chair, shifting a frame hanging there. The lone occupant looked up, made the sign of the cross, and went back to his reading. It was Father Kane. He was reading the Bible, murmuring to himself as he read. The priest didn't look any worse for wear, despite having been spirited away over the rooftops of London by three superhumans. I guess the seminary taught resiliency.

But that wasn't the weird thing—somehow, there were two of him. I saw the priest's physical form but it was superimposed with another figure being torn in opposite directions. One half was angelic and reverent while the other was angry and murderous.

I got up out of my cushioned armchair and moved closer to him. "Father Kane?"

His murmuring stopped. I noticed he was studying Revelation. Apropos, if a little morbid.

"Can you hear me?"

He looked up and I thought maybe I was in luck. Then he closed his Bible and the door opened. The person who came into the room would have given me a heart attack had I been connected to my body. Not the physical form, which was that of a woman in her thirties. She was not overly noteworthy in any respects: pretty but not excessively so, of average height and weight with straight, brown, shoulder length hair. She was so unremarkable that I could have passed her on the street without a second glance.

The superimposed vision, however, was something out of Wes Craven's nightmares. It had seven heads. Each was reminiscent of the woman's physical appearance but with some artistic flair that made my stomach crawl. One shifted between applying makeup and posing. Another wore a crown, arms overburdened by riches of every type. A third had red eyes and was in a constant state of libidinousness; eyes closed, panting. The fourth stared at everything and every person with longing as its green eyes dripped with bitterness. The next head was the most sickening to gaze upon. It was hideously overweight with yellow eyes and was constantly devouring a smorgasbord of greasy food and spirits. It shoveled them in, unconcerned by how much stayed in its mouth or dribbled down its puffy cheeks. If that was the sickest, what followed was the scariest. It was pure hate. This was the spirit of all the intolerance and anger. I felt the rage coming off it like a furnace. The last seemed almost out of place among its sisters. It lounged there, barely able to lift its head; annoyed at being disturbed by the others' raving, panting, or consuming. I had no doubt that I was staring at Euryale. The ever shifting image made me nauseated which, as a bodiless form, was saying something.

She stepped up to the priest. "Have you had a chance to think about what I said?"

"Yes and I still do not believe it to be the right course of action. Violence begets violence."

"What about the cruelty he is performing? Does that not warrant a response?"

"I can go to the authorities."

"He is the authorities. Do you think he cannot shift the narrative in his favor? Then there could be further punishments for her."

He closed his eyes. "The edict is clear. Thou shalt not kill."

"And yet, how many millions were butchered at the hands of the Church? The Spanish Inquisition alone disposed of nearly thirty thousand non-believers. What's one more for a good cause?"

He rubbed the black cover of the Bible on the table in front of him. "It is not my place to say who is to live or die. That is God's purview alone."

She circled around to the other side of his chair, a lithe finger tracing across his shoulders. "And, as a priest, are you not the hand of God in this world? Is it mere chance that placed this girl in your confessional? Or was it God pointing her to you so you could dispense his justice?"

"That is not how He works."

"How would you know? Isn't one of your mantras that God works in mysterious ways? What could be more so than a priest dispensing justice?"

His resolve was crumbling. I could see the conflict within him. Whatever this guy was doing to the girl was eating away at him. "Stay strong."

My words somehow reinforced his resistance, but that wasn't the only effect they had. The Tainted's eight heads all turned to look at me. The eyes of her physical form narrowed while the rest widened. Then the seven spectral heads all screamed at once. The strength of it hit me and caused whatever vehicle had brought me there to snap back like a window shade. I watched the manor recede as I was pulled at breakneck speed. I tried desperately to keep track of the terrain I whipped by. Within seconds, I was slammed into my body with enough force to send me across the rooftop and into the opposite wall—where I passed out.

Chapter Nineteen

"**H**E'S COMING AROUND."

I woke up in the hospital wing of the Covenant. I went to rub my face with my right hand, only to be reminded that it still didn't work. I had hoped that my ride on the metaphysical express meant I was back in the game.

"Fuck."

Tira stepped over. "What is it?"

"Nothing."

I was surrounded by all the Bishops in the house, including Francesca. The only one not in attendance was Edward Thorne. I sat up and a shock of pain gripped at my back. I sucked air through my teeth and moved more carefully but continued. Tira on my left and Hager on my right adjusted my pillows to help get me into a comfortable position.

"Thanks."

Hager put a hand on my shoulder which I couldn't feel. "How are you, my boy?"

"I feel like I was thrown against a brick wall."

Hager curled his lip. "Obviously."

I looked at Tira. "How bad?"

"Nothing broken, amazingly enough, but you will be a tapestry of bruises for a while."

"How did you find me? I didn't let anyone know where I was going."

Hager sighed. "Your impression of a battering ram loosened a stone which nearly hit me. I found you when I went to investigate."

"Thanks."

It was Hager's turn to nod. "Can you tell us how you were injured in such a manner?"

"I'll explain on the way. I think I have a line into where Euryale is holding up." Yanking at the blanket covering me, I stopped short, quickly pulled it back into place. I frowned at the team. "You guys really need to stop taking my clothes off."

I got dressed. An even tougher experience with back pain added on. It is amazing the things you take for granted. Pulling pants up one handed was doable, but frustrating. Getting them up to my thighs was no problem, but yanking them up over my ass took five moves instead of one. I maneuvered my dead arm into the sleeve of my Twin Pines Mall tee shirt like I was threading a needle with a strand of cooked spaghetti and pulled it over my head. I almost gave up on wearing socks. Almost.

I met the team in the briefing room. Soon-Li had run to the kitchens and brought me some food. I was ravenous, having felt like I hadn't eaten in days. Over the next few minutes, I described what I had witnessed in my excursion between inhaling two fried eggs, baked tomatoes, and something they *called* sausage but which bore no resemblance to the breakfast meats I was used to.

"How is it that you accomplished this without your powers?" Hager asked.

I swallowed the coffee I'd drained from the small paper cup, then put my napkin in it. "Your guess is as good as mine. But that's a problem for another day. Right now, I have a general direction where the priest is being held. That has to be our focus."

"Do we really think a man of the cloth is capable of murder?" Thorne asked.

"He's human. Plus, we've witnessed what men of faith have done of their own volition. It's not implausible to make an error in judgement for a good reason."

Thorne's face told me he was not on board with my views. I wasn't shocked and ignored it. He seemed to have spent an inordinate amount of time in his life being told that he was right and couldn't fathom a scenario where it would not continue to be the case. David had been difficult to win over as well. I had taken the time and energy to win him because we had a small team and were working to find John's father. He was oversight sent from the US Covenant headquarters in Philly. I'd needed his help as much as for him not to be a hindrance,

Edward Thorne was a high-ranking member of my larger team with no power to override my decisions or hamper my progress. I had read several leadership books since taking on this role. While I felt they would have helped my climb up the Walmart corporate ladder, they had limited use in battling the forces of evil. I could liken him to a defiant senior leader in a merger. These people were toxic to the overall mental health of a company. The suggested method for dealing with them was the axe because it would cost too much political capital on the off chance they could be won over.

I couldn't really just fire a Bishop, could I? Admittedly, it would be an enjoyable prospect and I took a moment to revel in the idea.

"I don't see how this plan could possibly work."

"Luckily you don't need to worry about it."

"What do you mean?"

"You're fired. Take yourself, your monocle, your stuffy attitude, and your annoying accent and get out."

"Christian?" Soon-Li's voice pulled me back into reality.

I blinked a few times to clear my head. "Sorry, I lost my train of thought."

She pointed at the screen. "This is an aerial view of London from our location."

I examined it for a moment. "Can you show me a view from the top of the tower?"

"I don't have one there," she replied.

John snapped his fingers. "I have an idea: Samson."

She smiled. "Perfect."

John got up. "Be right back."

He returned after a moment with a control pad which he hooked up to a tablet. Within a few seconds, we had an insect's view of a pad surrounded by grass that looked to be tree sized. The screen lifted above the lawn and quickly made its way to hover where I had been meditating this morning. As it passed over the wall, I saw the stone I had broken loose and I stretched my aching muscles. The camera was looking out over the pillars.

"Okay, that's good." Start panning around to the right."

The screen started rotating.

"Stop. Right there. Advance."

John eased the stick forward and the drone crept out over London.

"Can it go faster?"

John pushed further.

"Faster. Faster."

"If we go too fast, this whole thing will be a blur."

"That's what I want."

"Okay." He shrugged, then jammed the controller to its limit. The drone reached hyper speed in seconds. It was still not nearly the rate of travel that I had experienced but it gave a similar effect.

"Stop. What was that reflection on the right?"

Hager identified it just a heartbeat before Thorne. "Regent's Canal."

The Covenant head closed his open mouth with a grimace.

"Yeah, I think I remember that. How the light bouncing off the water contrasted with the surrounding city. It was a little closer, though. Can we back up and adjust?"

John made the correction and we were off again.

"Stop. I recognize that."

"Emirates Stadium," Thorne announced with a smirk. "Home of the Gunners. I got to see almost the entire Invincible Season."

"Wasn't that in Arsenal Stadium in Highbury?" Hager corrected.

I thought he would take offense but he just got a far off look in his eye and sighed. "Ah yes, Highbury."

We went on like that for twenty minutes; every so often readjusting the direction and finding yet another landmark before continuing the journey. All the while, Hager and Thorne tried to one up each other.

"I need to turn back or we may not have enough battery for the return trip."

"I think we have ample data. Soon-Li?"

"I agree. I have been plotting the points along the map. Now let's see if Confucius can come up with a list of properties to review."

"Great. Also, plug in that the course over London was approximately one tenth of the overall distance."

"Okay." Her fingers flew over the keyboard. "Done. It's running now."

"How long do you think it should take?"

"Not too long."

I frowned. "That is not a length of time."

Soon-Li flared her nostrils to tell me exactly what she thought of my request. "The geospatial analysis should be short. One to five minutes. However, the data retrieval and processing will take longer. Figure you have time to eat at McDonald's but not for a typical European dinner."

"Great."

She narrowed her eyes. "But there is plenty to call Marie."

I frowned back. "Gee, thanks, Ma."

"High praise, indeed."

"You know you are very difficult to insult."

She smiled in answer.

I returned to my office and pulled out my cell phone. They still worked down here, thanks to cellular repeaters placed all around. I stared at it for a few minutes, putting off the inevitable. I wanted to talk to Marie. In fact, I ached to do so. At least at home we could talk without a six-hour time difference screwing things up and it was only a two-hour flight on our jet for either of us to spend some quality time together. I understood when she took the promotion to Special Agent in Charge and I supported it. She was a born leader and she'd worked hard to get where she was. I was happy for her.

I also knew that becoming the first — well, second — Bishop commander was going to take a lot of my time. There were still factions that thought I was a fake, a fluke, or that I would lead us into another dark age. My days were split between finding the Tainted, managing the logistics of such a large organization, and strategizing on how to bring the rest of the Bishops onto our side. All of this, matched against her schedule, made carving out moments tricky at best. Add in the time difference and it became torture.

No, wanting to talk to her wasn't my issue. It was worrying her to the point where she might drop everything and fly over here. And no, that did not sound bad at all, which was the problem. I wanted her here but I didn't want her to feel like she had to come. It was a tightrope I wasn't skilled enough to walk.

I sighed and tapped the phone icon and selected the top person in my favorites. The one long ring we used in the US was strangely comforting after the two short bursts for UK calls. Man, I was getting sappy. Luckily, the Major wasn't in my head or I wouldn't hear the end of this.

She picked up and I inhaled in order to launch into my prewritten speech.

"Hey, Chris. Can I call you back?"

I heard shooting in the background. "Everything okay?"

"Team Two, move up. Team Three flanking positions. Yeah, everything's fine. Just a little distracted."

"I can hear that. No chance you're playing Call of Duty?"

"Ha, I would gladly get killed there to talk."

"Okay, call me when you get a second. I love you."

"You too. Fuck! Move your fat ass, Peterson, or I'll shoot you myself."

Marie hung up. Well, I definitely didn't worry her too much.

A knock came at the door and Soon-Li entered at my response.

"Done already?" I asked.

"I could ask you the same question," she countered.

"She was tied up."

"Hopefully not literally."

"What did you find?"

"Roughly three hundred estates."

"Three hundred? Can't you narrow it down?"

She gave me the *duh* look.

"That is narrowed down. Remember, you only provided me with a best guess trajectory based on a quick pass by a few landmarks. The variance becomes greater the further from London we look and you have no way to determine how fast you were going. These are the larger plots that have wooded areas on them within six degrees of your target area. Those equate to roughly a hundred and thirty-seven square miles."

"Shit."

"You're welcome. I sent you the files with pictures."

"Great. More paperwork."

Chapter Twenty

I TOOK MY LAPTOP outside to go through the pictures. I would've preferred to review them on paper, but printing out that many high-res photos would have taken hours. Plus, I didn't want to rescue humanity from the Tainted only to contribute to all of us perishing from global climate change in some save the whales but not the planet type of scenario.

Anyway, I was tired of being underground. So I found a cozy spot outside in the sun, another pleasant surprise. There was sun in the UK. I had no idea. From all the hype, I presumed it was twenty-four seven overcast. Next, I'd find out that it didn't always rain in Seattle. But I digress.

Going through pictures one at a time was mind numbing and made it difficult to stay on topic. Many fit the bill but the perspective was wrong. So it was hard to tell. It was like trying to recognize someone from the back or with those annoying masks on. They kind of looked familiar, but so did all the rest.

After a short while, I shifted my approach, separating them into virtual piles of possibilities and garbage. That took a few hours before I went inside to get lunch and recharge my computer. Another thing I found strange on this side of the pond was the midday meal. There seemed to be two schools of thought on it. Either they shut business down and had a three-martini respite followed by a nap or it was a supermarket meal. And I'm sorry, sliced cucumbers between three-inch squares of bread does not constitute a sandwich. Tira was in the kitchen already.

"Did you call Marie?"

"You guys are way too invested in my relationship."

"Is that a no?"

I ignored her and rummaged through the refrigerator for the makings of a real sandwich. "Yes, I called. She was… otherwise occupied."

"Bathroom?"

"Gunfight."

"That was my next guess."

I found various cold cuts that normal people would not combine. Since I was adventurous, I took a chance. In total, they built an adequate hoagie derivative.

"What are you having, a salad?"

"Cucumber sandwiches."

"Of course. Kind of reminds me of the first time we cooked together."

"Your first morning in the Covenant. I remember. You kept wanting to put bacon in everything."

"I was trying to make a good impression and bacon makes things better. How was I supposed to know you were a vegetarian?"

Tira smiled. "You did okay. By the end, I didn't think you were nearly as much as a pompous ass."

"Nearly?"

She popped a tiny sandwich in her mouth and, grinning, stayed quiet.

"Can I ask a question?"

Her mouth was full so she gestured for me to proceed.

"I thought we were getting off to a good start after that breakfast. Then, a short time later, you pulled me back from the edge."

Tira stiffened.

I continued. "For a while, you seemed angry with me. But I couldn't figure out what I had done."

We both sat at the table, in silence. She took another small bite. It grated at me but I let her take her time. I thought she was close to opening up and I wanted nothing to distract from that.

She sighed heavily. "It was about now."

I felt my eyebrows pulling together. "Excuse me?"

"The hunt for my sister."

"You got mad because you saw that we would be hunting her?"

Tira met my gaze. "No. I was angry because I saw that you would cause her death."

"Me?" It seemed impossible until I thought about it. The number of Converted that I had dispatched was growing exponentially. I was also slowly chipping away at the Tainted themselves, something that hadn't been done in the history of this war. I searched for words but could only come up with, "I'm sorry."

She shook her head and wiped at a tear. "No, Christian, I'm sorry." She reached out and put a hand on mine. "The visions and feelings I get from such a deep divining are mixed up and confusing. They leave me with baseline emotions, which I interpret. It was at a point when I didn't really know you. So I must have made a mistake. Knowing you like I do now, I'm sure that there is no way you could hurt her. You spend half your time trying to get us to be more conscious of how we use our powers."

My thoughts flashed back to the battle in the tunnels of New Orleans, where I faced a horde of Converted that had been more creature than human. I killed all of them without a second thought. She believed I couldn't do the same to her sister. I was not so sure. Even now, I was so focused on finding and stopping both Kali and Euryale that I wasn't considering the how of it.

"I get it. I wish you had talked to me but I don't know if that would have helped either." I put my hand over hers. "But I promise you, I will find a way to help her back."

Tira's smile was sad and she pulled back slowly. "I know you will find a path, Christian. I just don't believe she will be willing to walk it."

We finished our lunch in relative quiet. I walked away feeling good. While our relationship had been solid for a while, it was built on a rocky foundation. I felt a weight had lifted.

I picked up my computer and went back out to the courtyard to continue my search. This part would be the more time-consuming. I had to take all the potential matches and find them on the satellite feed before adjusting the viewing angles to match what I saw during my out-of-body experience. The first few took forever until I got into a rhythm. It was still a dog of a process. Soon-Li's AI could probably do it more quickly but I was doubtful how much it would actually save. I would have to find her, explain what I was trying to do and program the AI with the new information. Then I would still have to review each picture. It wouldn't feel like I was actively contributing. I wasn't sure if I could tolerate that. This was all going through my head as I lined up the next picture and stopped. I zoomed out to get a view from a higher point.

"Holy shit." I selected the pen tool and circled the house, then smiled. "Got ya."

"Christian!"

I looked up to find Francesca running towards me, my grin fading quickly based on her expression.

"What's up?"

"Hager's looking for you. There's been an attack."

"Dammit, Hager! Learn how to use a phone."

I closed my laptop and put it on the bench, then took off running after her. My arm flopped uselessly at my side but I did my best to ignore it. We passed through the black, iron gate and onto Cloth Fair. I followed her across the street and through the little alley lined with barrels which were exterior decor for the Rising Sun Pub. At the other end, next to one of the few remaining public phones, there was a car waiting with the back door open.

I didn't recognize it and tried to stop when I *did* recognize the woman in the backseat. Her twin sat in the front passenger seat. Ms. Deluca had already circled behind me in a blur and was shoving me the rest of the way. I tumbled into the car, not able to control my landing with one arm, and landed with my face in the lap of one half of the wonder twins.

"Ohhh, see? I knew you had a little fire in you," she purred.

As I righted myself, coming face to face with Francesca as she leaned into the car. She dug into my pockets and removed my phone, dropping it on the ground. I eyed her.

"Any specific reason you're betraying everything you swore to protect?"

"I'm not betraying anything. I'm getting rid of a cancer that is rotting us from the inside. One that has caused a rift in the Covenant not felt since Christ. We have no time for false prophets." She caught my expression. "What are you smiling at?"

"I'm picturing your face when I come back for you."

Her eyes went wide. Then she glanced at the twin next to me.

"He has a microchip in his right arm, which they can use to find him."

Before she closed the door, I said, "See you soon."

Chapter Twenty-One

"**G**IVE ME YOUR ARM," Psycho One said in a voice that conveyed she was going to chop it off or do a magic trick. I was leaning towards the former.

"See, there is a problem with that."

Her eyebrows lifted. "Do you remember the last time you didn't comply?"

"And that's where the issue comes in."

She seemed to have finally realized that my arm was in a sling. "Oh, what happened to the poor baby?"

"Some bitch stabbed me in the shoulder."

Psycho Two engaged from the front passenger seat. "Is that where I left my knife? I was looking for it. I don't suppose I could get it back."

"I'd love to return it, but I'm not sure you will enjoy where I put it."

Her sister, next to me, grabbed my arm and yanked it towards her. "Sounds like second date activities to me."

She pressed her thumb hard into the inside of my forearm. It was disconcerting watching the process while not feeling it. She found her target and flipped open a butterfly knife with a flourish of her other hand.

Front Seat Psycho purred, "I get tingles every time you do that."

Her sister blew her a kiss. Then, with a quick, precise movement like popping a balloon, stabbed me in the arm. I felt nothing. Blood pooled from the wound and the wonder twin slowly lowered her mouth to it. Her gaze never left mine. When she pulled back, it looked like she had put on bright red lipstick. She smiled, showing me the chip between her blood stained teeth.

"I'm gonna need a receipt for that."

Her smile widened as she pushed the button to lower the window and spat it out onto the street.

Her sister asked, "You are going to share, right?"

I wasn't sure what she meant until she leaned past me and locked lips with her, my bleeding arm still in her grasp.

"How about you two get a room? You can drop me off anywhere."

In answer, she yanked me in closer and let her have a drink from the tap.

"Do you have any Merthiolate or Mecuricome? 'Cause this might get infected."

The twin sucking on my arm came up for air and her sister regarded me with a smile that made me think they were out of antibiotic creams.

"I have something better." She traced her index finger along the wound. I could hear the sizzle and smelled burning flesh but I couldn't feel anything

"Ember, I presume?"

Crystal pouted. "I wasn't done yet."

"Don't worry, love." She leaned forward and licked the blood off her sister's chin, causing her eyes to roll back. "Euryale will have him bleeding again soon."

This led to more kissing.

"Seriously, I'm pretty sure there's a hotel up the road. I can just—"

I didn't even see her fist coming.

I woke up chained to the ceiling, hanging barely an inch above the floor. I wasn't sure how long I had been there but my left arm was already aching. The good news was that my right arm wasn't in pain at all. My mouth was dry and my head was a little fuzzy, so I assumed I had been drugged. Oh, and I was naked. Friggin' wonder twins.

I presumed I was in the same house I had visited that morning but couldn't be sure. It wasn't like I'd been given a tour. *There is a beautiful breakfast nook that overlooks the garden and here is a place that no medieval castle can do without; your very own dungeon, complete with skeletons.*

I jest, of course, there were no skeletons. Disappointing because I really wanted to do the *what are you in for* joke. My accommodations did have electricity in the form of a single bulb that dangled from the ceiling on a long wire. I didn't have time to ruminate on it further since I had a visitor. The thick steel door opened and Euryale came in, followed by Kali.

"In the several millennia you have lived, hasn't anyone ever taught you how to knock? God knows what you could have walked in on me doing."

Kali strode up, head held high, with an acidic smile. "Still so smug after we literally caught you with your pants down?"

"My pants are off so they can't be down."

I tried using air quotes, but it lost something in my current predicament. Apparently, Kali took offense because she drove her fist into my stomach. I saw it coming but she cheated by strengthening the blow with her powers.

"I'm going to enjoy this," she hissed in my ear,

When I could catch my breath, I whispered back, "By the way, Kamala, your sister says hi."

I wasn't ready for the next punch.

"That is quite enough, Kali." Euryale stepped up to me.

I stared her in the eyes and asked, "Was my outfit your idea or the pervy twins?"

"It was theirs but I can't say that I disapprove."

"This is some crew you have here: psycho killer, the porno twins, and the quintessential middle child."

"You talk big for a person who is naked and chained to the ceiling."

"And you don't look like Jack the Ripper."

"Jacqueline. Or at least I was at the time. I'm the one who whispered the name to the reporters back then."

"I would shake your hand but…" I wiggled my left arm in its chains.

"And you are the infamous Christian Bateleur."

"It's pronounced IN-famous."

Her expression never wavered. "I had heard that you had a problem taking things seriously. Quite different from your predecessor."

"Look around, you have me in a dungeon in what could be a castle in England. How am I supposed to take any of this seriously?"

"I see your point. Why don't we try something that will make it easier for you?"

She inclined her head towards an object to my left and Kali moved to retrieve it. It was a small, rectangular machine on wheels about the size of the personal shopping cart I'd seen the elderly pulling around. It was plugged into the wall by a long, thick cord and had a set of jumper cables, each with a natural sponge on the end.

Kali smiled the whole time she was setting things up. Then, as she reached behind me, I heard the squeaking of a valve. A stream of cold water rained down on me from above.

I repressed a shiver. "I appreciate the thought, but I already had a shower this morning. Plus, I didn't bring my Dr. Squatch soap with me."

A bucket of water hung off of the device into which Kali dipped the sponges. Then, careful to keep them apart, she flipped a hefty switch and turned a dial the size of her fist clockwise.

She stepped up in front of me. "This is no ordinary sponge bath—"

"You know what?" I interrupted, "I've had enough of your theatrical bullshit." I turned my attention to Euryale. "Let me guess. You want to know locations for all the Covenants and details about our troop movements and strategies. I'll cut to the chase. I'm not telling you shit." I met Kali's eyes, which were already sparking with anger. "Leave the monologuing to the experts and start the show."

The blood left her lips. Then she shoved both leads into my abdomen. My world went white and my body convulsed. My teeth clamped shut. Had my tongue been between them, it would have been bitten in half. I didn't vibrate as some movies would have you believe. I locked up. Every one of my muscles received the same command—constrict. They strained against my shackles and I felt like they would rip right off the bone. The pain was unimaginable and it was everywhere. Except my right arm, of course. Somehow, the lack of feeling there hurt more, I would have imagined smoke coming out of my hair if I could have formed a thought. I think I peed myself but I had no way to know for sure.

Somewhere very far away, I heard the word, "Enough."

It took a second to realize that it was Euryale. I was shocked—excuse the pun— that I had made the connection, but there was something familiar about her presence.

"I said enough!" A loud crack resounded off the walls and the pain suddenly stopped. When my eyes worked again, Kali was on the floor halfway across the room. One side of her face looked as if she had laid in the sun too long. The leads had fallen into a puddle, arcing like something out of a Frankenstein movie. The Tainted stepped through it without so much as a twitch and shut the machine off. Her eyes never left Kali.

"Your lack of control is shameful. If he dies before providing me with the information I need, you will follow him. And believe me, the pain that he has felt will be nothing compared to your agony."

Kali's eyes went from Euryale to me, a mixture of fear and anger behind them.

I was able to get my tongue to work and between gasps of air, I said, "See? Expert."

I thought Kali would launch herself at me again, but a quick glance at Euryale kept her on the floor. The Tainted cocked her head and Tira's sister slowly got up and walked out. Her stare told me we would continue later. Euryale turned to face me.

"Did you really think I would allow her to kill you?"

I was panting like I had just run a marathon or, more accurately, like I had stopped breathing for a while.

"It was worth a shot. Her sister has a temper. I figure Kamala's is worse."

She stepped up closer to me. "*Kali* underestimates you. She has manipulated scores of men and believes them to be simple creatures that think with their lust."

Reaching behind me, she shut off the water. I finally got my breathing under control, mostly.

"You think differently?"

With the pointed nail of her index finger, she traced a line down my skin from my chest to my abdomen.

"I have found that while many men fall under the umbrella of Kali's viewpoint, there are a rare few that do not. Of those, you find two types. Those who have spent their years advancing their brains; decades absorbing as much information as possible while they ignore their physical forms." She circled me, her nail still scratching across my flesh alarmingly low. "The others are quite the opposite, focusing all their efforts on perfecting their bodies while ignoring their minds." She stopped her inspection in front of me again, her warm hand came to a rest just below my navel. "The most rare, those truly exceptional few, balance their attention between both, not to compare themselves to anyone else, but to their former selves. Their only goal every day is to be better than the last."

Her finger traced the outline of my core muscles, weaving in and out of the patchwork across my stomach.

"You cannot tempt me. My heart and head belong to someone else."

My words seemed to have the opposite of their intended effect. She closed her eyes and bit her bottom lip. After a very awkward moment, she opened them again and let out a long breath.

"I know." She met my gaze. "You misunderstand me. I am not trying to seduce you. I am simply admiring a work of art. Attempting to memorize each brush stroke, each hue while knowing that, soon, I will have to destroy it."

She walked out without another word. Then the lights went out, casting me into total darkness.

Chapter Twenty-Two

I FELT DEPRESSION SURROUNDING me, like the pitch blackness in which I hung. I had been in dangerous situations but none quite so dire. We didn't get to the point of torture in Afghanistan—the physical part anyway. The torment of watching my friend's head exploding next to me while being heartbeats from the same fate, stuck with me even now. The pain of that experience had never left. It would be gone for a while, only to appear again without warning, but not without provocation. The sound of a balloon popping, the smell of goats (which is why I stayed far away from petting zoos) or hot arid air. They weren't always triggers, but those were things that had the potential.

But it wasn't the pain in my wrist or shoulder that plagued me; it was the visions. I couldn't make them stop. Usually, I was able to push them into the background by focusing on something else. Maybe I could turn the TV on and drown them out. Here, there was nothing else to distract me and my nightmare played on a never ending loop.

The new man entered the dusty hut. They argued. He pulled out his pistol. My friend's brains splattered all over me. The barrel pointed at me. The new man entered the dusty hut. They argued. He pulled out his pistol. My friend's brains splattered all over me. The barrel pointed at me.

I closed my eyes but the scene played against my eyelids. I opened them and the vision was cast in the darkness. Shaking my head, I growled in frustration. I tried replacing the image with one of the movies in my mind's library. They were there for this specific occasion. Some movies I could quote from beginning to end. I started with John Wayne movies. The duke staggers into a bar bleeding from his head and informs Joe that he's under arrest. A flunkie gets the drop on him from behind.

"Now, what are you going to do?" says Joe.

The sound of a pistol being pulled from a holster a shot rings out and a gun goes flying.

The next line is supposed to be Dean Martin telling Sheriff John T. Chance that he can do anything he wants. It was replaced by Josh's brains splattering on my face.

Okay, let's try again.

I started with another movie and got a couple of lines in before the nightmare reasserted itself.

Maybe we'll keep it light this time.

"He's gonna pinch my cheek. I hate that."

"Maybe he won't."

The gun aimed at me.

My breathing was coming in gasps and I felt I was losing my grip on my sanity. Yanking at the chains that held me to the ceiling caused me to swing. I needed a distraction but I was running out of ideas. I pictured Marie's face: the way her ears rose when she smiled. The sparkle in her eyes. Her scent as I cradled her in my arms. It was my ultimate happy place. The thought of a paradise sparked another idea. The one spot where I spent the most time in my head. I grasped the thread and started calming my breath. I focused on the place where all my powers started. Slowly, the meadow coalesced around me. Relief flooded through me like being hit by a cold shower and I dropped onto the grass, trying to control the sob that wanted to escape. I gritted my teeth until it passed, then exhaled as though extinguishing the candles of a centennial celebration.

It took me a few minutes to fully calm myself. When I did, I laid back and let the metaphysical sun warm my face. I enjoyed the feeling of my right arm again. I still didn't understand how this place worked but I wasn't going to analyze it now. It was a reprieve from the ghost of traumas past and, for the moment, that was good enough for me. I wasn't giving my curious nature a chance to break the spell.

I sat up, leaning back on my hands, and looked around. It was my normal spot on what would have been the shore of a large lake, but was still just a meadow. I tried to find my friend but she was nowhere to be seen. That might've been a good thing. The last time I saw the dragonfly, it took me on a journey to, well, here. I'd had out of body experiences several times on purpose. From what Adam had told me, most people could do it, but the ability to traverse more than a few feet away from your body was rare. I'd used it previously to travel from a rooftop in Miami. I'd gone across dimensions to a building on the other side of the city. We had thought it was the portal that allowed me to journey so far. But, based on the previous trip, that may not have been the case. Was it really only yesterday? Well, it could have been this morning, since I had no clue what time it was. The twins didn't leave my watch either.

This line of thinking gave me another idea. If I could travel from the Covenant to here, the reverse could be feasible. What good would that do? If I accomplished it, I wouldn't be able to communicate with anyone there. I would be a fly on the wall. At the very least, it was better than waiting around to be tortured.

The only flaw in this plan was in the process I used to step out of my body. I had to overlap my current surroundings with this meadow. I was not eager to reenter total darkness and the visions that may be waiting there. But I had a bigger issue with sitting on my ass when I could do something.

I stood up and raised my hands over my head. Taking a deep breath, I allowed myself to feel the restraints on my wrists. The physical world slammed back into place and I had to take a few more slow, deep breaths to stop the panic from encroaching. It took a few attempts to find the right balance. In the end, I centered myself midway between the meadow and the dungeon. Then, with purpose, I stepped out of myself and my metaphysical self dropped to the floor. I shook off the residual discomfort seeping into my shoulders and wrist.

Strangely enough, it was no longer pitch dark. I couldn't find any windows or other light sources, so I concluded it was a perk of this spiritual walk. Illumination was a necessity for my eyes to experience the world around me. Since I wasn't actually using them, apparently I was seeing reality as it was or at least how my physical form would see it.

"Okay, let's take a walk."

I walked through the door into the hallway. It was lined with doors of solid steel with reinforced hinges. Despite my tongue-in-cheek references, I was in a legitimate dungeon—and one designed to hold Bishops. No matter what, it would require a large amount of time and power to escape. I crept forward, looking for the stairs. Euryale had already caught me in this form before, so I didn't know how much she could naturally detect. I wasn't tiptoeing, but neither was I skipping.

I eventually found the stairs after picking the wrong direction first. The door leading to them was formidable but I passed through without incident. This place was extensive and I was not looking to take a tour. I just needed to find an exterior wall so I could figure out a way back to London. I heard voices and stopped dead.

"I don't see why we aren't torturing him right now."

It was Kali.

"Because you aren't seeing the big picture," replied Euryale. "You need to focus on the priest. He will be a powerful catalyst when he is turned."

I glanced around, trying to figure out where to go. My current state distorted the natural ability to determine where sound was coming from. I could run in any direction and bump right into them. Then I looked up. A fleeting thought had me considering the possibility that I could float. It was a logical assumption since I was currently incorporeal. I just needed to be fully confident in the theory for it to work. I closed my eyes—so to speak—and focused on becoming weightless. There was a technique Bishops used to reduce our rate of descent when falling. I grasped at that, believing myself to be lighter than air. Normally, my scientific mind would rebel against such notions, but that I was a disembodied spirit allowed for more lax interpretation of physical laws. I rose quickly up through the ceiling. Just before my feet exited the hall, I heard the voices from just below me.

"Hold it."

It was Euryale. I could perceive that same aura as when she stood in front of me.

"What?"

"Do you feel that?"

"I don't sense anything."

"I've been keeping my inner eye open since I found his spirit in the priest's rooms. You should do the same."

"He can't step out of his body from the position he's in. You need perfect calm and relaxation."

"And he shouldn't have been able to get to us from that distance either. Yet, he did. I'm not taking any chances so stay vigilant."

"Of course."

Their voices faded as I continued up through the multiple floors of the manor house. Ironically, the Tainted didn't think my visit should have been possible, either. Had I had not done it by accident already, it might have been a real roadblock to this entire process. I was amazed that they created fences around their powers as well. Humanity, and whatever offshoot we belonged to, are obsessed with defining limits. It was the steadfast adherence to those self-imposed boundaries that prevented humankind from moving forward. If we sailed too far, we would fall off the end of the earth or be eaten by a sea monster. Our imaginations are amazing. They can free us from our bonds or lock us away better than any jail cell.

But I digress. I reached the rooftop and tried to orient myself. Nothing looked familiar. No, that wasn't exactly right. I recognized the building from the outside as I gazed down into the courtyard. But I didn't get a clear indication of which direction I should be going. I peered up at the stars. I knew London was south. However, I had the same issue Soon-Li had mentioned, just in reverse. I could go that way and end up on the completely wrong side of the city. While I'd reviewed a map of London before we'd started out, I didn't have detailed street by street familiarity. It might take me all night to find the Covenant. What would happen when Euryale returned for our next session and I was only half in attendance?

In the past, I had snapped back into my body, including the most recent trip here. But I had never done it on purpose and could not guarantee success. That line of thinking, however, spurred a new realization. I was trying to instill physical laws into a very nonphysical experience. I remembered my encounter with the dragonfly. To reach it, I needed to move without moving.

Placing my hands on the parapet wall, I stared off into the Covenant's assumed direction. I fixed my vision on the place where I spent the most time: the bench in the courtyard. I thought about the smell of the trees, the flowers planted around their bases. I imagined the sounds of birds as they hopped from branch to branch amidst the nearby traffic on Long Lane and the feel of the breeze as it brushed my hair to the side. A loud gong rang out and I found myself sitting on that bench. The bells rang out the hour—one AM. The subtle lighting gave a soft glow to the area, bright enough for pedestrians to see while not disturbing anyone's slumber.

"That's convenient."

I jumped up and checked the seat, looking for the laptop that I had abandoned during the ruse that Francesca had played on me. It wasn't there. Not very surprising.

I made my way to the secret entrance since I didn't know to where the cavernous underground expanded. I wasn't inclined to experience sinking through layers of solid rock, clay, and soil only to find myself in the subway. Sorry, underground. I stepped through the wall and floated through the shaft down to the lowest level, then stepped out into the London Covenant.

I ran into Soon-Li almost immediately, walking briskly down the corridor.

"*Hey, Soon-Li!*"

She ignored me, of course, like in every ghost movie I had ever watched. I tried to grab her but my hand passed right through. I followed her into my office where Hager sat at my desk looking through papers and emails. My laptop was nowhere to be seen.

"*Hager, I know **you** can hear me.*"

He looked up at our approach.

"*Yes, see. I knew it.*"

"What did you find out?" His focus was on her.

"*Shit.*"

"The chip was coated with Christian's blood, which is no surprise.

The woman's saliva, however, was."

"Why don't you ask about my laptop?"

Hager sat back and stroked his beard. "Were we able to match it to anything?"

"The hair that Christian pulled out of one of the Twins."

"So, they have him." Hager sounded resigned.

I flung my arms in the air.*"Duh!"*

"Did we really have to go through all of this to prove it?" Soon-Li sounded annoyed.

I gestured to her. *"Yes, thank you."*

Hager continued to stare out into space for another moment before his eyes reengaged with her. "I was still hopeful that this was some impulsive ruse Christian thought up to draw them out."

Soon-Li plopped down in the other chair. "Yeah, that does sound like something he would do."

"My plans aren't that stupid. Most of the time."

"What do we do now?" she asked.

"Find my laptop. I drew a circle around the fucking building."

"I think we need to continue along the path he set out for us: find the house. Chances are that's where he's being held."

Thorne poked his head in. "Any news?"

I barked out a laugh. *"Oh, come off it, you know you're behind this."*

Hager replied, "They have him."

"Damn."

I had to admit, he looked genuine. *"And the Oscar goes to…"*

"I didn't think you would care," Soon-Li snapped.

"Ms. Yuan," Hager chastised.

"Oh, come on, Amram, he has been dragging his feet the entire time when he hasn't been putting up actual roadblocks."

"You go, girl!"

"I think I could use a walk," Hager said.

"I concur."

"What is it with you Brits? Everything revolves around walks and tea?"

"I do believe that China is quite fond of tea as well," Thorne pointed out.

Hager held up a hand. "A walk."

"What the hell is going on?"

They took a walk up to the bell tower, all remaining quiet until they got there. Well, except me, who just kept repeating the word laptop until I annoyed myself. They didn't seem to mind.

As Hager crossed the crenellations, he asked, "Is the sanctuary still in place?"

Thorne was already inside the square as he replied; "Yes, I check it periodically to make sure."

Soon-Li looked around, confused. Then, recognition dawned on her face. "Shèngpiàn."

Thorne nodded. "Very good, Ms. Yuan. The bastions were imbued with power upon its creation. Its existence is revealed only to the London Covenant Head when they take over. Few others know about this place."

"No shit."

"What does it do?" she asked.

"Several things, actually," Hager replied. "Most importantly, it blocks out human voices. No one outside the square can hear what is being discussed here."

"What about bugs?"

"What about bugs?" Soon-Li said almost at the same time.

I touched my nose with one hand and pointed at her with the other.

Thorne pointed as well. "This brick would glow if they were present."

"I didn't think any Bishop could infuse power into objects for hundreds of years."

Thorne shook his head. "It's electronic."

"Who had the forethought to do that?" Soon-Li asked.

The current Covenant Head inclined his head towards Hager.

"Huh."

Soon-Li smiled. "I should have known."

Hager looked uncomfortable with the praise. "Can we get on with it?"

"Quite right. I do apologize for the ruse."

Soon-Li placed her hands on her hips. "So, you have been intentionally obtuse and obnoxious?"

"Unfortunately, it was necessary that I seem not to fully support our leader."

"Why?"

"I believe the Covenant is compromised."

"By whom?"

"Francesca!"

"I'm not sure."

"For the love of God!" I threw up my hands in frustration.

"The fact is, while this location has many advantages, it is swarming with people. It could be any of the mass servers, tour guides, congregation, tourists, even priests. You name it."

"How about your right hand?"

"It is also why there aren't many Bishops here despite this being the European hub. I sent them all on missions far enough away as to limit the exposure."

"Hello? Captain Obvious knocking!"

"What about Francesca?" Soon-Li pushed.

"Yes, finally."

Hager shook his head. "She is an Angelic."

"Oh, I see."

"I don't see! Can someone clue me into why the traitor can't possibly be the traitor? This is like a friggin' reality show. Can I just banish her from the castle? Extinguish her torch? Pass her by in the rose ceremony?"

Soon-Li tapped her foot and stared at Hager. "Why didn't you tell me about any of this?"

"We needed it to seem real. Your reaction had to be genuine."

"What about John and Tira? Not to mention Major Mangine. He is ready to start raiding every house from here to the Hebrides."

"We will keep them in the dark a little longer."

"They deserve to know."

"Agreed. However circumstances do not always allow for people getting those things to which they are entitled,"

Soon-Li shook her head. "I don't like it."

"Which is why we chose to exclude you." Thorne grinned and I thought Soon-Li would throw him from the tower.

"What do we do now? This place has no cameras anywhere to see what actually happened." Soon-Li's long braid danced around as she moved, highlighting her frustration.

Thorne took on a schoolteacher's tone. "You can't see why we wouldn't want evidence of the comings and goings here?"

"Amram, your friend is about to lose a limb."

"Alright, you two, emotions are running high, but we need to focus on getting Christian back. That is the priority."

Hager's words started fading as I felt my energy draining. Exhaustion was creeping up on me, which aided me in stepping back into my body. I just let myself succumb to the feeling and I was back in the total darkness of my cell. I was too tired to let it bother me now and slipped into unconsciousness.

Chapter Twenty-Three

O PENING MY EYES, I found myself still surrounded by darkness. I couldn't tell what time it was, but from my grogginess, I don't think I had gotten more than a few hours' sleep. I was unsure if it was the pain from hanging that woke me or something else. I got the distinct impression that I wasn't alone.

"Is someone there?" My words came out gritty. I didn't know when I'd last had water and my tongue felt like I had just walked through the Sahara.

A flashlight switched on and I had to close my eyes and turn my head from the harsh light. The increased brightness told me that the beam focused on my face for a second. Then it faded while, I presumed, my visitor looked me over. I cracked an eye, trying to see who it was, but there were only shadows behind the light.

"You have the advantage over me in many ways. Can't I see who you are?"

"No."

I recognized the voice. "Why not, Father?"

A sharp intake of breath. "Are you like them? A demon?"

"So, you see them for what they are."

"Answer my question or I will leave you where I found you."

"No, Father, I am not like them." At least not while my powers were gone. I wasn't lying to a priest, really, Mom.

"Then how did you know I was a man of the cloth?"

"I recognized your voice."

"From when?"

"We met a few nights ago while you were being spirited away. Excuse the pun."

The light splayed on my face a second time, forcing me to close my eyes while he decided whether I looked familiar.

"Yes, I remember now. You are the one who crashed into my rooms and fought the twins. When I left, you were pinned to the floor with a dagger in each shoulder. You don't seem to have any sign of those injuries. So tell me again that you are not one of them."

Well, there went that ruse. "While I did have similar powers, I do not count myself among the Tainted."

"Tainted?"

"It's what we call them."

"What do they call themselves?"

I cocked my head. "I've never thought to ask."

"I have found that no one believes themselves to be the villain in their story."

"Would you consider setting off a dirty bomb in the middle of Manhattan to be the act of a hero?"

"What, that conspiracy theory from last year?"

"Say, Father, would it be possible for you to slide that chair over here for me to stand on? I would really like to release the pressure on my shoulder and wrist."

"Why, so you can escape and take me with you?"

"That sounds great but we wouldn't get far. I am in no condition to fight all the guards she's posted and, even if we were to get out, I doubt we would be free for long. As for your conspiracy theory, when you connect your current predicament to the stories you heard, is it really that far-fetched?" I considered his question about what they called themselves. "Who did they say they were?"

My eyes had adjusted enough to catch the distant look in his eyes. "Angels."

I barked out a laugh and it sent a shock of pain up my shoulder. "How many angels try to convince someone to commit murder?"

"Did you ever hear the tale of Abraham?"

"The guy who God told to kill his only son?"

"You see my dilemma."

"No, frankly, I don't."

He looked away from me. "Abraham's parable is about faith. Even to the very end, he believed that God would not let his son die. We priests must have that steadfast a belief that we are doing His will and we need to trust in that."

"Bullshit."

He met my eyes again and there was fire behind them. I pushed forward.

"The story of Abraham is a reminder to all of humanity that they can never know or understand God. That His plan is so far beyond our comprehension that we should all fall in line and follow blindly. Radical views like that, from every religion, have caused the most death in this world. It causes people to see others with different beliefs as heathens, savages, or infidels. It sows mistrust of anyone who doesn't look the same or pray to the same deity."

"The Church is not like that." I could tell by his voice that he didn't really believe what he was saying.

"You shall have no other gods before Me."

His eyes darted about. "You are trying to tempt me."

"They want you to commit murder. I'm just asking you to move a chair ten feet."

The priest looked at my chained hands. The straps around my wrists were similar to those found in a mental ward, padded with a leather strap to secure them. It wasn't for my comfort. Metal would rip skin and blood could be used as a lubricant to help escape. They were wrapped in a cut-proof material and had a steel ring sewn in with thick canvas. They were attached to a thick chain which looped through an eyebolt in the ceiling, then secured to a cleat on the wall. He could release me easily, but what I'd told him was true. Without my powers or help from my team, our chances were slim. I would need to go on one of my spiritual excursions to find a path out.

He seemed to come to the same conclusion. Giving me a wide berth, he dragged the chair over and placed it just close enough to me that I was able to hook my foot under it and pull it. I maneuvered it under me and stood up, taking time to balance myself. It didn't give me adequate slack to lower my arms completely, but there was enough to allow me to stretch the muscles and ease the pressure on my shoulder. I shrugged as much as the chains would permit.

"Having an issue with your arm?"

"A souvenir from my dance with the twins."

His eyebrows came together in confusion.

"A dagger severed the nerves."

"I see. Can you explain how you have recovered from the rest of your injuries so quickly?"

"I've always been a quick healer."

His eyes narrowed.

"As I said before, I had similar powers to the Tainted. I used those to stop their global terrorism."

"Had?"

"I seem to be having performance issues."

"Is everything a joke to you?"

"I find it makes life tolerable, especially during dark times."

His expression brightened, "Where did you hear that from?"

I glanced at him. This time I was the one confused. It was my standard response; something that had formed my entire perspective. I had never contemplated where it came from. I figured it was just part of my DNA. Now that the question had been asked, I tasked my brain with finding the answer. I discovered a voice behind it that wasn't mine. It only took me a few moments to connect it. My head twitched and I said the name with a mixture of wonder and joy.

"Father Murphy. Father Angus friggin Murphy."

The priest took a step back. "You know Angus…" He trailed off and the shock on his face turned to comprehension. "Are you Christian?"

I stared at him for several seconds before my disbelief transformed into a smile, then to laughter. It was one of those times something strikes you so funny that you cannot stop laughing. Then, when you think you've gained control, it starts the process all over again. I'm not sure how long it went on but, when I could finally speak, I confirmed his speculation.

"I am Christian Bateleur." I used my full name to show him I wasn't just repeating his own words back to him,

"I'm Father Kane. I thought you were in America. How did you end up here?"

"That is a long story."

He seemed to conclude that my circumstances were no longer warranted. "Let me get you down and find you some clothes."

"No, don't."

"But—"

"Nothing has changed. We still can't escape and freeing me will only put you in more danger." A notion occurred to me. "How did you get out of your room?"

"I am given free rein in the place. It is another ploy to make me feel that they are on the right side."

"How did you know I was down here?"

"I heard your scream."

My skepticism reared its ugly head. "Through the eight-inch-thick stone walls?"

"Not with my ears, but with my soul."

I wasn't sure if I totally bought that but I guessed it was no more implausible than the pill I was asking him to swallow. Then what he'd said before sank in.

"You are free to wander this castle?"

"So far."

"Can you tell me where the guards are? How often they patrol? Any other security details?"

"Only the ones that I see regularly. I haven't noticed patrols but I can look for patterns."

"Perfect. Now, walk me through the layout of this place."

"First things first." Giving the room a cursory search, he found an old rag, retrieved it, and wrapped it about my waist. "There. We were a little too eye-to-eye."

I laughed again and thanked him. Strangely enough, in this man's company, I felt better half naked and hanging from the ceiling than I had in a while.

✝

"I feel bad leaving you. I get the sense Angus would be unhappy with me."

"How do you know him again?" I was sitting on the chair now since Father Kane released some slack so we could talk more comfortably.

"Who doesn't know Angus Murphy?"

"Of course. But how did you meet?"

"Oh, he was a special guest lecturer at Allen Hall Seminary because of his many expeditions."

"His many..." I couldn't even form the words. My old friend never ceased to amaze me.

The priest checked his watch. "I need to get back."

I nodded and stood on the chair, raising my arms. He had made a small mark on the chain where it had been secured previously on my suggestion. Him talking to me and trying to get my confession was one thing. Releasing my chains would be suspect. The pain in my shoulder had miraculously disappeared and I almost didn't mind being strung up again. Almost. He moved the chair back to where it was but wasn't as careful with its placement since he wasn't attempting to hide his presence.

"Don't forget the rag." I inclined my head towards the cloth on my waist.

"Keep it. Perhaps we should say a prayer?"

I looked around. "I think we are beyond the praying stage."

"I would venture to say that this is the perfect time."

"All the same, I'll pass." I wasn't in the mood to forgive those who trespassed against me right now. I was more on the side of a forty day and forty night ass kicking.

The priest would not be dissuaded. "Would you mind if I blessed you?"

"Sure, I guess it couldn't hurt."

He pulled the chair over, stood on it, and made the sign of the cross on my forehead while mumbling. Then he got down and replaced it.

"Do you remember the message for Angus?"

"Yes." He looked back at me before leaving. "Will you be alright?"

"I'll be fine."

He frowned, forced a smile, and shook his head. Then he turned off the lights, plunging me again into total darkness. This was a welcome oblivion, however. I was bone tired and, despite the uncomfortable position, I drifted off almost immediately.

My dreams were a jumble, combining years and places into a montage of experiences. I was my current age in my childhood home during Christmas time with Hager, John, Soon-Li, Tira, my mother, and Angus. Hager and Mom sat on a love seat near the fireplace. Father Murphy stood to the side, sipping what appeared to be eggnog. The rest of us lounged on the floor opening presents like we were children. I ripped through package after package. The gifts included a Lego Death Star, the Cliffs of Insanity play set, and even a hoverboard right out of Back to the Future II. Each was another disappointment not fulfilling my genuine desire. Though, I wouldn't have been able to tell you what that was. I woke to the lights coming on.

"Who the hell put a rag on you?" Kali stepped up and ripped it off.

"I was cosplaying the crucifixion. That was my whole costume since I didn't have a thornbush to fashion a crown."

An evil smile grew on her face. She hauled off and punched me where the cloth no longer covered. To say I saw stars would have been the understatement of the year. I had an urge to vomit but I wouldn't give her the satisfaction. I couldn't even double over and protect the family jewels from another attack. I had to just hang there looking like I had to pee.

"When you can talk again, the name of the person who visited you will stop the next blow."

It took me a while but I finally managed to say. "The Keebler Elves. Not only do they make cookies but cover—"

That was all I got out before she made good on her promise. Carol Burnett once described child birth by saying take your bottom lip and pull it over your head. For those of you not familiar with being struck in the gonads, my best comparison would be to place your finger on an anvil and hit it with a ball peen hammer. Then do it to the other four. This time. I did throw up. But I missed her.

"Shall we try again?" I could tell by her tone of voice that she wanted me to give her another smart-ass answer.

"You're right. It wasn't the elves. It must have been the Care Bears."

I clenched whatever muscles still worked, awaiting the next blow. But it never landed. I opened my eyes cautiously, in case she was waiting for me to watch my punishment. Her arm was mid strike and I could see her struggling against an invisible force. Behind her, framed in the doorway, was Euryale.

"That's quite enough of that."

She waited for Kali to relax her stance before releasing her with no physical acknowledgement that she had done so. "The priest was the one who visited our friend."

"I told you we shouldn't allow him to wander free."

"*We* didn't. I granted him access to show him we are trustworthy. It wouldn't be necessary if you had turned him faster. He is the last element we need before my ascension."

"That and his cooperation." Kali hooked a thumb at me.

"That is inevitable. However, I am losing confidence that the priest will succumb to your charms."

"No man has ever resisted. This one is no different."

Euryale brushed away her statement as trivial. "Words spoken confidently do not make them true. I am starting to get the idea that it was your incompetence that caused the failure in New York."

Anger flared in Kali's eyes. "I did my part. It was Baldemar who couldn't even handle one old Bishop."

"So you have said. Fortunately for you, I trust him less than I do you." She stepped up to me and ran her eyes over my naked form, lingering at points. "You don't seem too much the worse for wear. Almost like you got a good night's sleep."

"Do you think he is faking being powerless?"

She ran her finger over the scar on my right shoulder. "No. Of all the experiments I have done through the millennia, no bishop has ever been able to control their healing. They run dry doing so, when leaving the injury would keep them in the fight. Once we eliminate the source of their powers, they will be unable to continue this useless struggle."

My eyes widened for a heartbeat before I could get them in check. Euryale smiled up at me.

"Yes, I know of the sacred pools. What we have always lacked was a vulnerable person who knew the location of all the Covenants."

Kali frowned. "Why would you tell him?"

"Look at him. There is nothing he can do. I will break him, then I will keep him as a memento." She circled me again, her hand trailing across my buttocks, finally resting on my thigh very close to my manhood. She bit her lower lip. "I'll enjoy their savior pleasuring me after leaving their organization in ruins."

There it was again. It was a scent, at least that was what I connected it to. There was an acrid odor like when you light a match but this also had undertones of decay that clawed at my gag reflex. She tapped my stomach.

"But let's not rush the fun."

"Lady, and I use that word extremely loosely, I'm an Army Ranger. There is nothing you can do to me that I haven't been prepared for."

Her smile got broader and her eyes actually twinkled with mirth. "It's adorable how you think that is the case."

She pulled a nine-inch kitchen knife out from between her breasts, of all places. My breath caught. She thought it was out of fear but it was recognition. Having spent time analyzing the two other relics that had the power to kill a Tainted, it shone for me like a beacon of light from fog laden waters. The passage from the French poet echoed in my mind:

> *Separated from them at the time of their rebirth,*
> *Cursed to carry their humanity with them,*
> *A vessel for the vestige of what they were,*
> *A commination for their failure,*
> *A catalyst for their demise…*

I watched it. Studied it. Euryale once again mistook my attention for fear and smiled.

"But for now, you know how I have a soft spot for blades and I absolutely love a man with scars."

She dragged the sharp edge slowly across my abdomen. I could feel the knife pulling at my skin, slicing through its layers. Pain radiated from the area and my stomach muscles tightened reflexively, my jaw clenching. I focused on how it felt as it touched me, trying to separate the pain from other feelings. I needed to memorize everything I could, to use when I got my power back.

She examined her handiwork. "Yes, that will be a nice one."

Through clenched teeth, I said, "You didn't even ask me a question."

She met my gaze. "I found that my subjects are more receptive when they have a baseline for their suffering. It will only increase from here. Now then, where is the German Covenant?"

"Fuck you."

"Later. Right now, I want a location. Let's keep it easy. You don't need to give me a street address, just a city."

I remained quiet but kept the curse in my eyes. She placed the knife in the groove of the first cut she'd made, then looked into them again. I narrowed mine in answer.

"No?"

She dragged the knife again even slower. The raw nerves, already vibrating from the last slice, screamed in protest and I had to nearly bite my tongue from doing the same. I put her out of my mind and pictured Marie's face.

"Are you seeing this? He's a tough one. Not even breathing hard."

Kali shook her head. "I don't know why we have to play these games. Can't you just pull it out of him?"

"Maybe. But it would not nearly be as fun and he would be mindless at the end of it. I want him to retain his talents."

"Thank you."

Euryale turned to me, beaming. "You see, he is already coming around to my gifts."

"No. I was wondering who could have screwed up those twins to that degree. Now I have my answer."

Her smile transformed to anger in a fleeting second and the knife flashed, cutting a deep line across my ribs. I managed to keep my smile in place. Though I wasn't sure how much I was selling it.

Three hours later, I gave her a city.

Chapter Twenty-Four

"**M**ARIE!"
          I jerked awake, my demons driving me from
          sleep. I must have passed out at some point during
my "conversation" with Euryale. It was, once again, pitch dark. There
are few things more disorientating than waking up to complete darkness. Even in the dead of night, there is moonlight and starlight. When
one awakes in their own room, the light from an alarm clock or LED
casts a soft shimmer coating dressers, nightstands or the bed itself in
places. I knew where I was. The pain in my shoulder reminded me
of that much. But I couldn't connect myself with a location. Couldn't
even investigate by touch to get my bearings.

Panic slipped in around the edges of my awareness. I took a few
deep breaths, pictured Marie's face, connected with my serenity field,
and stepped out of my physical form. All the pain and discomfort
I was feeling dissipated. I desperately wanted to look at my body to
see the extent of the damage the bitch had done, but I knew doing
so would only induce a wave of dizziness and nausea, putting me out
of commission for a while.

Ain't nobody got time for that.

I had broken down the previous night and given up the name of
a German city. It was the wrong city and she knew that. Apparently,
she had some information and wanted to catch me in a lie. Her plan
worked perfectly and the level of pain she inflicted on me after it
caused me to pass out. I think. The point being, I was running out
of time.

As a Ranger, I had to go through SERE training—Survival, Evasion,
Resistance and Escape. Torture, while barbaric, has a method which
is based on the idea that all humans will break. The only variable is

how long a person can hold out under questioning. That adage about the frog and the frying pan? It's bullshit, but it is an effective process for forcing information out of a prisoner. The art, if you'll excuse that word, of enhanced interrogation is one part pain and one part anticipation. If it's all waiting, then fear is reduced; like a child who is always threatened with discipline, but never receives it.

If suffering is slowly built up, there is trepidation about what is coming. In anti-torture training, we endured increasing levels of pain and discomfort. They never pushed it so far to cause bodily harm, since they still needed their soldiers to do their job. But they could make it very uncomfortable for extended periods. I knew I would break, eventually. I just had to hold out long enough for the cavalry to arrive. But that meant they had to know where I was.

Thanks to Father Kane's description of the building, a tour was no longer necessary—except for one place. There was a chamber at the far end of the dungeon, locked with a key as opposed to just a bolt. That was my first stop. I walked through my cell door and went right. Most of the doors were made of wood but this one was steel. Passing through it, as well, I followed a stone spiral staircase leading deeper into the earth. I was getting the idea that every Tainted had the same taste in decorating. At the bottom was a large open room, though far from empty. It was lined with beds. There must have been fifty of them. All were the same.

Each was occupied by a person who was completely naked. There were no sheets and no blankets. It was warm to the point of being uncomfortable. They were all strapped down and had more tubes coming out of them than a Borg. Fluids were being pumped into them on one side, along with what looked like antibiotics. There was an additional chemical I would need to look up later, along with a feeding tube. On the other side was a catheter, colostomy bag, and, finally, a slow drip of their vital fluid into an air-tight plastic sack. I didn't think I needed to research the drug anymore. I was pretty confident it sped up hemoglobin production. This was a blood farm.

I walked up to the nearest patient. She was a woman in her thirties who looked like she had been athletic at one point. The deterioration of her muscles told a story of how long she had been here. As bad as I believed this nightmare to be, it was actually worse. She was awake, staring wide eyed at the ceiling; her focus dancing around as though watching something. I realized it was a fly that was buzzing about. I thought the insect might be a form of entertainment, but her expression held a tinge of fear. Then I realized how distressing it would be to a person unable to move to have an itch that she couldn't scratch. Her mouth was partially open because of the feeding tube. A nice moist place for a bug to seek refuge.

My breathing quickened and my teeth ground together. Without thinking, I reached out and snatched the bug in the air, crushing it and tossing it to the floor. The woman's eyes relaxed and I thought a small smile crept onto her face. The fact that, to them, joy came from a fly not landing on them made me even angrier.

Fly?

I found where it lay, still twitching as electrical impulses danced through its final moments until they, too, fizzled out. I had physically interacted with the real world. It was something I had done in the past but I had assumed it was part of my powers. It never occurred to me I might be able to do it without them. Hell, I didn't even know how to do it on purpose. I needed to figure it out, though, because a plan was forming. But time was slipping away.

There was one more item on the list to check out before I headed to the Covenant. Looking up at the ceiling, I willed myself in that direction. I drifted past several floors until moonlight greeted me. During my last excursion, I had focused my attention on the front of the building but Father Kane said he kept hearing a ruckus coming from the back. I walked to the other side, only realizing afterward that I could have floated possibly faster and more easily. I didn't know if that required more energy. More experimentation would be needed when I got myself out of this. I found a low part of the crenelations and looked out over the grounds. If I'd had any food in me, or a stomach, I would have thrown up.

Chapter Twenty-Five

OW AFTER ROW OF tents lined the grounds behind the castle. Euryale had an army ranging in the thousands. She had enough people to overpower any Covenant and, eventually, she would have all the locations, as well as whatever secrets I had. All the shelters were camouflaged so that aerial photos wouldn't show obvious signs of a military presence. It must have been why I hadn't noticed it before. I could see plenty of activity so estimated that it was still early in the evening.

There was a section of the camp set apart, like its own little fiefdom. A ring of tents forming a large opening. I thought they might be officers' quarters but those are generally located in the center for protection and ease of communication. Why would they be separated? I felt my heart stop in my body six levels down as the realization struck me.

I hopped over the wall and floated down, angling towards the remote encampment. I followed a group of servants that were walking towards them, carrying three large coolers between them.

"No," I said to no one as I trailed like a ghost haunting the grounds. I had put two and two together, but prayed I was wrong.

A space between tents formed an entrance where the small parade filed in. The cooler bearers seemed nervous as they crossed the threshold, entering the open ring. There was no one around. The great circle was barren. The grass had been demolished, vast clods of soil ripped up as though a great battle had been held here. The servants placed their burdens on three raised platforms. They had the look of shrines with ancient symbols carved into them. Just off to the side hung a large gong. A felt covered mallet dangled from the frame.

Once the coolers were in place, all but one of the bearers headed directly for the exit. The last grabbed the mallet and struck the gong which echoed through the grounds. Silence fell. All activity from the other camp stopped; the ringing of the forge hammer, the loud but indistinct rumble of conversation. Even the birds and the insects seemed to feel the foreboding and quieted their calls. He struck it twice more, then took off at a run.

I stood next to the coolers, both afraid to know what was in there, confident in my prediction, and dreading its conformation. Slowly, one by one, tent flaps opened. What stepped out were things from nightmares. In my short time in this world, I'd seen Converted who looked like average humans, their powers provided by a perverted ceremony and a vampiric habit. They were less powerful than the typical Bishop but, in numbers, could prove formidable. Earlier that year, we'd uncovered a chemical process that used the blood of a converted Bishop to create a wave of lustful puppets that could be controlled by the Tainted. They were stronger than Converted, but unstable. Most recently, in an underground arena, we'd come up against a group of Converted that were turned *hard*. This referred to a process that left them as little more than mindless fighting machines that would attack anything, including each other. Finally, there were demons like the soccer mom; more powerful than a Bishop and nearly impossible to kill by normal means. They were rare and took years for the Tainted to develop.

These, however, were totally different. These…creatures looked to be a mix of all. Some were thin and wiry with a sense of dread emitting from them like stink off a garbage truck. Their hair grew in tufts, splotched around their bodies. Others were completely hairless and massive, as if I had walked into a bodybuilders' competition. Their skin was leathery and scarred. The last bunch were of typical size and stature, but looked as though they had just walked out of an inferno. Cracked flesh the color of ash gave the impression they might disintegrate at any moment. They all made their way out of their tents, pushing each other to be the first. The lids were ripped off the coolers, revealing bags of blood stacked to the rims.

Each walking nightmare took a bag and stepped off to the side while downing it. The hulking creatures tore off the tops and tossed them back like they were in a beer chugging contest. The wiry ones sliced them open with a razor-sharp nail and sipped at them as though they were in the middle of a cocktail party. Most disturbing, however, were the burned ones who each ran a finger over the top of the plastic so it melted away. The contents within were steaming hot by the time they brought it to their gray, cracked lips, savoring it like hot chocolate on a wintry day.

In total, there were near to a hundred of each type. I turned away from the sight and hurried back towards the castle. This was bad. Beyond bad. My attitude took a hit and depression swept in. These were creatures we couldn't fathom, didn't know how to combat, and they outnumbered the Bishops we had on our side five to one. I didn't see a way we could win this battle. I pictured our troops getting overwhelmed by the superior numbers and slaughtered by these inhuman creatures Euryale had created. My team would be caught battling multiple enemies with varying powers. Then I pictured those people in the lower dungeon multiplied by a factor of ten— whole towns being turned into blood farms for the evil that was growing.

I was far enough away now that the disgusting sounds of the creatures devouring the bags of blood faded. My head started spinning and I felt the tug of my body. The stress was interrupting my ethereal walk and I had to focus so as not to be slammed back into my physical form. My army training kicked in.

Don't try to solve every problem—just the one in front of you.

The problem in front of me was communicating with my team to let them know where I was. And I thought I had an idea, if I could touch the real world again.

Chapter Twenty-Six

A MRAM HAGER SAT AT his desk going through reports for the army of the Bishops. He knew it was busy work, but he had run out of ideas. Having gone through every location on the list, nothing stood out. They'd narrowed it down a little more based on the description Christian had provided, but without him, there was no way to tell which property it was. This is where he would usually come up with a hare-brained scheme that had about a three percent chance of working, but somehow always did.

Well, he wasn't Christian. He absently twirled his white curly side locks of hair and thought, *not Christian in any sense*. Amram smiled at his own attempt at a joke and more at the face he knew their new leader would make at it.

When had he become so dependent on the man? It was barely a year ago when he'd gotten the notification that a very old initiate had just inherited his powers. It was luck that the priest officiating over the marriage had been privy to the Bishops and an acquaintance. Was it luck? It was something that he had puzzled over for hours since the battle in the streets of New York.

If Christian's mother hadn't died months before his First Holy Communion, he would have followed the path that every Bishop had for the last thousand years. He would've grown up being taught the same rules and restrictions on his abilities that the rest of them accepted as fact. Under those conditions, would he have been able to see past what was to what could be? Would he have found the power to banish not one, but two demons? Stop time to save Tira? Open a portal? Discover how to kill a Tainted?

No, it appeared as though Angela had been right all along. Her death was not only part of the plan, it was the pivotal point that let

Christian see beyond the Bishops' own shortsightedness. It was a loss, though, that had plagued him every day since. Then to be banished out of the boy's life completely, only to get the occasional word from Angus. After a time, even he'd struggled to keep a connection with the boy— with Angela's boy.

He pulled out his phone which unlocked via his face. He thumbed the photos app, tapped on his favorites, and selected the first one. Angela was as beautiful as always. Her sparkling blue eyes shined like sapphires and the wrinkle around her nose when she would scrunch it filled him with more joy than any little thing had a right to.

Hager heard something, a faint scraping noise. He shut off the phone and slid it back into the pocket of his black suit. He looked towards the door, but didn't see anyone. Amram got up and walked to the entrance, sticking his head into the long hallway, but found it empty. Soon-Li was working on her AI program, trying another algorithm to puzzle out the location. She busily pulled up satellite feeds from various agencies to scour the area for anything that might give them a clue. John was tinkering with one of his contraptions and the Major was drilling his squad for whenever he got the word. He stepped back into his office to seek serenity in his portable rock garden, but instead it made him frown. There was a thick line in the sand crossing the neat ridges left from the rake. When had Christian done that? Vexing him was one of that man's greatest pleasures. Hager assumed that, with everything going on, he had not noticed until now.

He stalked over, picked up the small rake, and redrew the lines, creating order once again. Replacing the tool, he stroked his beard and moved to sit. The faint scraping noise came again and he stopped, poised halfway into his chair. Hager looked around, suspicion etched in creases on his forehead. He was just about to finish his descent when his eyes caught sight of his rock garden again. Another line in the sand disturbed the harmony and itched at his patience.

"What the devil?"

How had he missed that? The answer hit him like a smack across the face. He wouldn't have. Nor would the first have gone unnoticed with how often he sought balance from its granules and stones. There was only one person who would constantly throw disorder into his life.

With barely a thought, he called upon his spectral vision. It was something he rarely used, since it generally revealed little. This time, however, he saw a translucent finger sticking out of the serenity garden. He followed it up to the owner's face.

Christian dusted off his hands, grinning like the Cheshire Cat. "It took you long enough.

Chapter Twenty-Seven

H AGER WAS FINALLY STARING at my face instead of through it.

"Christian, how are you here? Where are you? Do you have your powers back?"

"Spirit walk. In a minute. No."

"An out-of-body experience at this distance?"

"Hager." My tone wasn't harsh, but it was firm.

He stopped and blinked.

"I'm not sure how much time I have. However I'm doing this, it is physically draining and I could pass out anytime."

Hager nodded.

"Close the door."

His substantial eyebrows knitted together, but he did as requested.

"Francesca has betrayed us. She handed me over to the Tainted."

"We know. We found your laptop in her room. Destroyed."

"Not an issue now. Got a pen?"

I rattled off the coordinates stuck in my brain since that day in the garden. Hager finished scribbling and met my gaze.

"Hang on. We're coming."

"Not yet."

Confusion became etched clearly on his face. He dropped into his chair as I outlined what we were up against. The troops, the Hyper-Converted, and the blood farm.

"Dear Lord. We don't have nearly enough available personnel to combat a force of that size. Half of them are deployed in other skirmishes around the globe. I knew getting involved in the symptoms of this disease was a bad idea."

"Hager, not the time. While we can't overwhelm them with

numbers, we can out strategize them. The linchpin, though, is we
need more Bishops. There aren't enough on just our side to handle
this. You've got to convince some of the opposition to join us for this
one battle. They can go back to ignoring us after that. But if Euryale
is allowed to continue building this army, there will soon be nothing
we can do to stop her."

"I will get them there if I have to drag them myself."

"I know you will. Pull up a map of the coordinates."

He did so and turned the monitor to face me.

"Here is the plan." I laid it out for him. Where the troops should
be stationed, and how I wanted them to get there. I also outlined a
special request with detailed specifications.

"You're insane."

"No argument there."

"This will take days to put in place. All while you are being tortured."

"I've had worse."

Hager curled his lip and tilted one eyebrow— a physical representation of *bullshit*.

"Fine, I'll manage. Apparently, she has too many irons in the fire
that are keeping her busy most of the time, and she takes too much
joy in the questioning to leave it to someone else. Our sessions are
unpleasant, but are not going around the clock. We need the element
of surprise or this battle will turn into a final stand."

Hager's face was lined with worry. "Understood."

"One last thing."

"Name it."

It took me a second to organize my thoughts. The notion had been
with me since I had been shoved in the car, but now that it was here,
I wasn't sure how to convey it.

"This is the stupidest plan I've had yet and I am completely devoid
of power. I am not sure if I can make it out of this one."

"Don't be daft. Your plan of jumping out of a plane without a
parachute was much more foolish."

I smiled at him and he smiled back.

"At any rate, I wanted to express how much your help and friendship have meant to me over the past few months. I could not have done any of this without you."

Hager folded his hands behind him and arched his back, taking on a haughty air. "No, I expect not."

I squinted at him. "I'm trying to tell you—"

"Yes, well, don't. You are not very good at it and I do not give you permission to die."

"Please listen. I need you to tell Marie that I love her and I'm sorry that I put her through all this for nothing." Hager's statement finally sunk in. "What permission? I outrank you. I don't need your permission."

"You may outrank me in the Covenant, but I am still head of this family and you would do well to listen to your grandfather."

I had another quip on my tongue that was quickly forgotten. I stared at him for several seconds and he met my gaze without flinching.

"I'm sorry, what?"

"You heard me." He was practically panting. "You listen to me, you big pain in my ass. We have all spent the last year underestimating your power. Time and time again, you have shown us that we make our own chances, our own luck, and control our own destiny. Don't you *dare* give up on me now. We are coming and you will damn well hang on until we get there, or so help me God, what that Medusa has put you through will be nothing compared to the shitstorm I will let loose."

Chapter Twenty-Eight

I IMPARTED THE KEY elements of my plan to Hager—my grand-father—before I passed out. That was weird to say. I always felt a bond with him, even when he was just a pain in my ass. I wasn't sure why he hadn't told me before. It may have made my transition easier. But maybe that was it. He did revel in making my life more difficult.

Once again, I only got a few hours' sleep. This time I didn't have the benefit of Father Kane's visit to ease the pressure on my shoulder, and it felt like it would be ripped off at any moment. We'd both thought that chancing a second long visit would be a mistake. I woke to the pitch darkness, which no longer triggered me. I guess I was too tired to be traumatized.

I hung there for hours, waiting for my next round, Every minute seemed to last a year. My body was a mass of cuts of varying depths. They weren't visible in the dark, but I felt each one. My skin itched as the blood dripped down. I thought I could feel infection seeping in, but maybe it was my imagination. I pictured the raw edges of each slice; the redness growing in a circle around it.

I must have slipped back into unconsciousness because, the next thing I knew, a cold blanket was covering me. Then suddenly, my body was on fire. My skin screamed from everywhere at once and I shook with the pain. The lights came on and my eyes were added to the inferno. The wave of pain subsided and, after a few seconds of blinking, I could distinguish a shape in front of me. I thought it was Tira and that my rescue had arrived faster than I'd expected. But it was Kali standing there with a brown bottle in her hand, holding it up as though selling the newest rage in skin care. It took me another second to realize what it was—hydrogen peroxide. Well, on the bright side, at least I wasn't actually on fire. Yet.

"Thanks for the wake up call. I hope you didn't get that from the minibar. They charge an arm and a leg for a bag of peanuts. Also, while you're here, can I file a complaint? My pillow was so thin it felt nonexistent. Plus, there is a draft coming from somewhere."

Kali narrowed her eyes in a way that seemed to say that I wasn't funny. But I knew that couldn't be right. "Do you know what today is?"

"Is this one of those cognitive tests? Did I hit my head?"

"It's a special day."

"You need to return some video tapes?"

"It is the day that you will reveal the locations of the Covenants."

"See, I thought that was on the twelfth of kiss my ass."

"I will give you this, you have stamina."

"Let me guess, nobody resists the machine?"

She punched me in the stomach.

When I was able to talk again, I said, "I win."

Euryale came gliding in as though she were at a fashion show. "Ahh, I see our guest is awake."

"Oh good, it's bring your psycho-sexual partner to work day."

"Are we feeling cranky today?"

"Not at all. I love just hanging around."

"Splendid. Shall we begin then?"

"Let's. But I have to warn you, I'm a bit ticklish."

Euryale smiled and pulled the old kitchen knife from behind her back. I focused on it. Though I'll admit that there was fear mixed in this time. Stepping up to me, she drew a finger over my cut-ridden body. The simple process was incredibly painful as her digit tugged at loose skin. I clenched my teeth and tried not to let it show. She appeared to select a spot, and tapped it a few times as if to say, yes, that's the one. Then she lifted her knife.

I wouldn't give her the satisfaction of turning away from the pain. My focus shifted from her area of attention to staring her down. She had selected an angled cut from yesterday. Placing the blade at the apex, she drew it down slowly. Pain danced on the already raw skin and I fought to control my reaction. Her slice formed what looked to me like the rank insignia for a Private. To the rest of the world was an upside down "V." Then she carved a second that connected the two points of the shape, creating a pretty accurate isosceles triangle. She leaned back a little to admire her work.

"What do you think?"

"You wear too much eye makeup. Oh, sorry, did you mean the shitty triangle?"

She reached up, wiping away the blood flowing from the new wounds, then grabbed the tip between her fingers. Realization of what she intended to do hit me and my eyes went wide. She blew me a kiss and yanked the piece of skin off.

I couldn't hold back the scream. The agony was unlike anything I had experienced yet. I struggled against my bonds, causing my whole body to rock. In my throes of torment, I caught sight of the Tainted. Her eyes rolled back in her head and she bit her lower lip, breath coming in gasps. As the searing agony and shock receded to a sustained pulsing, I got my breathing back under control. She took a deep breath. Her smile was euphoric.

"Now then, the city."

I didn't have a sarcastic quip. The hours of movie lines permanently emblazoned on my gray matter now eluded me through a fog of pain, loss, and anger. I met her stare and said simply, "Fuck you."

She shook her head. "You know, there are much more sensitive areas of the skin. And the first time I was gentle, ripping it off like a bandage. Pulling it off slowly is a completely different experience. Or I could use little, jerky motions, sending many shocks through you like those you just felt. And the shape of the patch influences the intensity as well. Circles, squares, rectangles, rhomboids, but my favorite is the octagon. Oh, the screams *that* elicits from my guests. It's time consuming with all of those small cuts, but worth it."

I gained control of my breathing enough to speak. "I normally don't agree with using the 'C' word, but I believe I can make an exception for you."

Her smile held actual amusement. "Do you know some of the most sensitive skin…" She used the knife point this time to trace a line from my missing patch of skin down my abdomen, crouching as she reached my thigh and shin before finally resting on my foot. I attempted to kick her in the face, but she caught it easily and held it in a vice grip. She stood again, my ankle in hand, and tapped my sole with her knife. Her wicked smile reached her eyes. I tried to struggle, but it was useless. My ankle might as well have been trapped in cement. She began her work and I started screaming again.

Chapter Twenty-Nine

I HAD PASSED OUT several times during that session. Each time, they woke me with a peroxide bath; occasionally following it with a bucket of water to keep the pain from knocking me right back out again. I was starting to crack. I knew it—could feel myself slipping. The thought of telling Marie I'd broken was what kept me from the edge. I would spend hours in the dark, waffling back and forth, trying to rationalize giving her some information—not all of it, maybe one or two answers. Give her enough to stop the agony just for a while. Help was on the way and we were going to take her down. What was the difference if she had a little intel? She would take it to the grave after I shoved that knife of hers into her eye socket. I would do it as slowly as she did when carving off sections of my skin. She'd watch the blade get closer, feel the pressure on her pupil building, then slicing through down to the cornea.

"Stop it. You are starting to sound like them."

Yeah, well, what of it? I'm tired of constantly doing the right thing. Watching as they butcher and torment the weak. Take people from you. They need to pay. Who will they take next? Marie?

"Turning into one of them is not the answer."

It saved John, Adam, and Terrance down in the catacombs under New Orleans.

The battle came back as clearly as the day it happened. The portcullis slammed shut, barring our escape. Grunting and scratching sounds echoed off the walls as twenty or thirty of the most powerful Converted we had ever faced closed in on us. By the time I finished with them, their blood painted the walls and coated the floor.

"It's not the same."

NO? How many did we dispatch down there? Not just kill. We ripped them apart with our bare hands.

"We defended our friends."

Really? Is that what you are telling yourself? How much power did we wield in that battle? Even more in the aftermath when Baldemar tried to bury us alive. Do you honestly think that we couldn't have gotten through those bars?

"I…"

We wanted to kill them. Ached to do it. Let loose the anger and frustration and point it at the enemy. It's what humanity has done since we crawled out of the mire and declared ourselves lords of all we surveyed. They are different, therefore they must be evil. Destroy them before they contaminate us with their tainted ways. Why fight it?

My head drooped down so that my chin touched my chest as I closed my eyes. Though with the depth of darkness in the cell, it made little difference.

What was happening to me? Could this be how the Tainted were created? Was the story of the Devil creating them just another parable written by flawed humans to put themselves on the right side of history? Humans. Could we even call ourselves that?

"My son? Are you alright?"

Color danced behind my eyelids until I opened them. It was a priest. I recognized him, but I couldn't connect the dots. Where was I again? I tried to move and pain shot through my one shoulder. His name appeared through the fog: Father Kane. He'd covered his flashlight with a cloth, dimming the light so it didn't blind me like the first time.

"What are you doing here?"

He crept forward. "This was when you told me to come back."

I heard him, recognizing each word, but the meaning of them all together eluded me.

"What?"

"Three days ago, you said you had a plan."

It took a great deal of concentration, but I finally grasped what he said. "I only arrived three days ago."

"No, you didn't. You got here six days ago. I visited you twice. The second time you told me you had a plan and that I was to come back when I got the signal, but you wouldn't tell me what that was." The priest stepped up close and ran the dull light up and down my form.

"Dear Lord."

I wasn't sure what he was on about, so I followed the light's progress. My body was a geometric patchwork of missing skin. In places,
more had been removed than held the rest together. It all dripped and
oozed. I couldn't really feel it anymore. At least I didn't think I could.
I tried to shrug, but lacked the energy to manage even a twitch. For
all I knew, my position may have cut off my circulation and caused
my other arm to lose feeling.

The priest pulled the chair over, put his flashlight down, and slowly
lowered me into it. Pain shot through me where my skin touched the
seat, which answered my previous question. I still felt all of it, but
apparently my threshold had shifted. I had a new normal.

"I brought clothes. Sorry, but I only had the white robes that go
under my vestments. They had provided a set for me, though I'm not
sure what they expected me to do with them."

He helped me into them. Each movement was a struggle. My right
arm was still useless and my left wasn't much better. Every gesture sent
a shock of pain through me until the anticipation of moving filled me
with dread. Somehow, he got the robes on me. They became immediately stained with my blood. It felt good and strange to have clothes
on again. Painful, too, since the fabric rubbed against my wounds.

"Why can't I remember any of that?"

"I don't know. But you did mention that they may start trying to
pry information through some magical means. You warned me that
you might not be all there when I returned."

That sounded familiar, but I still couldn't recall the conversation. I
tried to ask something else, then lost the mental thread. All that came
out was, "Thirsty."

"Of course."

He found a glass on a shelf, which I also recognized. Flashes of
memories came where either Kali or Euryale would pour water down
my throat with that grimy glass. Father Kane did his best to clean it
with only his hands in the dirty sink. Then brought it over. I nodded,
not quite able to voice my thanks. It took all my energy to lift the cup
to my lips. The water wasn't cold, nor particularly pure, but a frosty

beer couldn't have tasted any better to me.

"Slowly. I'm not sure how long it has been since you had a drink and we don't want your body rejecting it."

The hydration was helping. My brain cleared a little and my stomach growled. I took it as a good sign. It took me a few more sips to get out my next question.

"What did I ask you to do… when you came?"

"Get you down and help you escape."

"Did I think they were… just going to let us leave?"

"I wondered that as well. But you said not to worry about it. When I heard the signal, I figured it out."

My head perked up. "What was the signal?"

Kane frowned. "It sounds like a war going on out there."

Everything came flooding back. The glass fell from my hands and shattered on the hard floor.

"I don't suppose you brought shoes?"

He hefted a pair of leather sandals.

"Really? White robes and sandals?"

"It's all I had."

"Of course." He helped me slip them on, which created a whole new experience in pain. Then he practically lifted me to my feet. My legs hadn't held my weight in a while, but after a few false starts, we were able to hobble forward.

"Who were you talking to?"

"When?"

"When I first came down, I heard you arguing. I couldn't make out what you were saying, but the other voice sounded very guttural."

I glanced over at him, then refocused on walking.

"That was just Smeagol."

The sounds of battle made themselves known as we climbed out of the dungeon level: gunfire, explosions, and the din of humans doing their best to exterminate each other. We weren't close enough yet to hear individual voices, or rather, screams— at least none that were outside of my head. Each step was agony and it took all of my concentration and willpower to take the next one. If you've ever had a pebble in your shoe, you know how little it takes to make walking uncomfortable or even painful. Imagine walking on feet where half the skin has been carved off. Luckily, the sandals were tightly strapped in place or the blood would have caused me to slip right out of them.

We reached the main floor and the noise level rose. The sounds of fighting outside became more distinct so I could pinpoint where they originated. I caught the occasional order being yelled or a scream of pain, but nothing was clear. This was an enormous house and we were in the middle. Most likely, the voices we heard were coming from inside. It was worrisome, something I knew we would have to deal with. I was hoping I would have enough strength to when the time came. But no such luck. I didn't see her when she walked into the room, but I heard her clearly enough.

"You."

Kali's voice dripped with anger and hatred. I looked up from the floor where my focus had been. She was splattered with blood, probably from throats that she'd been cutting. Her eyes narrowed and she flexed the fingers that gripped her curved knife. Then she attacked.

Chapter Thirty

O
NE SECOND SHE WAS across the room, the next she stood in front of us. She batted the priest away like a rag doll and grabbed me by the neck, lifting me free of the floor despite my height. I saw Father Kane crash into a table before rolling off of it and out of sight. I hoped that he would be out of her mind as well, but Kali's vindictive side ran deep and I didn't think she would just abandon the job of finishing him off.

She smiled at me and the malice behind it actually sent a shiver down my spine. "At last, I get to kill you."

"Like you killed Morty?" It was difficult to get the words past the fingers around my throat.

"Who?"

"Old man. Whitehall. New York."

"Oh, that guy. Yeah, he was fun to play with. I made him think he could beat me with his little knife and slow reactions. I was about to kill the sniper and let him watch when you all pulled up and started tromping your way through the trees. I decided that you watching him die would be even better. I stayed just out of sight. The anguish on your faces was priceless."

"How could you?"

The question didn't come from me, but from behind me. I knew the voice, so different from her carbon copy holding my life in her hands.

"Ah, my sister has arrived just in time to watch her savior die."

Tira repeated her question.

"How could I what? Kill that old man? Easy. You will see in a moment."

"How could you turn away from your family? Go against everything we believe in?"

Kali's face displayed just how stupid she considered the question to be. "This war doesn't matter. Only power matters."

"How can you say that? Our house has dedicated themselves to helping humanity."

"And what has it gotten us? Nothing has changed. This war has been going on for centuries. The humans don't even know it exists—that we exist. They just go about their stupid, pointless lives, ignorant of the sacrifices being carried out on their behalf."

"We don't do this for recognition."

"Bullshit. Your useless degrees weren't for you. They were to impress Daddy. His perfect little girl. I built an empire, made billions of dollars, became the richest, most influential woman in the world. Was he proud of me?" Kali spit on the floor. "That was how much he cared. Brushing off my greatness to dote on his angel. The next Bishop. The one to carry on the line. Nothing I could do would measure up. Well, now I will end it all. I'll do what no Tainted has ever been able to do, kill off the Bishop lines."

"Do you think that will make our father proud?"

"I am not interested in making him proud, only scared. Remorseful. I want him to feel his failure. Know that it was because of him, that his actions and inactions led to the fall of the Bishops."

Tira shook her head. "You are so lost."

I had a front-row seat to Kali's every expression and she was radiating contempt.

"Lost? I see the truth that you have denied."

"I deny nothing. I'm fully aware my path is partially Father's doing. I know his wants and desires have shaped my perspective. His vision laid the foundation for who I am."

"You see? Like me, he made you what you are."

"No. He may have shown me the path, but I'm the one who walked it. I decided what direction to take, which fork to follow. I chose the more difficult road, to learn continually, to make more of myself with the clay he had given me."

"For him."

"No, Kamala. For me. That is where you became lost. You forgot that you were not serving his goals, but yours; seeking his approval and deciding if he was proud or disappointed. You perceived his responses as uncaring, callous. You believed that he treated me differently. I tell you now you are wrong."

"How would you know?"

"Because he manipulated me the same way. I could never live up to your accomplishments. 'Look at what your sister has done without any power at all. See all she has built with nothing but her mind and ambition.' I presume Matrika heard much the same message."

I watched doubt creeping into her eyes. "Father said that?"

"Daily. He pitted us against each other to motivate us. Mother told me, it was what his father did to him and his siblings."

"You see? It's his doing. He made us what we are."

"You're wrong. I molded myself into the person I am. It was not his choice. Contentment came easily then."

Kali's eyes narrowed. "His manipulation made me into this."

Tira shook her head again. "Your decisions led you here. Your need to be the best. All because you were jealous of your sister who got everything she wanted because she was born six minutes before you.

"You want to know what I saw? My two sisters got to go out to play while I trained. You could have friends and boyfriends while I studied. You two were free to choose what you did with your life while I followed the path predetermined for me the second I was born. I watched Matrika build a family and a career while I earned another degree. The difference between you and me, sister, is that I chose to make the best out of the cards *I* was dealt. Look at all the destruction you have wrought, the lives you have taken and the life that you abandoned. It was all because Daddy didn't pat you on the back enough. Now that is just sad."

I hung there by my throat, watching Kali's face go through a myriad of emotions. If you had asked me an hour before if a person who killed as many people as she had, consumed their blood, and plotted the downfall of humanity could experience shame or remorse, my answer would have been no. I would have said that someone that far gone had nothing left to connect those sentiments to. And I would have been wrong. I watched them all etch themselves upon her face one after the other; along with anger, frustration, malice, desperation. She had forgotten about me, focusing only on her sister. When her eyes filled with hate, I knew the conversation was at an end. I had been storing up my energy for one desperate move. Grabbing her wrist with both hands and with all the strength I had left, I swung my legs around her neck. I understood what it meant for me, but I wasn't trying to defeat her this time. I just needed to distract her. Pain bloomed in my chest and she released her hold around my throat. I dropped onto a small table, which smashed from my weight. I sat there unable to move, and barely able to breathe, watching the short, high-speed struggle.

It took Tira three moves. Kali was on the floor, her other knife sticking out of her chest. Their angled position, along with my neck craned against a chair, gave me the perfect view of a scene I didn't want to watch.

She looked confused as she mouthed the word, "How?"

"Your strength was an illusion. Every Bishop you faced knew who you were and wasn't willing to use deadly force against you. I've come to the realization that Kamala died many years ago. She was Kali's first victim and I have just avenged her."

The woman who was Kamala Gupta was still alive when Tira turned her back on her and came to my aid. She dropped beside me and packed bandages around the knife Kali had plunged into my chest.

"Shit, Christian. Why did you do that? I could have taken her out without you."

"You... could have mentioned that... in your exposition."

"I would have if I'd known you would do something so stupid."

I gave her an incredulous look.

"Yeah, I know. How would Christian Bateleur not act heroic and foolish? Now shut up so I can delve you."

I shook my head.

"What do you mean, no? I need to see how bad this is."

"Bad."

My words smacked her. "You have to do something."

I gave her the best 'What would you like me to do?' expression I could muster.

"Find your power."

"Little… late."

"Bullshit, Christian. I believe in you. We all believe in you. Every Bishop we could find is here, all fighting for you. Sides don't matter anymore. You've done it. You have given us hope."

I was slipping into unconsciousness when that word triggered something in me. My eyes snapped open, but Tira didn't react. I stood up out of my body and glanced down at her, cradling my unmoving form. It would have been very disconcerting if not for that thick pink line running from her to me. A single link connected us. Then others were added one or two at a time. They multiplied like the beginning of a rainstorm. Hundreds of lines came from every direction. I followed them, an apparition floating along. They led me outside to the fighting. Each ended at one of our team. I floated higher, getting a better view of the battlefield. From above, it looked like a large, complex, pink tree, with all its roots ending at my limp form deep inside the house.

I focused in on my extended family scattered across the front line. With each strike, each step, each shot fired, they said the same thing.

"For Christian."

One Converted attacked Hager, spewing fire. My mentor pivoted, somehow redirecting it around him and back at the creature. The impact sent it flying into its compatriots. "For Christian."

A brute took on four armed men, slow but menacing. Bullets and knives seemed to have little effect on it. Then a crack rang out from a distance and a high caliber round pierced his eye. The beast roared. A second crack sounded. The back of its throat exploded. It fell to its knees, then onto its side.

"For Christian," I heard clearly in Jelena's voice, despite the vast space between us.

John, knife in hand, was a blur, taking enemies down left and right. Each slice of his wicked blade was punctuated with a distinctive cry, "For Christian."

Soon-Li stood surrounded by the enemy but completely unfazed, The bodies of her attackers formed a perfect circle around her. Anyone who took a step inside that ring lost a limb or got skewered. She was in constant motion, the blade flashing in the lights, the long tassel spinning on the other end. On her back, she wore my mother's sword. She had brought it with her. With each slash of her ancient weapon, I could hear her whisper, "For Christian."

Off in the distance, a military unit pushed forward, breaking the defensive lines. The Major stood on a small hill, windmilling his arm to urge the troops forward. He lifted his rifle and fired, taking out an enemy combatant as casually as swatting a fly before he continued driving the team. His lips spoke words of encouragement to them, but what I heard was, "For Christian."

It took me a few seconds to realize that these were not verbalized but thoughts. They were spiritual gifts, the embodiment of hope. And they were all flowing right to me. I just had no idea how to use them. I felt the connection to my body slipping away.

I hovered there watching everyone else fighting while I was useless. Worse still, the lines were starting to waiver. For every Converted they dropped, two more took their place. Their positions were stalling and they began losing ground. I witnessed Bishop after Bishop fight till their wells ran dry. Speranza battled next to a much younger man who I guessed to be her son, Antonio. A fireball shot his way and he deflected it into a group of Converted. His sleeves caught fire and he dropped to the grass to put them out. His pained face told me the deflection had taken the last of his power.

What followed were three more attacks by each of the Mega Converted. Speranza dashed in front of the man and stopped the next fireball in mid air. It hovered there for a second before she sent it flying back to its origin, mowing down the enemy. Another brute lumbered towards her, winding up with a war hammer half her size, and swung it in a sideways arc. She cartwheeled over it, wrenching it from his hand. Then she brought it up under his chin hard enough to launch him into a tree, impaling him on a broken branch ten feet up. A speeding demon zipped in and drove a long, serrated dagger into her chest. Before dropping to the ground, she reached out and grabbed its head in both hands. I heard its neck snap.

"No!" her son yelled.

My heart screamed out the same denial. He dragged her limp form back as other Bishops took up their places, I watched in horror as the ripples of pink wavered and dimmed. They were losing hope.

"So, he's dead." I heard Euryale's voice through my body. She was in the room with us. Instantly, I was there, but still hovering over the scene.

"He's not dead!" Tira yelled.

"If not, he will be soon. By my hand."

"You'll not touch him. I won't allow it."

The Tainted laughed. "Little girl, there is nothing you can do to stop me."

She pulled her butcher's knife from inside the folds of her clothes and approached menacingly. With each step, her image shifted, taking up more of the room. Each stride made her a more frightening figure, displaying the essence of her existence. She thrived off of the fear of her victims and gained power from their terror. Tira was afraid, but not for herself. She feared for me, for the rest of our team, for the people who were powerless to fight this force. Entwined with all of that, her hope continued to flourish. That line became thicker and thicker, flowing directly into me.

But it wasn't helping. I still lie there, my breathing becoming shallow and labored. I tried to think how I could tap into it, but nothing came. Desperate, I stepped into my serenity field, hoping for some representation I could connect with to utilize the power I felt but could not access.

The meadow was green and flourishing, but the well of energy had disappeared completely. I was fresh out of ideas and time. Dropping into the grass, I tried to think. I believed that somewhere in the mix of my thoughts, emotions, and memories, an answer lay waiting. But my mind was merely being bombarded with movie lines.

"Carpe diem. Seize the day, boys."

"You miss one hundred percent of the shots you don't take."

"I am not afraid of storms, for I am learning to sail my ship."

"Fear is the mind-killer."

"Failure is not an option."

"Pray to God."

Wait, what?

Could it be that simple? Hager's statement, what seemed like a lifetime ago, came back to me.

"*There is also a hypothesis that large-scale communal focus on something can affect the physical world. Prayer groups may actually work, just not in the way they think.*"

I stood up and took a deep breath. I knew this needed to be more than just words. This had to establish a connection with the rest of the people who prayed, creating a single voice out of millions. One call. One acknowledgement that something existed that was larger than the sum of the whole. I pictured it in my head and I was there again in the pew next to my mother as the priest offered us the opportunity to join together in the words our savior gave us.

"Our Father, who art in Heaven, hallowed be thy name."

I recited the words still emblazoned in my mind, heart, and spirit. But they had meaning now. They were not a connection to a deity full of love or wrath, but an alignment to every other person on the planet saying the same words, focusing on the same thing—hope. Their hopes ranged from the recovery of a sick loved one to a new toy. The object didn't matter; it was the emotion of it, the focus, the faith. My powers stirred in me as I ended.

"Amen."

Then, more words were there, coming to me just as easily as those I had said a thousand times before.

"Blessed are You, Lord our God and God of our ancestors, God of Abraham, God of Isaac, and God of Jacob."

I knew it to be the Jewish standing prayer, but couldn't tell from where that knowledge came. Simultaneously, other parts of me began reciting the Islamic Surah Al-Fatih, the Gayatri Mantra from Hinduism, and the Buddhist Metta Bhavana. I was not connecting to one religion. I was a beacon for all.

I felt rather than heard the roar of the floodgates opening. I opened my inner eye and saw a tremendous flood barreling through the meadow. It carved a great swath of earth where my lake used to be. When the water settled, it was no longer a still body of water; it was a massive fast-moving river.

"No, you can't have him."

Tira's voice broke in, telling me that the Tainted and our deaths were close. I walked up to the water's edge and placed a foot firmly in its path. Power like I had never felt flowed through me, almost carrying me away. My back arched. All of my muscles tightened and, with my head aiming skyward, floodlights of energy burst from my eyes.

Then I was lying on the floor in the mansion. Tira was no longer next to me, but locked in combat with Euryale. They both moved like lightning, but it was clear to me who had the advantage. I watched the battle in slow motion, seeing five moves ahead and knowing when and where she would strike. Attack, counter, block, counter, *stab*.

Euryale's butcher knife stopped centimeters from Tira's neck. It was the second time since we met that I prevented a blade from severing her choroid artery. They both turned to gape at me. Moments ago, I was presumed near death. Now I was staying the Tainted's strike, held in the firm grasp of my *right* hand.

Chapter Thirty-One

W ITH MY LEFT HAND, I casually pulled Kali's knife from my chest; feeling the itch as the wound healed. That discomfort was nothing compared to the missing patchwork of skin knitting itself back into place. The Tainted stared at me as though my very existence offended her.

"That is not possible!"

"It would seem that you are incorrect." My voice had an echo to it as if I stood in a deep canyon. She yanked her hand away and put some distance between us. I let her, wanting to keep Tira out of harm's way. While she was a formidable opponent, she was no match for one of the Tainted. I wasn't sure I was either, based on my past performance. This time, however, I had an idea that may turn the tides on the entire war. Some might have even called it stupid. Euryale didn't seem overly confident either. Like the typical bully, she turned and ran. Tira moved to follow, but I caught her arm.

"Leave her to me. You go help the troops." I went to check on Father Kane.

"Are you sure? You didn't look so good just a minute ago."

He picked his head up from behind the coffee table. "Is it safe?"

To Tira I said, "I'm great." To the priest, I asked, "How are you?"

"I've had worse during choir practice."

"Remind me not to attend any of *them*."

"How have you healed? You could barely walk."

Tira crossed her arms. "She's getting away. And why are you dressed like Jesus? Becoming a little full of yourself."

I marveled at her turn around. "Euryale's not going anywhere. Father, show my friend the door you told me about. Tira, before you go back out into the fray, there is a dungeon filled with patients that we need to secure. I don't want them sacrificed."

She frowned at the statement but said, "Okay." She inclined her head in the direction Euryale had gone. "Can you handle her?"

"I think so. She is someone who hides in the shadows and attacks from behind."

"She knows you are aware of her vulnerability. She will not give you the chance to use it against her. You surprised Uji and Anton. She is ready for you."

"I have a thought about that, too."

Father Kane got to his feet and Tira stepped in to take his arm. She gave me a pointed look as if to say, *Well?*

I blurred out of the room. I followed her scent, which I now understood to be the clawing odor of fear. Everything I had been feeling over the past week was coming together. It led me outside into the battlegrounds.

The scene was chaotic. The attack plan I had imparted to Hager had been to hit them on multiple fronts so they would have to spread out their troops. It had been working, but the team was buckling. We had broken the line at several points and they now fought in confused pockets, making it difficult to determine allies from enemies at a quick glance. For all the complaining the Major did about the uniforms, they allowed me to distinguish the two fighting forces.

I turned away from tracking Euryale for the moment. The one constant with the Tainted was that they had time on their side. She wasn't about to take a chance getting caught up in an endeavor on the verge of failure. Being immortal had its advantages. She could just hide out for a few decades and start the whole process again. I couldn't allow that., but I had to make a pit stop first.

I needed a bird's-eye view of the area so stepped out of myself and rose above the battle. It took very little time to find Soon-Li, like spotting a tornado in a field of leaves. It required real willpower to not just sit up there and watch her flowing from form to form, her blade a blur as it slew opponent after opponent. But I had work to do. Not to mention a brute had noticed me standing there immobile in front of the house and was making his way towards what I'm sure he believed to be easy pickings.

I popped into my body as he strode up with all the confidence of a heavyweight champion in a bar fight. He cocked his arm and threw a punch with all his weight behind it. I let it land. I was curious to see what this new source of mine could really do. Okay, and maybe a little cocky.

I reinforced my skin. The force of his attack reverberated through my jaw and down my spine. His strike tossed my head to the side, but did very little else. The confusion of my reaction read plainly on his face. I rubbed my chin.

"Not bad." Then I smiled. "My turn."

I moved faster than he could react, pushing his still extended fist out of the way and jamming my palm into his shoulder. Falling backwards, he windmilled his arms. One leg came up for balance, just as I planned. Grabbing his massive ankle in both hands, I lifted him in the air and slammed him to the ground. Then, yanking him up again, I whaled him back down on the other side of me. I repeated this two more times for good measure. The creature was alive, but he was out of the fight. I leaned down next to his ear and whispered, "Puny brute."

I blurred away towards where I had seen Soon-Li, reveling in the constant flow of power coursing through my body. She was engaged with a pair of Claws McGraws, a name I came up with on the spot. She didn't look like she was having a problem, but a Burnie was winding up with one of its fireballs. I zipped in next to her, manipulating the surrounding air into a shield. The ball of fire smashed into it and flames wrapped around us. The blast hit the clawed creatures and she dispatched them while they recovered. The Burnie decided to find easier prey.

Soon-Li grabbed my shoulder with her free hand. "Christian! Are you okay? We were worried we may be too late."

I smiled. "I'm great."

She narrowed her eyes. "I had it covered, you know."

"You're welcome."

She unstrapped my mother's sword from her back and handed it to me.

"Looking for this?"

"As a matter of fact, yes."

"What's the plan?"

"I help you turn the tide in our favor, then I'll go after Euryale."

She glanced at my bloody clothes, "Should I come with you?"

"No, you're needed here."

Another of the brutes came into range and I kicked it in the chest, sending it flying backwards twenty feet into a tent, which collapsed from its bulk.

Soon-Li glanced past me at the carnage I had wrought, raised her eyebrows, and frowned. "Yeah, I guess you're okay by yourself. One last question."

I gave her an impatient look.

"Why are you dressed like Jesus?"

I sighed and blurred out of there, wondering if I should take time to change. My first concern was for Speranza and her son. Two Bishops I wasn't familiar with were defending Antonio, who cradled his mother's body. Having seen one fall, the force that had descended upon them was large and trying to push past the line. I blurred in faster than any of them could track and became a tornado of death.

Durendal was true to its name, slicing through opponents almost as if they weren't there. I slashed the arm off a Burnie who was about to throw a fireball, then kicked him into a nearby tree. A few more flicks of my wrist and two of the Claws McGraws were reeling, I grabbed a Brute with my free hand and launched him into a cluster of military units who were pushing their position. A final enemy was taking cover behind the same tree I had hurled the Burnie into. He poked his head out to send a magazine of bullets our way and it exploded with the crack of a rifle.

Images of my friend's brain coating me flashed through my mind and threatened to pull me down, but they passed just as quickly. The speed and veracity of our attacks pushed the enemy back and provided the small team with some breathing room. I looked up to where I knew Jelena to be keeping overwatch and gave her a few hand signals, ordering troops to this location. Less than a minute later, thirty soldiers came jogging over, pushing their way through the enemy line I had broken.

"Set up a defensive perimeter."

The officer saluted and moved to make it happen. Stepping over to Antonio and Speranza, I put a hand on his shoulder as tears streamed down his face.

"I'm sorry."

He looked up at me. "She gave her life to save mine. I'm not ready for her to be gone."

"I know, but we need to mourn later. We still have a job to do."

Antonio shook his head and buried his face in his mother's neck. "I'm tapped out."

I released a flow of energy from my river of power into his shoulder. He jerked and his eyes went wide. It only took a few seconds for them to begin shining with an inner light.

"How?" was all he could manage.

I smiled. "The gift of prayer."

I filled up the other Bishops who each gave me similar expressions of awe.

"Keep moving forward. This is not over yet."

I zipped from area to area, helping the push and refilling the bishops who were drained or getting there. Mostly, I was just showing my face. There was too much going on to get to everyone, but I wanted to show them I lived—that hope was alive. Then that acrid odor hit my nostrils again and I knew it was time to finish this.

I followed her trail to a portable cabin buried deep in the woods. She was coming back out, a large duffle bag hung over one shoulder, and had changed into traveling clothes. She was so focused on what she was doing she didn't even notice me.

"Leaving so soon? And after you made me all those promises."

She gave a start and tried to cover it up. "How did you know where I was?"

"Your aura."

She smiled, but I could sense the fear under it. "And here I thought my charms weren't working."

"Please don't confuse it with a compliment. It's more like the stinking draft out of a slaughterhouse."

She narrowed her eyes. "I will need to work on that next time."

"There isn't going to be a next time, this time." I considered that for a second and then nodded.

"Brains, talent, and a sense of humor. Maybe I should take you with me?"

"Maybe you should give up now. You're not a fighter, you're a manipulator. A nymphomaniac serial killer that preys on fear and strikes from the shadows. You can't walk around without a bodyguard."

Something tickled my memory and I got a bad feeling. The air thinned and a concussive blast threw me sideways into a tree. I bounced off and fell to the ground but managed to keep hold of my mother's sword.

"Was he talking about us?"

"I think he was. It sounds like us."

I picked myself up, brushing off leaves. The twins stood in the clearing, dressed in green camouflage. One's pattern a direct contrast to the other.

Euryale tied her hair up into a knot. "Perfect timing as always, ladies. Shall we eliminate this bother once and for all?"

"Are you sure we can't take him with us?" one murmured seductively.

The other snuggled next to her sister, her chin on her shoulder while one hand caressed her abdomen. "That sounds heavenly."

"Sorry ladies, I'm in a monogamous relationship. Plus, there is just a little too much crazy going on here."

"Alright, death is almost as much fun."

Without warning, they blurred in opposite directions, coming at me from both sides. Short swords appeared in their hands and they slashed at me—one high, the other low. I jumped, flattening my body into a spin parallel to the ground between them. The air moved around me from their blades' proximity. They followed up with a second slash, but closer together this time. I blocked the blows with the flat of my sword, which still rested on my forearm.

The twins switched to alternating their attacks, forcing me to put in double the work just to keep the blades at bay. One would slash at my face, then the other would stab at my stomach. They found an opening when one feigned a stab that I attempted to block. Then they both kicked at my chest simultaneously. I was knocked back off my feet and slid a good distance before backward rolling to a defensive stance.

"Oh, he has other hidden talents, Ember," said one.

"I'm getting fanny flutters, Crystal."

"Do you ladies ever give it a rest? Seriously, how do you even think with the blood constantly trapped in your crotches?"

They each blew me a kiss, then attacked again. They were a formidable pair and fought as if they had one brain. Midway through the next set of attacks, they added supernatural assaults of concussive explosions, ice shards, and fire balls. I was forced to switch between powers so rapidly that I struggled to keep up a defense. I was breathing hard when Euryale joined the fight. She had been circling the battle, caressing her wicked butcher knife. The twins' attack pushed me towards her. Then Crystal froze the ground under my feet while Ember hit me with a blast. Euryale slashed me across my side and Ember followed up with an ice storm that pelted me with razor sharp barbs.

I could protect myself to a point, but it took a lot out of me. I had finally tapped into hope and it looked like I was going to die before I could pass on the information. How is that even possible? What the hell was my problem? I had access to a font of energy that no other Bishop had ever connected with and I was worse off than I had been before; still clueless about the limits of this source or what I could do with it. It wasn't the same, didn't react the same way or have the same elements to it. It was like going from driving a sports car to flying a plane. Some concepts were similar, but more were vastly different. I was stuck battling two high level Converted and a Tainted with a sword and a small bag of tricks.

I looked down at myself. The white robes had been burned and ripped to shreds from the barbed ice crystals. I grabbed the piece that had the most fabric left and tore it off. So there I stood. All I needed was a Stetson and I could be the naked cowboy. I received several cat calls from the three women who were trying to kill me and I asked myself again how I'd ended up here.

I had to figure this out before they burned, stabbed, or froze me to death. Taking a deep breath, I sought the calm of my inner serenity. The peaceful meadow now had a wide, fast-moving river cutting a path through it. A buzzing sound tickled my ears. I looked around for the dragonfly but it was nowhere in sight. I wasn't really there, not even in my mind. I was harnessing the feeling that the field gave me. The place centered my being. It was in that calm that Soon-Li's voice came back to me.

Stop battling with the sword and become one with it.

Whether it was the meadow, the situation, my new power, my mother's sword, or a combination of all, that statement finally made sense. It clicked like a puzzle piece fitting into the gap that seemed ill formed for it. I sank lower in my stance, my purpose solidifying. I smiled at them and blew them a kiss.

They attacked all at once. Ember threw a fireball while closing the distance. Crystal hurled spiked balls of ice. I used power to push each just far enough out of the way that they passed by without harming me, impacting the trees behind me. One tree exploded into flames and the other crystalized where the ice ball struck it, as though it had been soaked with liquid nitrogen. Both crashed to the ground as the three women reached me, blades flashing.

My mother's sword sang as it cut the air—parrying, blocking, and slashing. It was a blur, moving almost with a mind of its own. The harder they pushed, the faster it moved. Euryale stayed in the background, throwing supernatural forces at me like I had never seen. Wind focused into a ribbon so sharp that they cut through anything in its way. Spears of ice simply appeared as she spun until she sent them speeding at me. I had been wrong. She was not weak at all, but all of her attacks were ranged.

The twins began alternating their weapons strikes with their powers as well and I fought against the heat and ice attacks, all the while feeling that I had somehow manifested this battle from the mural on my Miser Brothers heating and cooling business van.

One used an elemental attack while the other slashed at me. I was dodging, parrying, and blocking for all I was worth. The sword was an extension of my body. I could feel its metal right down to the tip. When I sliced or stabbed, I could tell exactly how far the steel was from my opponent's skin.

The tide turned suddenly when I found an opening. My fight had brought me in close and I slipped in between the twins, facing Ember while Crystal stood behind me. We were so near each other that it was practically a lover's embrace. I anticipated their reaction, a slight hesitation at the intimacy. I looked into Ember's eyes as I reversed my sword and pierced her sister's heart. Shock danced across their faces. The fear and pain that followed were not for herself, but the thought of spending the rest of her life without her sibling. She didn't have to wait. A heartbeat later, I sent a foot long ice spike through hers. I wasn't entirely sure I was going to be capable until the thing formed. They both fell backwards.

Euryale staggered back at the shock. There was no anger or loss in her expression, but there was fear. The buzzing I had heard from my inner place still went on in the background until I finally recognized it for what it was—a drone. It was the updated version John had been working on. Then a rustling arose from woods around the small clearing coming from multiple directions. I barely gave them a second thought. My focus was on Euryale's knife. I studied it while I wiped Crystal's blood from my sword.

"This changes nothing. You can't beat me. I am death. I am the creature in the shadows that everyone fears. The thing under your bed. Your every nightmare come to life."

Hager stepped out into the clearing. He was holding a phone, which lit his features from below.

"I am not afraid of you."

"Me neither." Soon-Li appeared a short distance from him, cell also in hand. It dawned on me then that they had all been watching a feed from the drone.

She was followed by Thorne. "Nor I."

They came in groups after that. Adam stood alongside Jelena, who had a sniper rifle leaning on her shoulder. Tira stepped out, crossing her arms, and John slipped his knife back into its sheath. The High Council, together again except Speranza, emerged.

"We are not afraid."

Ima from the Miami Covenant appeared and next to her—My heart stopped. It was Marie. She smiled at me as though we had not been away from each other. "I am never afraid when I am near Christian."

The river of hope that was flowing into me churned and frothed like the rapids in my field. I gazed one last time at the knife held in her iron grip, then met her stare. "You are nothing but a scared, pathetic creature to be pitied."

I turned my back on her. I could feel the rage like a furnace from behind me. With a great roar, she blurred forward. I spun so fast that the leaves lifted into a whirlwind and my mother's sword severed her head. Her whole body stopped like it was frozen in place. I peered down at her as she looked up at both me and the rest of her body. Her lips moved, confusion clear on her face. Then black smoke started pouring out of her neck. It didn't shoot skyward. It oozed down to the ground, creating a noxious-looking mist that hovered there. Then it pooled together as though it were attempting to reassemble its host.

"Not today," I said.

I held out my palm and a light so bright exploded that it outshone the brightest day in summer. It flashed out, forcing the black ooze to shrink back into Euryale's body. Everything fell silent and the night crept back in to claim its property. It took a moment for our eyes to adjust even with supernatural assistance.

I turned to Hager. "Did you bring what I asked?"

He called out to the Major, whose team came running in with two steel cases. One was a small square, slightly larger than a hatbox and fitted with a clear plexiglass front. The other was the size of a short, more claustrophobic coffin. Each had multiple locks and chains. I picked up Euryale's head and stared at her. Her expression shifted back from anger to fear. I said nothing before slipping it into the box. Mangine and the team placed her body in the other crate and the two were secured.

"Airtight?" I asked.

The Major said, "As requested."

That done, I turned to the crowd now gathered around me. The Bishops, as one, all dropped to their knees.

"NO!" I bellowed.

The few remaining birds in the area all departed. All the Bishops looked abashed.

"Enough bending knee. Enough bowing to ancient ways that no one really understands. You are not my children. You are my brothers and sisters. You will not fight for me, but by my side as equals. Only then can we rid ourselves of this scourge. Only then will we be truly free to live our lives as we choose."

I drove my sword into the ground and stepped up to Hager, holding out my hand. "Will you join me, brother?"

He looked up at me, took it, and rose to his feet. "I will that, grandson."

Chapter Thirty-Two

OUR CASUALTIES WERE WHAT could be deemed acceptable, though for me they were anything but. Thirty-three military men and women were dead, as well as three Bishops. Two of those I didn't know, in addition to Speranza. Those heroes saved fifty-eight people, including me, and stopped a reign of terror that would have killed thousands.

Now, we walked up a hill during the predawn of Northern Italy bearing the former leader of the high council's sarcophagus between us. Her children and grandchildren followed in silence. I was amazed at the vast family she had created despite her responsibilities. She had six kids; three boys and three girls. Each of those had a few of their own, and many of that generation had little ones of their own. They were not all here. I had met them during the public wake. Hers was one of almost forty that I'd attended in a brief space of time. This ceremony was strictly for those in the know, which meant her immediate family and a few of theirs. Her husband was in his eighties and still climbed the steep hill with minimal effort. There were a few friends, probably those she helped along the way.

Her sarcophagus was carved from a solid piece of granite. One side outlined her lineage from her mother, all the way back as far as was recorded. Her name was etched in the top left, then the names ran from left to right and down eight lines. The earliest relative was simply a round shield. His or her descendant had added a sword behind it and their successor entwined them with white lilies. The decorations continued for another two generations before names appeared. They were in a language that was unrecognizable to me for about another seven successors. After that, the names looked to be in Latin, then later what resembled the more modern forms of Italian. There were one hundred and twelve ancestral tiers carved into the stone.

On the other side were depictions of the key points in the family's history, including her rise to leader of the now defunct High Council. By her feet was the crucifixion, as seen through the eyes of Fra Angelico. At her head was the crest of the Bishops.

The lid was plain, bearing her name followed by the inscription "defender of the faith." Further down was "The Song of the Dardanelles" by the Italian Poet Gabriele D'Annunzio.

RISE, O BROTHERS, IN ARMS AND IN SPIRIT,
FOR THE EARTH CALLS FOR YOUR VALOROUS SOUL.
BLOOD OF HEROES, SPILLED IN SACRED BATTLE,
IS THE SEED OF FREEDOM'S ENDURING GOAL.
FALL, IF YOU MUST, AS THE SUN DOTH DESCEND,
INTO CRIMSON SEAS OF ETERNAL GLORY.
YOUR NAMES SHALL ECHO, UNYIELDING, UNENDING,
IN THE HEART OF OUR NATION'S STORY.

Finally, from what would have been her waist down, a thick sheet of highly polished steel was affixed. Nothing was written on it. It held no adornments and sat on a one inch wide steel frame, giving a gap of a few centimeters between it and the stone below. The gap was filled with a sheet of foam not too dissimilar to what would be found under carpets.

We reached the peak of the hill with a sheer drop overlooking the small vineyard that the De Angelis family owned and ran. At the top sat a stone mausoleum with thick, glass doors facing the glorious view. A dais sat off to the side and we placed the sarcophagus on top, also facing the vista. Subtle lighting had been arranged so that we could see each other in the early morning.

Family and friends formed a semi-circle around her while her pall-bearers stood as honor guard to either side in reverse rank; showing that, in death, we are all equal. Father Murphy stepped forward and stood at her feet.

"I have known Speranza for twenty-five years. We met during

Desert Storm. I was a young traveling missionary and she was leading a group of Bishops against one of the Tainted driving the conflict. We had different views on how things should be handled. I thought we should take a more passive approach and she was, well, Speranza."

A ripple of muted laughter went through those in attendance and her husband bobbed his head, smiling, and wiped at his face.

"We call ourselves defenders of the faith no matter what that faith entails. Whatever your beliefs, you are steadfast in your knowledge that you were put on this earth to defend its inhabitants. It is ingrained in your DNA. Speranza took that role very seriously, right down to her last breath. Many warriors dream of meeting death on their feet instead of growing old. We write songs about it. Heck, even Bon Jovi wrote one."

More chuckles.

"But Speranza did what few others have been able to do. She accomplished both. It was not the only dichotomy she maintained. I have never seen a better example of living life to the fullest than the family that stands here today. She was proof that you could be more than one thing." Father Murphy sighed deeply and tapped the sarcophagus twice. "She will be sorely missed."

That was my cue since the honor guard faced the family. "Orders, hup!"

We slammed the inside of our fists to our chests and turned to face the departed. Then we started singing the Bishop's Lament, written centuries before. The first verse was sung by all standing at attention. As it ended, Antonio stepped up. The Bishops from Rome's Covenant fell in line behind him. At the end of the first line, Antonio, with tears streaming down his cheeks, drove his fist into the steel plate. The sound echoed off the surrounding hillsides in the cool, still morning air. It left a perfect imprint. He slammed the same fist to his chest in salute, tried unsuccessfully to choke back a sob and moved to stand next to Father Murphy so he could witness the rest. There was a long queue. The end of each line of the song was punctuated by another Bishop's strike, leaving a further imprint and sending its own echoes through the valley again like a giant, slow metronome. This went on for several minutes.

The second verse was repeated until the last of us had their turn.

There were so many Bishops in attendance, I wondered if there would be room for everyone. This was my third funeral of this type. All were large, but none came close to this. Everyone wanted to honor such a legend. When the attendees had finished, the honor guard strode up one at a time, adding their fist prints to the rest. My turn came. When I approached the metal plate, my breath caught. The indentations from all the other Bishops had covered the panel except for a space in the center in the shape of a Bishop. I met Antonio's eyes, who inclined his head and motioned to the only open area.

They had done this on purpose to show their support. At this time, that should not have been about politics or leaders or even the war. It touched me deeply and I almost missed my cue. Then I rammed my fist into the belly of the Bishop and left an indentation so deep that going any further would have cracked the granite top.

Antonio saluted with his hand to his heart and I repeated it back to him. I took my spot back up and we all sang the third verse. At its completion, silence once again came over the area. I heard him step up to where she rested and run his hands over the imprints. He took a deep, shuddering breath.

"I wanted to thank everyone for taking the time to be here for this. My mother would have been so proud. Not because so many are here for her, but that you came together despite your differences or grievances, like we did for the Redemption Battle."

It was what they were calling the attack on the castle.

Antonio continued. "She died how she lived her life, full speed ahead. No regard for herself, but with a determination that she would leave this world better than she found it. I think we can all agree, she succeeded. We may have a hole in our hearts this day, but we can revel in the thought that Heaven has gained another angel."

He stepped back and Father Murphy double tapped his leg. I turned to face her and the rest of the bearers followed suit. We lifted the thousand pounds of rock without effort and guided it onto a pedestal inside the mausoleum, facing the glass doors, where she could enjoy the view. It seemed a fitting place to spend eternity.

Chapter Thirty-Three

THERE WAS ONE OLD-FASHIONED cell deep in the bowels of the London Covenant. There was no bed, no TV, and no nightstand as was in the more modern versions that were at the higher levels. Those resembled guest chambers that doubled as holding cells for the few prisoners that we "entertained." This was more like the place I'd been held during my stay in the mansion and just being near it made my shoulder twitch.

This chamber had been built to hold one of the Tainted in case we were ever successful in capturing any. It had gone unused for hundreds of years, until now. Hager and Thorne were to either side of me as I unlocked the door and pulled it wide. Francesca sat on the wooden bench built into the wall, legs and arms crossed, back stiff, and her chin aloft.

I stared at her for a few moments. "Angelic," I finally said.

Her demeanor lost some of its resolve.

"Hager had to explain it to me. Though I should have worked it out on my own. To be fair, I was naked and hanging from a chain when I first heard the term as well as being in the middle of a spirit walk spanning over a hundred miles." I moved in closer and sat next to her. "A disciple of Sparanza De Angelis. One who has been personally trained and mentored by the great woman herself. The oldest living Bishop on the planet and the wisest and talented for generations. Or at least, she was."

I leaned in and whispered in her ear.

"She's dead."

She reacted as if I had slapped her, rearing back to stare at me. I didn't meet her gaze.

"She was killed in the battle to release me. Her last act was to give her life to protect her family. I thought you would like to know."

"I did what I believed was right. Speranza was blinded by prophecy and outdated views. Your generation and those before it have screwed up this planet and just keep plowing forward without any regard for the devastation you leave in your wake. Then you come in and divide the few of us remaining who are trying to make things better!"

"You mean like Nathan?"

This was another verbal slap.

"Yeah, he found me after the battle. Word had gotten to him of your betrayal and he came to your defense. He said that there was no way you would do anything like that. It turns out that he was also an Angelic and had worked closely with you until the trial that had changed everything. He had left you behind to join me in Manhattan. Then it all clicked. If I was no longer there to follow, Nathan would come back to you."

She lowered her head.

"Did you ever tell him how you felt?"

Her hair shimmied as she shook her head. "Why bother? The regulations prevent marriage between Bishops. It would reduce the line of defense." The last was said with venom. "Nathan was all about rules."

I gently took her hand. She presumed I was trying to comfort her. I clipped the titanium bracelet around her wrist and pinched the clasp between two fingers. A lick of power heated the metal and melted it into a solid piece, searing her flesh beneath it. She yanked her arm back with a hiss of pain and anger. The wound healed quickly. She moved to grab the bracelet with her other hand, but I caught it and held her tight.

"Gentlemen?"

Hager and Thorne stepped in and grabbed her by the arms, pushing her against the wall.

"What are you doing? Stop! Get off of me!"

I placed a hand on her chest as she struggled in vain. I found her well of power and drained it. The cry of anguish that she expelled was heart wrenching. Few Bishops ever let themselves run dry on purpose. The feeling of loss that accompanies the lack of power is devastating. I felt nothing for her. I probed her arm until I found the subcutaneous chip and ripped it from her with another small ribbon of power. She screamed in pain as it tore her flesh on its way out. I didn't heal her. I wanted her to have a permanent reminder of what she'd lost—what she betrayed.

I held it in front of her eyes as I crushed it into powder. "Francesca Deluca, you are stripped of the title Bishop and, with it, your access to the holy waters. You are free to roam the lower levels of the Covenant with notable exceptions, but you will never leave here while the Tainted are still a threat."

I nodded, and the two men released her. They filed out and I followed.

"You can't do this!" she screamed. "I deserve a trial."

Thorne turned. It was the first time I saw genuine anger on his face. "You deserve death! It was Christian that saw fit to show mercy."

We left her in the cell, the door still open.

"Are you sure about this?" Hager asked.

"I gave one of the Tainted a second chance. How can I deny her the same? Only time will tell if she embraces it."

"You have been avoiding me for too long, Christian." Hager barged into the lab, with Soon-Li and John on either side.

"Come in."

I waved them over to the table where I'd laid both the knife and my mother's sword next to each other.

"You cannot keep a person in that state. Not even one of the Tainted."

Hager's voice was rising, showing just how agitated he was. Who could blame him? I looked over at the steel case in the corner. I didn't notice the banging anymore as her body fought to find her head so she could make herself whole again. Euryale's eyes never stopped darting around the room as she stared through the plexiglass front. I imagined she was searching for some way to escape. Her expression shifted from anger to fear. It never once registered regret or sorrow. I kept it covered with a blanket while I was not in the lab, kind of like a pet bird.

I returned my gaze to the two blades. "It is not a situation she will have to tolerate for much longer."

"Can you at least tell us what you're doing?"

I looked over at him, "Haven't you figured it out yet?" Narrowing my eyes, I answered my own question. "No, you still refuse to look past the limitations you've been taught your whole life." I refocused on my work.

Soon-Li crossed her arms. "Since you have evolved past us, how about you lower yourself to our level and explain it?"

Why would she say that? Couldn't they see I was doing everything for them? For all of humanity? I was trying to wipe out the disease that had plagued the world nearly from the beginning and they were being petty. Maybe they were jealous. After all, I was doing what none of them were able to do in thousands of years. Shrugging off the thoughts that had been gnawing at me, I finished the final examination of my mother's sword. I picked it up and flipped it around before I caught it by the blade and thrust it towards Soon-Li.

"How about I show you instead?"

She glanced from me to the handle and back, then reached out tentatively and grasped it. I kept eye contact as I smiled. Then I stepped over to the steel box containing the head and ripped the lid off its hinges with a screech, metal bits flying in all directions. Reaching in, I pulled it free. Her eyes bounced around like ping-pong balls as I placed the Tainted's head on the table. Moving to the large trunk which lay on the floor, I broke the two massive padlocks with a twist of each hand. The chains slid off and I grasped the two latches.

"Christian, what are you doing?" Hager's voice was strained.

"You're right," I said matter-of-factly. "We can't keep her like this."

"You can't just let her out!" Soon-Li practically yelled.

"Free her, don't free her. I'm getting some mixed signals."

"Think about what you're doing, bud." John's tone was calming, as if trying to talk someone back in the window of a skyscraper. I regarded them and sighed.

"I have. In fact, I've thought of little else for the past week. It was my focus with each slice of her knife. With each cut, it was my only objective. With each patch of skin she removed, my resolve solidified. This was my end goal."

I flipped up the latches and the top shot open. The thick black smoke sought the head like a snake lunging for its prey. Euryale's body stood up, taking on a regal pose as though she expected everyone to bow before her. I grabbed her around the waist and pulled her from her small prison, placing her torso in the center of the room and holding it tight. Her flesh still felt warm against me and I shivered.

Soon-Li's eyes were wide. "Christian, this is crazy."

My smile widened. "Yeah, isn't it great?"

The smoke pulled the head back into its proper place. Immediately, Euryale started screaming. "I will have you all begging for your lives for this! I'll torture you until you give your children to me to stop the pain!"

She writhed in my grip. It was like trying to hold an octopus. I planted my feet and steeled myself against her.

"The heart Soon-Li. Aim for the heart."

Her doubt melted away and her face hardened. She pulled the blade up parallel to her body. Then she rolled it around her before she plunged it into the Tainted's chest. The screech that burst forth shattered glass all over the lab and the black smoke shot from the wound like a geyser. It circled us, finally coming to rest in the corner, where it reformed into a dark, hooded figure. In its hand, it held a long scythe. Soon-Li tracked its movement as she stood still facing it. The smoke creature raised both hands and shot forward, screeching.

"The sword will protect you!" I yelled.

She switched to a defensive stance and held the blade like a shield against the attack. The form struck it and dissipated. Everything fell quiet. The body in my arms turned to ash and dropped to the ground. I could see the harsh words forming on Hager's lips until the full meaning of what had happened dawned on him. He looked from Euryale's remains to the weapon in Soon-Li's hand.

"How?"

I smiled at him and said simply, "Hope."

Chapter Thirty-Four

MARIE AND I SAT at the top of the bell tower in Great St. Barts. Our feet hung over the sides and dangled into the open air.

I wasn't good at this. I struggled to find words to tell her how I felt without making it sound accusatory or needy. Plus, I wasn't sure if she had the same problem or was just trying to figure out how to let me down easy.

I finally went with the blatantly obvious. "I missed you."

"I know. You told me. I missed you, too."

"How is the case going?"

"Fine."

"Are you liking your new position?"

"Oh Jesus, Christian."

"What? I don't know what to say."

"Say you're hurt that I haven't made time for you. Say you're angry because I have been blowing you off."

"I don't want to fight."

"No one wants to fight."

"Why don't you just tell me why you have been avoiding me?"

"I haven't been avoiding you."

"So then, why has it been so long since we talked?" I heard my volume getting louder and tried to modulate it, which just made me sound fake.

"You were a prisoner for a while, with no way for me to contact you." Marie's tone was defensive.

I tried not to sigh, but it came out anyway. "I meant before that."

"Remember my new job?"

"How could I forget?" I knew the statement was unhelpful. "I feel like I did something wrong."

"Did you?"

"Not that I know of."

"I should hope you would know if you did." She was in attack mode now. I wasn't even sure if she realized what she was saying as she shot jab after jab.

I took a deep breath. "I get the feeling that you are mad at me for something I did, but I don't know what that is."

She shook her head and mashed her lips together. A tear escaped and she wiped at it like it stung. "You didn't do anything."

"Well, something's bothering you."

I rubbed at my shoulder. Marie caught the motion.

"Is there a problem with your shoulder?" There was an edge of concern in her voice.

"It's nothing."

Now that we were communicating, I didn't want to get distracted.

"If it was nothing, you wouldn't be rubbing it."

"It's a remnant of my fight with the psycho twins."

She turned to face me.

"What does that mean? Is it a scar?"

She seemed almost excited by the prospect.

"No."

Her face fell.

"It's more like a mark?"

Marie's head jerked up. "Take off your shirt."

"We're on top of a church."

"Take off your shirt or I'm going to throw you off this bell tower."

"That's a little—"

"Christian!"

"Fine."

I peeled off my Jurassic Park t shirt. She pulled out her phone and clicked on the flashlight to banish the night, aiming at the space between my shoulder and right pectoral muscle. Etched there in the place where Ember's knife had penetrated, the skin off color, was a cross. I would have called it a coincidence, but it was too deliberate.

The edges were perfect right angles. And I could have been imagining things, but I could swear that when I looked closely, I could see the outline of a body. She traced her finger over the mark that sparked a longing in me. I had ached for her touch for months and now it felt so good I wanted to weep.

"Oh, Christian."

"It doesn't hurt. Kind of tingles, though."

She launched herself into my embrace so that I had to grab the wall to keep us from tumbling over the side. I didn't know what the hell was going on, but at that point, I really didn't care. Marie was in my arms and that was all that mattered. I felt her shudder and realized she was sobbing.

"What is it? What can I do?"

She pulled away, tears streaking her face.

"Speak again, and I'll shoot you."

Marie and I were lying in my bed deep under the church. We had barely made it there before we ripped the clothes off each other. Now she lay across me, her head on my chest and one leg crossing mine. I traced my fingers over her shoulder and kissed her hair, feeling happier than I had been in months.

"At the risk of breaking this awesome spell, can you clue me into what just happened?"

"You were pretty good for not knowing what was happening."

She bit playfully at my chest. I smacked her naked ass. My long reach was a nice advantage, being so much taller.

"Fine." She punched my stomach before she rolled over, reaching for her clothes. I thought she was getting up to leave and immediately fished for words to fix whatever I had done. She pulled out a piece of paper in a zip-lock bag and threw the pants on the floor again. She handed it to me and nuzzled back into her previous position with a contented sigh. As such, she missed my confused look.

"What is this?"

"Open it, silly."

I did. The paper felt old and familiar as I removed it from the plastic. I unfolded it and immediately recognized my mother's flowing handwriting. I sat bolt upright, knocking Marie off me.

"Hey!"

"Sorry." I met her gaze, but she was still smiling. "This is my mother's letter."

She nodded.

"I can read it?"

She nodded again. Her smile widening.

I unfolded it the rest of the way.

To Her,

First, let me say that it is very nice to meet you, so to speak. I wish we could do this in person. I only catch glimpses of what you look like and I am still in awe. And frankly, a little jealous. But I guess I should explain.

If Christian has handed you this letter, then you know how special he is, in more than just his personality. What he may have also told you is that each of us has a speciality. An area of extreme expertise that sets us apart from the rest. Mine is foresight. I have the ability to see the future. It sounds cooler than it actually is. Most of the time it confuses things and I don't really understand my visions until afterwards. Sometimes, however, insight accompanies them. These are critical divergences in the course of history. Defining points in a person's experiences that decide the direction of their life.

I'm telling you all of this because I've had such a vision concerning you and Christian. I don't know any easy way of saying this, so I will just say it. Christian is going to be put through an ordeal. I don't know the details of it, but I do know that it will have two possible outcomes. He will either get through it and be stronger for it or he'll be turned and betray everything he holds dear. He'll be converted into the enemy he fights against, only much worse. The one thing that will help him through it is you.

You are his lifeline. You are his true north. Without you, he will become lost. I'm sorry, but it gets worse. You cannot tell him about this. If he knows, he'll find a way to avoid the situation and all will be lost. He needs the strength that this trial will provide him to weather the coming storm. I won't sugarcoat it: this is going to be bad. Really bad. And he needs you to be the lighthouse that guides him home.

So why am I telling you this? Because you are about to be given everything you have worked your whole life for. While I know you love Christian, your brain and your upbringing will tell you to break up with him so you can focus on your career. I am asking you not to do that. At least not yet. Not for my son's sake, but for the world. I'm sorry to make this request and I'm sorry to ask you to keep this secret. It will be a wedge between you two that will cause even more pain.

There is one more thing. If he turns, you will be his first victim. However, if he makes it through unscathed, he will be forged into the steel that will banish the Tainted forever. Like all who make it through the crucible, he will be marked. Look for that mark and you will know. One final note, in that moment when you see the mark, you will know what you truly want. I am sorry to ask this of you.

May the glory of Easter and hope of rebirth guide you.
Angela Bateleur

I read it again. I rubber-necked between Marie—who was still smiling for reasons I couldn't figure out —and the letter. Finally I let out, "What the fuck?"

I jumped out of bed and started pacing, repeating the same curse over and over.

"Christian, I'm not sure what you are freaking out about. You made it. The mark proves it."

"Great, thanks. That's helpful. I almost go full-on Darth Vader and no one bothers to let me know. But, hey, you made it through, so all's well that ends well."

"I couldn't tell you."

"I know! I read it. Dogs and cats living together. I get it. I'm still pissed. And why the hell are you still smiling?"

"You apparently read over the best part."

"What, the part where my mother knew I was going to be tortured for a week and didn't give me a heads up?"

"Read the last line again."

I looked at the page. "I'm sorry to ask this of you."

She gave me the *you're being stupid* face. "The one before that."

I read it and my breath caught. I looked up at her and her smile turned mischievous.

"I just quit my job."

She pulled back the sheets invitingly. I tossed the letter over my shoulder.

The End.

Get Exclusive Content From
W. J. Grupe Jr.

If you have enjoyed this book, I would really appreciate if you would leave a rating and a review.

If you haven't already, check out the first two books in The Tainted War series, Awakening, Unworthy, and Heretic

Sign up for my newsletter to stay up to date with everything going on .

Visit me on Facebook, Instagram, Twitter, and Linkedin.

Get the John McCaw novella and learn how he came to join the New York City Covenant of Bishops.

Available exclusively on my website:

www.WJGrupeJr.com.

Acknowledgments

As always I need to start out by thanking my family. You are still my biggest supporters and I couldn't do this without you. But specifically:
Marie- Always my alpha reader and biggest cheerleader.
Kristina & Will - My semi-unpaid staff. Money cannot buy the support you guys provide, but that doesn't mean I shouldn't try.

Special thanks to:
Lawrence Mangine for his help with the military elements,

my beta readers Jim, Marguerite, Jen, Lawrence, and Sarah for their insights,

my editors Mark Stay and Liv Mammone that kept me focused on my voice instead of others;

www.ingramcontent.com/pod-product-compliance
Lightning Source LLC
Chambersburg PA
CBHW070452260626
47161CB00004B/1275